ALSO BY BETH BROPHY

Everything College Didn't Teach You About Money

MY
EX–BEST
FRIEND

A Novel of Suburbia

BETH BROPHY

SIMON & SCHUSTER
New York · London · Toronto · Sydney · Singapore

SIMON & SCHUSTER
Rockefeller Center
1230 Avenue of the Americas
New York, NY 10020

SIMON & SCHUSTER and colophon are registered trademarks
of Simon & Schuster, Inc.

Designed by Lauren Simonetti

For information about special discounts for bulk purchases,
please contact Simon & Schuster Special Sales:
1-800-456-6798 or business@simonandschuster.com

Manufactured in the United States of America

10 9 8 7 6 5 4 3 2 1

Library of Congress Cataloging-in-Publication Data
Brophy, Beth.
My ex-best friend / Beth Brophy.
p.   cm.
1. Washington (D.C.)—Fiction. I. Title.

PS3602.R646M9 2003
813'.6—dc21   2003042847

ISBN 0-7432-4422-2

ACKNOWLEDGMENTS

I'm grateful for the many people who lent their editorial advice, technical expertise, and encouragement. Any glossing over of the facts to fit my fiction, or outright errors, is my responsibility, and no reflection on them.

I especially want to thank:

Philippa Brophy, whose talents as an agent are exceeded only by her generosity as a sister.

Alice Greenwood, whose keen editorial insights made the crucial difference.

Chuck and Susan Freed, and Carol Bloomberg, for giving me a room of my own, many years ago, to start this project.

Two very smart doctors, Angela Knox and Robert Siegel, for pivotal plot points that rely on years of medical training.

Patent attorney David Forman and photographer Linda Creighton for allowing me to vacuum their brains for details related to their professions.

Louie and Ralph Dweck, my current and future best friends, for their daily nurturing of my spirit and advice on all matters, literary and otherwise.

Betsy Streisand, Jill Rachlin, Barbara Inkellis, Bob Garfield, and Noreen Wald for helpful suggestions, and bolstering.

My parents, Shirley and Milton Schrenzel, for always telling me I could accomplish whatever I set out to do.

Acknowledgments

At Simon & Schuster, many, many thanks to my editor, Sydny Miner, who gets it done in the way every author hopes, to David Rosenthal, for taking a personal interest, and to Kerri Kolen, for her thoughtful editorial comments (and her exceptional taste in men).

Lastly, but not least, my love and gratitude to my husband, Arthur, who never let his skepticism that I was pushing rocks uphill stand in the way of his support, and my daughters, Ariel and Lily. They are my reasons for everything.

For Arthur, Ariel, and Lily

MY
EX-BEST
FRIEND

ONE

It begins like any other ordinary workday. I'm in my cubicle of an office at *Nationweek,* too busy to notice my view, a narrow slice of downtown K Street. In clear weather, from a certain angle, you can see the White House, but on a gray, rainy spring day, like today, I'm not missing much, mostly backed-up traffic and people in trench coats hurrying to their next appointments.

Inside, I'm drowning in paper: overflowing files on my floor and desk, a stack of the day's half-read newspapers at my feet, an in box stacked precariously and ready to tip at the slightest movement. I'm trying not to spill my black coffee on anything crucial—the fact checkers hate it when the source materials are too stained to read.

Although I hate computer jargon, I'm in my usual working-mother multitasking mode: phone cradled under one ear while I type at the computer, writing one story for business, editing an education piece for the social trends section, rearranging the boys' nursery-school car pool, and calling friends to guilt them into providing homes for a litter of eight gerbils. The queasiness in my stomach is an acute reminder of my promise to Allison.

"I will be at your recital by five," I told her confidently this morning.

"Don't forget the cupcakes," she reminded me.

By noon, my neck and shoulder muscles were tighter than my prepregnancy jeans. Finally, at 4:15, mumbling about an appointment, I duck out of a cover-story meeting and race to the parking garage.

Despite the drizzle, the traffic is light as I head to Bethesda along Massachusetts Avenue. After years of this commute, I automatically zip past the mosque, the Brazilian and British embassies, and the vice president's house, barely registering the sights.

My first stop is a bakery in Bethesda. I am unprepared for the Lydia sighting that awaits me. As soon as I'm inside, the smell of vanilla and cinnamon reminds me that it's been more than eight hours, and four cups of coffee, since my sole meal of the day, a meager but virtuous bowl of bran cereal. I intended to run out for a salad at noon, but the phone never stopped.

As I stand at the counter, I restrain myself from ordering a fragrant cinnamon roll—about half a million calories. I impatiently glance across the narrow, crowded store. Only the back of her head is visible, but I know instantly that the woman in the black raincoat paying for the six-grain bread is Lydia Finelli. My stomach lurches and my heart rate rises to the level of forty-five minutes on the elliptical machine.

No doubt Lydia has spotted me, but will pretend she doesn't see me. We've only run into each other a few times over the last five years, but that's her pattern. There's no way she's getting away with this.

I stride over, giving up my place in line. "I thought that was you, Lydia. Hello," I say, managing a neutral tone.

"Claire. Oh, hi," she answers as if seeing me for the first time. "How are you?"

"Fine. Ooops. My cupcakes are ready. See you around." No need to linger. I made my point: I'm not invisible. I've got nothing to be ashamed of, no reason to avoid a simple greeting in a public place.

I pull out my wallet. Lydia pats me on the shoulder and waves good-bye as I wait for change. A small victory, I think, walking briskly in the rain to my Camry, and sliding the bulky cake boxes into the front seat. Too bad I lost the war.

The neon clock on the dashboard flashes 4:53. The rain will slow me down but, if I make all the lights, I'll only be five minutes late. As I turn the key in the ignition, I hear a light tap-tap-tap on the window. Opening the window, I lean out, catching a few drops on my face. This time I register Lydia's appearance. Still exceptionally pretty, but she doesn't look well. Pale complexion, gaunt face, the lines around her mouth more pronounced. Her blond, curly hair has been expertly cut and highlighted, but it's not as thick and shiny as I remember.

"Claire, it's such a coincidence to see you. Really. I've been thinking about you lately. A lot." She hesitates. "Listen, is it okay if I call you?"

"It's always been okay, Lydia," I say evenly. "My numbers at work and home haven't changed. I have to run. Allison hates it when I'm late." I touch the cupcake boxes for explanation.

"Of course. I won't keep you. I'll speak to you soon. I mean it."

I back out of the parking spot carefully. Sure Lydia will call. That's as likely as the Publisher's Clearinghouse van driving to my door with the ten-million-dollar check. As likely as a Hollywood producer buying the rights to one of my magazine stories and turning it into a movie of the week. Lydia will never call and I know it. She hasn't dialed my number for five years. Wait until I tell Aaron about this encounter.

The light turns green and I drive off, leaving my former best friend of twenty-three years, the person who once shared the most intimate details of my life, including the play-by-play of my lost virginity, standing alone on the curb in the rain.

* * *

A few days pass, and thoughts of Lydia return to the back of my mind, the repository of the unresolved hurt and angry feelings that have accumulated since she dropped out of my life with no explanation soon after our thirty-fifth birthdays.

Naturally, her disappearance didn't happen overnight. It took me months to realize Lydia was dumping me for good, a process punctuated by me dropping by her house at odd times, hoping to talk, and dozens of unanswered phone messages. When Lydia was home, she would invite me in, but act politely distant, as if I were a pesky neighbor, then recall an urgent errand she had to run. Resentment, denial, hurt, grief, I felt them all, in various combinations. I still do, although with less intensity.

Gnats have nothing on me in persistence. I pursued her like an elusive source until her final snub. When she didn't return Aaron's call, announcing the twins' birth, the door in my heart finally slammed shut. I was too mad to try again, replaying in my head her pregnancy with Colin: all the times I held her head over the toilet, brought her ginger ale or peppermint tea, and drove her to doctor appointments because Matthew, then a lowly intern, couldn't leave the hospital.

For six months, maybe more, I had vivid dreams about Lydia at least a few times a week. Not that I clocked much sleep between nighttime feedings and diaper changing. I longed for some closure with Lydia, but not enough to make any more overtures myself.

The Thursday after the bakery encounter, on an otherwise uneventful workday, as I'm rewriting my lead for the third time, the phone rings.

"Claire Newman," I say curtly, anticipating Tim, the annoying editor who has already nagged me twice about a story that is not due until tomorrow morning.

"Claire, it's Lydia. I know you're mad at me but don't hang up, please. Just hear me out, okay?"

Common sense dictates slamming the phone down but, as usual, my curiosity overrides it. "I hate mysteries, Lydia. How could I possibly hang up when the biggest puzzle of my life is about to be solved?"

"Look, I know I owe you an explanation, big time. I promise you'll get it. But, for now, I need your help." She pauses. "I'm in trouble. I know I gave up my right to your friendship years ago. But, in a strange way, you're the only person I can trust now."

"Trouble? What do you mean?" It doesn't really surprise me that Lydia can still push my buttons.

She hesitates again. "It's complicated. And I'd rather tell you in person. Please, Claire, I know I don't deserve it, but give me one more chance. Please. I'm appealing to your big heart." Her tone is soft, placating.

I'm intrigued. For Lydia, this constitutes groveling. To her, a simple request for help, like asking a dinner guest to bring a bottle of wine, is the moral equivalent of panhandling. She's not inclined to admit that she needs help, ever, especially from me, a person she views as not quite as competent as herself, but luckier. Proud and self-contained, she's my polar opposite, which is what drew us together and caused tension in our long friendship.

We were so close as kids, shared so much history, that it hardly mattered to me that, if we met as adults, we'd have practically nothing in common. All our common memories is why I tolerated her inconsiderate behavior for so many years. Losing Lydia would be like losing a chunk of my past.

Sure, she was smart and funny, but so were a lot of women. Yes, I loved going places with her, especially to museums where she'd drag me through obscure exhibits and dazzle me with her commentary. However, I didn't remain loyal to Lydia because of her interesting views on art history or her gracious entertaining, and certainly not for her political views, which grew alarmingly more conservative each year.

Until it actually happened, I never imagined the day would come that we would stop being friends. It was as unthinkable as not inviting my alcoholic uncle to Thanksgiving. So what if he passed out in the bowl of creamed onions before the rolls were served? Family is family.

So, I do exactly what Lydia, who knows me as well as anyone, would predict. "I'll come by Monday on my way to work. I can be late and skip a few of those boring planning meetings," I hear myself say. "See you then." As I hang up, I notice my hands are trembling.

Trembling hands holding the phone, the brand of black-leather wallets in the pockets of the terrorists who blew up the World Trade Center, these are the sorts of details we traffic in at *Nationweek,* America's second largest newsweekly.

I'm not one of those journalists who regrets not going to law school or medical school, or who dreams about owning a little newspaper in rural Cape Cod, or who wants to quit to drive car pools and be a fulltime PTA volunteer. Which isn't to say I don't occasionally suffer from the usual work–home conflicts, or feel a twinge when our kids sneak downstairs to our nanny's basement bedroom for a good-night hug in the evenings when I'm home from work.

I joined the *Nationweek* staff twelve years ago as a business writer, single-mindedly devoted to climbing the masthead. Gradually, my priorities changed, an inevitable result of marriage and motherhood. I juggle lots of balls, but I don't want to drop any of them. I've made my uneasy peace with my double life as a journalist and a mom. Some days, I worry over shortchanging my kids; other times, I cut a few corners at work but, on balance, it works out okay. If I ever slow down long enough to take a yoga class, my mantra will be: "Perfection is the enemy of the good enough."

There's no question that my husband, Aaron; Allison, nine; and my four-year-olds, Max and Zach, come first, although I still care how many cover stories I write versus anyone else, whose title comes above mine on the masthead, who's getting a bigger raise. It's mostly residual competitiveness. I've crashed enough cover stories, broken enough news, gotten enough heavy hitters to call me back on deadline to have built up a pretty big account in the goodwill bank, and my editors cut me lots of slack for soccer games and class trips.

And, financially speaking at least, I could quit if I wanted to, although it would put a noticeable dent in our household spending. We tend to value convenience over frugality, as time, not money, is our scarcest commodity. Aaron's a partner at a top patent and copyright law firm that practically prints money, and he spends much of the week trying cases out of town.

I had second thoughts that day about agreeing to Lydia's request. But, like most reporters, I'm a relentless snoop, and Lydia was counting on that. One riddle I never solved is why Lydia bailed on our friendship. It's a phenomenon harder to explain than how my life became the caricature often portrayed in *Nationweek* and other trendy magazines: the women who complain too much, who have everything they've dreamed of, except the time to enjoy it.

Lydia, despite her degrees in art history, and her long-ago promising career as a museum curator, took a different route after her son Colin was born a dozen years ago. She abandoned her career and wholeheartedly embraced home and hearth. I suspect her change in direction was related somehow to our rift. Anyway, that's one of my many theories on the subject.

More on that later. What I'm trying to explain, or rationalize, is that, at the time, Lydia's phone call seemed like a gift—one of life's rare opportunities to tie up a loose end. I didn't realize then how one phone call could set in motion a series of events that would eventually transform so many lives, including my own.

Unable to sleep Sunday night, I wander into Allison's bedroom. Surrounded by stuffed animals and Beanie Babies, she's snoring like a barnyard animal, a trait she inherited from Aaron. I pull up her quilt and stroke her thick brown hair. I leave her door open just a crack, the way she likes it. Down the hall, the boys are sprawled in their bunk beds, inert as deflated soccer balls. I kiss the tops of their matching red heads, whose color matches my own.

Without thinking, I touch my forefinger to Max's wrist, then Zachary's. Taking their pulses is a habit that began with nightly forays into Allison's nursery, commando attacks against sudden infant death syndrome. When she turned two, I gave up pulse checking after reading somewhere that premature boys are at the highest risk for SIDS. Comforting news, at least until the twins arrived a month early, weighing barely five pounds each. Until they were eighteen months, I got out of bed two or three times a night to check their pulses and watch their little chests move in and out. I don't share all of my phobias about the children with Aaron—if he ever turns against me he could have me committed—but, every so often, when he comes with me to kiss them good night, I catch him looking as I hold their small wrists and silently count. He knows exactly what I'm doing.

The weekend flies by in the normal blur of soccer games, birthday parties, and errands. At odd moments I reflect on Lydia and her mysterious troubles. Divorce, illness, a reversal in Matthew's prosperous neurology practice? Not likely. MRIs certainly weren't getting cheaper, or brain tumors more rare. Or was Lydia's problem more specific to our friendship? Something that only I, in my new role as savior, can fix?

Monday morning, I'm so distracted during the four-mile drive between my house and Lydia's that I barely hear *Morning Edition.* How is Lydia going to behave? She wouldn't dare act aloof after begging me to come. Or would she? Probably she'll act polite and formal and force me to endure too much small talk before she warms up. I hope she's made coffee. Zach's crisis over his missing lunch box had eclipsed breakfast. Not that I expect Lydia to offer me so much as an English muffin. She has no interest in eating. Caffeine is her primary food group.

I pull into the driveway, behind Lydia's navy blue Volvo, which must have replaced the white station wagon. A few years ago, I stopped driving past their house periodically, finally realizing that turning down their street was unlikely to yield any clues about why Lydia dropped me. Those stealth drives made me feel like a stalker.

I smile, noticing a black Mercedes coupe has been added to their fleet, parked behind Matthew's beloved Porsche. Lydia used to scorn such flagrant displays of materialism, but they must be rolling in it now.

I ring the doorbell. No answer. I ring again and wait a few minutes. No footsteps. I turn the knob. The door's unlocked. Should I just walk in? I weigh the awkwardness of barging in against Lydia's invitation to come over. Should I call her from my cell phone in my purse? What the hell. I turn the knob.

The house is quiet. I'm right on time, but maybe Lydia has overslept or is in the shower. Slowly I take the stairs to her bedroom, noticing no coffee smells emanating from the kitchen. "Lydia," I call tentatively, wondering if she will be offended by my boldness. Maybe I should go back outside and knock harder. Or use my cell. No, I'm already inside. And I'm an invited guest, not a burglar.

Her bedroom door is closed. I open it, gasp, and freeze against the door. I hear a high-pitched shriek and realize it came from me. It takes only a few seconds to achieve full comprehension.

Lydia has an impeccable excuse for not answering the doorbell. She's dead.

Two

The second I see her pale, listless body, I know. Yet another part of my brain is in control, giving the orders. Lydia's lying on her back in bed, eyes open. Her muscles look stiff, especially in her face. Running to her side, I grip her wrist. No pulse. Icy hands. The grayish cast of her rubbery skin is a major clue that it's too late for CPR, but I blow air between her white lips, and pound her chest. The stiff wax doll isn't coming back to life. Her bones feel as brittle as a piece of matzoh, as if my lightest touch will shatter them into pieces.

Although my body is moving, my mind has been shocked into a protective fog, at least for a few minutes. Then, I come out of it, noticing the frayed hem of her nightgown and the tiny missing button on the neckline. A heart attack is my first thought. Or an accidental overdose. Finally, surveying the scene, the peaceful bedroom, no sign of a struggle or forced entry, I accept the reality that Lydia's death was no accident.

"Why, Lydia? Why?" I sob. "Why didn't you wait for me? I was going to help you. You knew that." I wonder how long she has been dead, if I could have saved her by arriving earlier. It doesn't seem likely that she could have died after Colin left for school. Then why wouldn't he have found her this morning, hours ago?

I snap into crisis mode. First I call 911 on my cell. Then I run to the kitchen, where the list of emergency numbers is neatly tacked on the bulletin board. I leave an urgent message at Matthew's office and locate Aaron on his cell.

I notice a paper taped on the refrigerator door and walk over to read it. A suicide note from Lydia? No, it's a list under the heading "Avoid Food or Beverages with Tyramine. Could Interact Dangerously with Medication. Don't Eat or Drink: . . ." The list contains about forty foods, including some of my favorites—chocolate, caffeine, several types of cheese, bananas, avocados, Chianti, and sausage. Curious, I open the lid of the trashcan, hidden out of sight in the cabinet under the sink, just where it used to be. I'm not surprised by the contents: rinds of Brie and Camembert, crumpled foil from Lindt chocolate bars, the end of an Italian salami. It appears that Lydia killed herself by gorging on forbidden foods.

I dash upstairs to the bedroom and stand on the pale, plush carpet beside Lydia's bed, clutching her limp hand, crying. None of this makes sense. Why would Lydia ask me for help, then kill herself hours before I got there? Did she want me to find her? Hadn't she hurt me enough? Now she was dead, leaving no hope of ever setting things right between us.

The blare of the sirens grows louder. I touch Lydia's forehead for the last time, then open the door for the paramedics.

Thursday morning, inside the dark church, I squeeze Aaron's hand, and try to focus on the priest's words, not the high ceilings, the stained glass, or the cool marble floor. The nightmarish irony isn't lost on me: Through Lydia's death, I've finally been taken back into the fold. Under the circumstances, unfailingly polite Matthew had no choice but to invite me to the funeral mass.

Lydia is dead. Dead. It's been a few days but I'm still in that numb, altered state where daily life occurs in an out-of-body sort of way. I narrate events to myself, play by play, as if I'm a sports commentator. From my trance I can recognize the comic overtones to the tragedy: Lydia, who presented herself to the world as the perfect wife and mother, offs herself by combining prescription antidepressants with foods guaranteed to interact lethally with them.

That's Matthew's explanation.

I could hardly believe what he told us, last Monday night, after Aaron and I returned to the Finelli house. Matthew led us into his study, away from Colin and the throngs of sympathetic neighbors and friends, and gently revealed Lydia's various bouts of depression; the long list of failed treatments—Prozac, Nardil, individual counseling, group therapy, alone, and in assorted combinations. The depression wasn't hard to believe. Lydia was the queen of mood swings, and always had been, even as a teenager. But suicide? Giving up usually wasn't an option for Lydia, which is why I never understood how she quit our friendship.

Father Kelly's saying something about Lydia not being in her right mind, which must be his kind way of reconciling his duty to say something soothing with her suicide. I wonder if he really thinks she's lying in a state of eternal sin. Despite being an agnostic Jew, I hope not.

I locate Matthew in the front row, surrounded by a sea of dark suits. He places a protective arm around Colin. At twelve, Lydia's son's childhood is permanently revoked. I glance away from the statues of Baby Jesus.

Sallie, Lydia's mother, sits on Colin's right. Her eyes are red and swollen, and she looks shrunken, and more fragile than I had remembered. When we met earlier on the church steps, we hugged each other and cried. I had missed her terribly these past years. She always approved of me, was forever inviting me to sit with her and talk, especially in the days when I wouldn't give my own mother more than a sentence or two at a time. The habit of talking with

Sallie survived my most sullen teenage years. I wonder if it's any consolation to her that Vince was spared the grief of mourning his beloved only child. A three-pack-a-day man, Lydia's father died of lung cancer almost a decade ago.

Many of the faces look unfamiliar, a further reminder of how far apart Lydia and I had grown. Despite the distance that had grown between us, my tears haven't subsided for days. If only we had had more time to fix our friendship.

"A pillar of the community," Father Kelly says.

Lydia's across-the-street neighbors, Randall and Karen Kline, are on my right. Randy is a psychiatrist in private practice; Karen is a caterer. They weren't my favorites among Lydia's acquaintances; he was nice enough but Karen struck me as slightly standoffish. We make eye contact, and I'm reminded of how their middle daughter and Colin used to ride their bikes up and down the Finellis' driveway, training wheels gliding along the smooth surface.

I feel mildly guilty about how Lydia and I used to make fun of Karen's catering skills, often calling each other after we returned home from parties. "How does she poach the flavor out of salmon?" I asked Lydia once.

"She doesn't use real fish, only gelatin. It's less fattening," Lydia had replied. But judging from Karen's splotchy face and the balled-up tissues in her hand, she and Lydia must have grown closer.

". . . raising money for refugee families," Father Kelly continues.

Lydia would have been mortified. Father Kelly is practically comparing her to Mother Teresa. Looking around to see if anyone else is registering a similar reaction, I notice a clump of well-groomed blondes dressed straight out of a Talbot's catalog. I wonder when Lydia fell in with the velvet-hairband crowd. They looked like professional moms, a type I dread, women who chucked thriving careers to devote themselves to their children, bringing to motherhood the same zeal they once used for strategizing corporate mergers or organizing international conferences on global warming.

These women had a way of bringing out my worst insecurities—making me question whether my children will be permanently scarred by too little time spent in Mommy and Me groups, or why I didn't schedule biweekly eyebrow-waxing appointments.

". . . a gracious hostess who welcomed friends and neighbors to her table."

Everyone but me, that is. He's not embellishing too much in that department. My eyes rest on the back of Jill Browner's head, a few pews up, sitting alone. She probably hasn't hooked up with anyone in the five years since I've seen her. Jill and Matthew had been lab partners in medical school and remained close. Lydia was very fond of her. In the days when I was a regular at Lydia's parties, Jill and I often retreated to a corner to catch up. We always vowed we'd call each other and make social plans, but we never got around to it, permanently stuck in the more-than-acquaintance, less-than-friend category. Jill used to head a team of medical researchers studying Alzheimer's disease at the National Institutes of Health. Then, during the booming eighties, she started her own biotechnology company, Theragenics Inc., in Gaithersburg, Maryland, raising funds from venture capitalists eager to place their bets on promising research. Matthew was an investor. Her company was mentioned a few times in the business pages of *The Washington Post* and *The New York Times* in the last year or two, proof that her work is attracting national attention.

When I knew her, Jill rarely dated or went out with friends. Her social life consisted of going to parties at the Finellis. Lydia, who tightly controlled her family's social calendar, included Jill on several occasions—birthday parties, the annual New Year's Day brunch, summer barbecues. Unlike me or Lydia, or the other women in their forties whom we knew, Jill possesses no outward signs of vanity. Her dark, shapeless clothes hide a trim figure toned by daily jogging. Her once shiny brown hair is streaked with gray, and she wears it long and lank around her shoulders. Not a smidgen of makeup accentuates her hazel eyes. "With those bones, she could be beautiful," Lydia used to lament. "If she only got a good haircut. And bought some decent clothes."

"Right. If she colored her hair and shopped at Saks, and stopped being poor, dateless Jill, how many times a year would you invite her over?" I had countered. "Once, maybe twice?"

". . . whose home reflected the love and care she lavished upon her family."

Father Kelly is hitting his stride; now it sounds as if he actually knew Lydia and her exacting standards of personal hygiene and housekeeping. Lydia carried good grooming and neatness to fanatical heights. Trained at Sallie's knee, Lydia regularly climbed onto her dining room chair to dust the chandelier with a toothbrush. She wore pantyhose under her well-pressed jeans. She never took Colin to the kiddy pool before undergoing a complete body wax. As misguided as Lydia's perfectionism could be, I understood it, even though my tendencies in that direction were marked by lying awake at night wishing I had made a few more phone calls on a story, not by how much my kitchen floor could use another coat of polish. Lydia and I used to poke fun at each other, but neither of us ever expected any changes in what we obsessed over.

For as long as I knew her, Lydia's self-discipline about appearances never wavered. As a teenager, she squeezed lemon juice in her hair every summer to lighten it (Sallie outlawed peroxide) and lived on a can of Tab and an apple a day for a few days before an important date. In hindsight, I realize that Lydia's washed-out appearance at the bakery should have tipped me off that something was terribly wrong.

My eyes settle on Matthew, wearing an impeccably tailored charcoal-gray suit. As he turns to whisper something to Colin, I see that his face is a portrait of anguish, his mouth drawn tight and his eyes puffy. Pleasant looking in a lanky, boyish way, with sandy hair and green eyes, Matthew obviously has discarded the last remnants of his preppy wardrobe. No more faded denim shirts hanging out of worn khaki pants, or dilapidated Topsiders on bare feet.

Matthew's European suits, like his Mercedes, must be part of the evolution that started a decade ago, when he began making a big deal out of what wine we drank with dinner. Not that I'm throwing any stones at materialism. I eagerly held out my glass for whatever he was pouring. No reason a liberal social conscience can't co-exist with an annual clothing budget that exceeds the gross national product of a third-world nation. I chastise myself for noticing details like Matthew's clothing at a time like this, instead of listening to the service. I can't help it, though. Taking mental notes is as natural to me as breathing.

". . . devoted to a marriage that grounded her to her family and the wider community." It certainly looked that way. What was the source of Lydia's mysterious "trouble"? A faltering marriage? Did Lydia continue to puncture Matthew's little pretensions, or had she given that up?

"Why use an English word when a Latin one will do?" Lydia once joked during brunch, interrupting Matthew's convoluted, neurologist answer to my question about migraines.

"For Claire, the Latin expressions are free of charge," Matthew had replied, with one of his disarming smiles. My mother's words echo: "She's a doctor's wife now. That's why she dropped you." I had rejected that explanation as too facile. I couldn't imagine the old Lydia, with her working-class roots, transformed into a snob.

". . . her son, the light of her existence."

I can barely bring myself to look at Colin. I hadn't laid eyes on him since he was seven. A young man now, he's still the male version of his mother, right down to his cornsilk hair, dimpled chin, and extralong eyelashes that I couldn't achieve with two tubes of mascara. The pain he must feel brings tears to my eyes. I choke back a sob, imagining my three having to make their way in a world without me. I wipe the tears away, and Aaron tightens his grip on my hand.

The priest's genuinely soothing words were having little effect on my anger and grief. Clearly Lydia was deeply troubled, enough to take her own life, an act I find unfathomable, and as a mother, unforgivable. How could she do this to Colin? Without so much as a note? She must have remembered, as sharply as I do, our high-school heartthrob Buddy Nolan.

Valedictorian of my brother Rob's high-school class. Student-council president, track star, National Merit Scholar, Buddy was Holly Dale North's version of male perfection. Lydia and I had enormous crushes on him.

When we were in eleventh grade, a few months after Buddy had departed for Yale, his mother Jeanette, former president of the PTA, den mother, and church volunteer, closed her garage door, sat in the front seat of her station wagon, and turned on the ignition. Buddy's father found her body when he came home from work. Sallie railed for days about Jeanette's selfishness toward her model son. "That lovely boy is going to think it's his fault. It will ruin his life," she predicted.

Within two years, Buddy dropped out of Yale, hitchhiked to California, and eventually moved to Maui, where he kept himself in coconuts and marijuana by selling overpriced puka shell necklaces to tourists. Perhaps he was perfectly happy in his tropical paradise, but Sallie considered his descent from the Ivy League a waste of a human life.

No matter how muddled, confused, or depressed Lydia had become, I didn't understand how such a vigilant mother could purposefully inflict Buddy's fate upon her own precious son.

"... her good works will live on in our memories." Father Kelly is wrapping up.

Aaron puts his arm around me and we walk back to the car, neither of us speaking. Blinking back more tears, I gaze affectionately at my husband, a rare Nancy Reagan moment. Not once has he uttered, "I told you so," one of my favorite phrases in the English

17

language. Although I'm too upset to be thinking clearly, Aaron's warning to me about not getting involved with Lydia again turned out to be entirely on the money. If only I had listened to him I would have been spared a lot of grief.

Aaron spent hours on the phone trying to locate Rob, in case he wanted to fly in to pay his respects. We Newmans are big on rituals, hardly ever missing far-flung weddings, bar mitzvahs, or other milestones. Aaron carefully explained Lydia's death to Allison—the twins never knew her—and called my parents while I sobbed in the bathtub. My parents were upset, but Lydia's death barely registered with Allison, who no longer had a mental picture of her. I've seen Allison more emotional over the death of a character on *Buffy*, her favorite show about a vampire slayer.

Not that my refusing to meet Lydia would have changed anything. She'd still be dead, but I wouldn't have been intimately connected to her death. I would have heard about it second- or third-hand, or read her obituary in *The Washington Post*, from the safe remove of my kitchen table. I could have imagined her death in an abstract way, rather than replaying the scene in her bedroom, over and over again in slow motion.

Walking to the car, I clasp Aaron's hand until my knuckles hurt. Here I was, on the verge of learning the answer that had eluded me for years, the reason Lydia ended our friendship. Instead, Lydia took the insult one step further, leaving me with a more perplexing question: How did the Lydia I knew so well, in five years, turn into a woman bereft of hope, a woman who gave up on life?

THREE

Aaron at my side, my stomach in knots, I ring the Finellis' door-bell for the obligatory condolence call. It's our turn to exchange banalities with other ill-at-ease friends and relatives. A lingering dread supercedes happy memories of times spent under this roof. My usual defense mechanism of covering deep emotion with sarcasm has kicked in: I can't help thinking that nothing spoils a place's ambiance like discovering a dead body on the premises.

"Claire, Aaron, thanks for coming," Matthew says, pulling me to his chest for a bear hug. Clusters of people are standing around the understated beige-and-white living room, speaking in hushed voices while balancing coffee cups. Lydia's decorating scheme is a stark contrast to our house, where we favor blues and green, preferably in dark shades, to camouflage stains from spilled food and apple juice.

Aaron and I join some neighbors near the couch and introduce ourselves. Matthew wanders around, shaking hands, mumbling greetings, trying to pick up threads of conversations. Without Lydia's social cues, he seems as lost as a child on the first day of camp.

Colin's standing near the dining room table with a friend.

"Colin, I've missed you so much," I whisper, squeezing his hand. He looks at his shoes, refusing to meet my gaze. Mindful of Allison's admonishments about "PDA," her shorthand for public displays of affection, I restrain myself from putting my arms around him, and hope he doesn't misread this as a lack of affection. I steer the conversation to school and sports until Aaron joins us, offering Colin a plate of cookies.

"I'm going to find Sallie before I inhale those brownies and hate myself," I say. I'm lying; I've barely eaten in days, another example of my only proven method of weight loss, the heartbreak diet.

"Colin, you have to promise to come for a visit very soon. It's been a long time, too long, and we need to get reacquainted. What do you say?"

"I'd have to check with my dad, I guess," he mumbles. I can't read whether he's glad to see me or is politely trying to push me away.

"I'll call you, okay?"

"Sure, Aunt Claire," he says, turning his back and walking in the other direction. So he does remember what he used to call me.

Sallie's in the kitchen, measuring coffee into the filter, showing less emotion than a hired caterer. But as soon as we hug we both start crying. Then I help her slice cake onto platters. After a few silent minutes, we chat about her bakery, my kids, Holly Dale, how Matthew and Colin are coping. We're just warming up to a more intimate talk when Aaron strides in. Kissing Sallie on the cheek, he points to his watch.

"Sallie, we have to go home," I say. "We promised the kids. Can I see you again soon?"

"Sure. Come back in the morning. Matthew and Colin will be gone by eight-thirty."

"Okay, around nine, after I get the kids off."

We both understand that Lydia will be the topic of tomorrow's conversation. Aaron and I say our good-byes to Matthew and find

Colin in the den, deep in conversation with a hunky guy I noticed at the memorial service. Major movie-star good-looking, he has shiny blue-black hair and eyes so blue I suspect they are tinted contact lenses. His powerful chest and muscled thighs are obvious under his standard-issue navy blazer and khakis. He couldn't be more than thirty-two.

"Colin, we're leaving now, but I'll call you and your dad about coming over in a few days."

"Sure. Aunt Claire, Aaron, I'd like you to meet my soccer coach, Roger McCaffrey."

"Nice to meet you." McCaffrey pumps my hand vigorously. No glint of gold on his ring finger.

"Claire Newman. And this is my husband, Aaron Willentz. We're old friends of the family. You sure don't look old enough to have a son Colin's age," I say. In our neighborhood, fathers and mothers of team members are the customary labor pool for coaches.

He smiles, displaying perfect teeth. "I don't. I'm not a parent. I'm the gym teacher at Colin's school. Lydia, uh, Mrs. Finelli, was a big help to the team." I bet Lydia wasn't the only mom vying to schlep oranges and jugs of water to soccer practice. McCaffrey's eyes dart around the room, looking for an escape route. I wonder how anyone that handsome could be so ill at ease.

"Aaron, I'll be right back," I say, ducking into the downstairs powder room. On my way out of the bathroom, I notice two women, practically clones of each other, blocking my path to the front door, where Aaron is waiting. Both have streaked blond hair and are wearing black pantsuits with a patch of brightly colored T-shirt sticking out of the jackets (one in fuchsia, one in lime green). Between them, there's enough jewelry to start an auction on the spot: diamond rings, diamond tennis bracelets, and clunky gold earrings. Lydia and I used to call this look the "full Potomac," but that was before she had friends who actually dressed that way.

"I can't believe he had the nerve to show up here," says Lime

Green, in what was intended to be a whisper. She's looking straight at Roger. "Look at how he's fawning over Colin. It makes me sick." They must be mothers of Colin's teammates.

Fuchsia speaks low enough that I have to step closer to make out her words. "Well, he was a close friend of Lydia's." She shoots a knowing glance at her friend, who replies, "A very *close* personal friend."

Their implication is clear. "Excuse me," I say, stepping past them to reach the door. "Let's go. Now." Taking Aaron's elbow, I guide him out the door. These two are dishing about Lydia at the very place where they are supposed to be paying their respects. They're probably jealous that Roger paid more attention to Lydia than to them. If they are typical of Lydia's new friends, the ones she took up with after dropping me, I should be grateful that she had cut me off. That's what I tell myself as I get into the car, taking tissues out of my jacket pocket to blow my nose.

It's not Sallie's nature to sit around idly and dwell on her troubles. Not when there are chores to do, dinners to cook and freeze, floors to scrub. She answers my knock wearing a smock over her black dress, hair tied back in a scarf. In her seventies now, she looks more vulnerable than the forceful woman of my youth. Her middle has thickened—whose hasn't?—but she's still a beauty, her thick chestnut hair streaked with white and pulled back in a neat bun. She's midway through cleaning out Lydia's closets, and her efficient bustling signals that she doesn't intend to let grief slow her down.

"Sallie, isn't it painful to go through Lydia's stuff this soon?" I put my arms around her. There were times in my life when I felt closer to Sallie than to my own parents, who were wrapped up with each other, and their friends and their careers. My father was a high-school principal and my mother a history teacher, and they were often at meetings and conferences, leaving Rob and me to our own devices. I loved the attention from Sallie, especially because I could return to my own freewheeling household whenever I felt like it, unlike Lydia who couldn't escape Sallie and Vince's watchful supervision. Part of Lydia's reticence, I've often thought, comes from how hard she had to fight during adolescence to maintain a zone of privacy that her parents couldn't penetrate.

"Of course it's painful. Where does it say that life isn't painful?" Sallie blinks back tears. "But, I'm going home in a few days, after I straighten out the house. And help Matthew hire a housekeeper so Colin won't be alone after school."

Her plan surprises me. I assumed she'd stay in Washington indefinitely. Her husband's gone, after all, and she has installed a trusted neighbor's son-in-law to manage the bakery, in preparation for her retirement.

"So soon? I thought you'd stay awhile. I was hoping we'd get to spend some time together. To catch up. You haven't seen Allison in years. Or met the twins."

She shoots me a look I remember from adolescence. Loosely translated it means: Your parents may be too naive to know, or care, that you cut school today, but I see a lot out of my living-room window and don't you forget it. "You're right. We do have lots of catching up to do." She lowers her voice as if speaking forbidden thoughts. "I never understood. What happened? You were so close. To all of us. Colin used to ask: Where did Aunt Claire go? When's she coming back?"

So, Lydia had made me out to be the neglectful friend, the one who vanished.

The situation requires tact, never my strong suit. How can I make Sallie understand? I can't tell her the complete truth without pointing a finger at Lydia. Nor can I say anything that will add to Sallie's pain.

"Sallie, I'm going downstairs to make tea. Be right back. Then we can talk."

"Just let me finish this pile." She's folding a stack of Lydia's shirts and pants. "Matthew's going to bring these to a shelter on Saturday. Want anything? Some of this stuff has hardly been worn."

"As if I could fit into a size six anymore. But thanks for asking."

"You had three children. What do you expect?" Was Sallie making an oblique reference to Lydia's failure to produce further grandchildren? I don't respond to the comment.

We drink the first cup of tea in silence. I think about Lydia's spirit hovering around the gleaming white kitchen. The KitchenAid blender, once used for concocting potent margaritas at summer cookouts, is on the drain board. "That old blender brings back memories," I say.

"Older than Colin and it works like new. I made carrot soup in it last night," Sallie says.

I nibble one of the home-baked almond biscotti Sallie puts in front of me. "Remember my idea to market these nationally? You told me that no one but old Italian ladies would eat them. Boy, were you ever wrong."

"I know. I think of you every time I see them selling for fifteen dollars a bag. You and your business ideas. By the way, Rob sends his love. He's sorry he couldn't make it to the funeral. He was out of the country and it took a few days for us to connect."

"How is the Hollywood tycoon?" she asks. Her affection for Rob is genuine and predates his unlikely and wildly successful career.

Nobody who knew Rob in high school would have predicted his path to Hollywood mogul. A classic underachiever, he spent most of high school stoned, playing his guitar with his band, staying up most of the night, and failing many tests. He cut classes, talked back to teachers, and was suspended at least twice. Thanks to my father's connections, and excellent SAT scores, he was admitted to a small liberal-arts college in Massachusetts that specialized in students who listened to their own inner beat.

Junior year, after a romance that ended badly, and tired of the arctic winters, Rob hitchhiked to Los Angeles instead of returning to school after Christmas break. The only job he could find was in the mailroom of the William Morris Agency. At night, he played with the new band he joined. At gigs he met other aspiring musicians and singers. Folk singer Laura Cardinal, who had a string of hit albums twenty years ago, almost became my sister-in-law. The rock band Crow were his roommates for awhile. Rob eventually worked his way out of the mailroom by representing his friends and their friends. By the time he was twenty-six, Rob owned his own hip talent agency, Newman Creative Associates, Inc. A few years later he had earned the first of his many millions.

Sallie waits expectantly for me to mention Lydia.

"Sallie, you know how much I loved Lydia. How intertwined we were for so many years. How I wouldn't have survived high school without her. I don't know what she told you about the last five years, how hard I tried to save our friendship, how many times I called her before I finally gave up . . ."

"My daughter wasn't much for talking. Especially the last few years, but she called you last week, right?" Sallie has heard all about me finding Lydia that morning.

"Look, Sallie, all I know is what Lydia said in that phone call. And it isn't much. But, maybe, if we put our heads together, we can figure some stuff out. Because, for the life of me, I can't understand how Lydia could have done this. I don't care how much she changed. She was such a devoted mother. How could she have killed herself?"

"She had problems," Sallie says, "but I don't have to tell you, she was no quitter. Remember when she broke her leg and kept telling the physical therapist to work her harder, just so she wouldn't miss playing in that silly tennis tournament?" She continues. "So, tell me again about the last time you spoke to her."

I repeat, in detail, our last conversation, starting with our chance meeting at the bakery. Our conversation meanders and before long we're in a delicate area: Lydia's fertility problems.

"She didn't intend for Colin to be an only child, right?"

"They tried for years. No luck," Sallie confides. "And Lydia was against medical intervention. Too invasive and unnatural."

"That surprises me. Lydia and Matthew were medically sophisticated. Why didn't they adopt?"

"They weren't interested. Especially Matthew. One perfect son is good enough for him, he always says. Why mess with a stranger's gene pool? Once Colin turned about six or seven, Lydia said she was done, that she couldn't face all the baby stuff again—the colic, the sleepless nights, the spitup. She talked about her freedom. But that was nonsense. Lydia loved babies."

"Maybe that's why she dropped me. You know, I was pregnant with the twins when she stopped talking to me. Maybe Lydia could deal with me when I had a career and no kids, or a career and one kid, but not a career and three kids."

"You mean she was jealous?" Sallie's tone is highly skeptical. I have to admit it would take a powerful amount of envy to knock out a twenty-three-year friendship. Nothing short of an ax murder would have led me to drop Lydia. That's why her behavior was so incomprehensible.

So, I drop the jealousy talk. This is no time to bring up that particular theory. Anyway, I don't mean that she was overtly jealous. Not exactly. If Lydia had wanted a career, she could have gone back to work at any time. Her jealousy, if it could be called that, was more implicit. Maybe it was getting harder for Lydia to maintain her slight air of superiority around me. For most of our lives, she held the lead on that internal scorecard that women, even the best of friends, perpetually tally: Blonder. Thinner. Better grades. She bagged a husband (a doctor, the jackpot) and achieved motherhood years before I did.

And maybe that was the problem. In our twenties, Lydia staked out domestic life as her turf. No one would have guessed that in our thirties, in mere output alone, I would have trumped her.

And I had my career, too. In Washington, being a journalist is considered prestigious, exciting, fun. Which it is sometimes, when you're not frantically trying to reach people who won't call you back. Or have an hour left to artfully write a story around holes in research that you hope no one will notice. Or when you're sitting around endlessly, waiting for an editor's revisions, when all you want to do is get home before your kids go to bed so you can kiss them good night.

"Sallie, I always knew Lydia was moody—the way she ran hot and cold. Matthew mentioned the other night that she was suffering from depression. When was she actually diagnosed?"

"She was in therapy, and on medications for, oh, five or six years."

"Why didn't she just tell me? Maybe I could have helped." I already knew the answer. Lydia was a good listener, and generous with advice. However, when it came to talking about her own problems, the ones deeper than her troubles with Colin's teacher or how her father-in-law had snubbed her at Christmas, she wasn't the most forthcoming.

"When Aaron and I were with Matthew the other night, he mentioned an earlier attempt, er . . ." I can hardly bring myself to utter "Lydia" and "suicide" in the same sentence.

"The first time she tried to—well, you know it was nothing more than a call for help. It happened about three years ago. After that, I was afraid to say what was on my mind, the way I used to. We avoided painful topics. Like your absence. I'm sorry, Claire." Sallie pats my hand.

"Tell me about that first time. From what Matthew told me the other night it sounded so unlike her."

"A cry for help. Completely. That's all. She didn't mean to kill herself. Pills. A whole bunch of them. Colin was spending the weekend with me in New York, and she knew Matthew would be home within the hour. The whole thing was so stupid," Sallie says.

27

"What made her try that time? Were she and Matthew fighting? Or having financial problems?"

"A few months before, her psychiatrist had taken her off Prozac. Something about the side effects. It was before she started taking the Nardil, which seemed to be helping. I thought she was pulling herself out of it. Then this." She put her head down on the table for a few seconds.

Like me, Sallie found Lydia's suicide particularly ironic. Lydia, who barely ate, had eaten herself to death by ingesting foods like wine and cheese, which interact harmfully, and sometimes fatally, with Nardil. Lydia knew that overdosing on Nardil would take longer to finish her off than mixing the foods and her medication. Her death couldn't have been an accident. The police had already ruled that out, based on the food wrappers they found in the trash and interviews with Lydia's psychiatrist. Matthew had told Aaron and me all about this stuff the other night.

"She was a walking textbook on depression and its treatments. That's what I don't understand. She knew those foods could kill her. This time, she must have really meant to do it," Sallie says, tears streaking her cheeks.

"I guess I still don't understand why she was so depressed. What do you think?"

Sallie shook her head. "Who knows? Maybe her brain chemistry. I blame myself. I should have tried harder to talk to her, but I was so afraid of upsetting her."

"Come on, Sallie. It's not your fault. Lydia was an adult. You think she was disappointed about not having more kids?"

"I think so. Matthew disagrees."

I grab at the opening. "You know I always thought they had such a great marriage. A united front. They never argue or fight the way Aaron and I do."

"A little screaming never hurt a marriage. It's healthier to argue than to hold everything in. Remember me and Vince?"

Sally and her husband had been yellers. It used to embarrass Lydia. She'd hide out at my house for a few hours, helping me with my math homework or watching television. "Too noisy to study," she'd say, grinning. It was an era before kids nervously thought divorce every time their parents bickered.

"Lydia knew we liked to make up in the bedroom, so she used to go to your house for awhile."

"Sallie, I'm only forty. I'm not ready to hear that grown-ups like you and Vince, or my parents for that matter, ever had sex." I change the subject again. "When Lydia wasn't well, when she was depressed, why didn't you or Matthew call me? I could have tried something. Didn't you trust me?"

"I wanted to. So many times. I even dialed your number a few times and hung up. But you know how proud Lydia was. She didn't want you to know. She said you were too busy, working and traveling, that you had your own family to take care of. Matthew felt strongly that we should respect her wishes. So, I went along." Sallie sighs. "Obviously, we made a mistake. No one could have failed worse than we did."

Unlike her taciturn daughter, Sallie doesn't mince words, yet her silences are as telling as her words. I fill in a few blanks around what Sallie's careful not to say. She doesn't dwell on Matthew and Lydia's marriage, for instance. My heart goes out to Sallie, so burdened. "Sallie, if you don't mind, I'm going to poke around a little, talk to some of Lydia's friends about her last few months. I probably won't discover anything that will help us understand it, but I'm going to give it a shot. Maybe it will make me feel less helpless."

Sallie looks relieved. "I wouldn't mind at all. Finding things out is your job. I know you're good at it."

So, it's settled. We make a pact: No need to tell Matthew about my poking around. It may upset him.

Not knowing exactly where to start, I ask Sallie to mail me a copy of the autopsy report. I think I saw someone do that in a movie once.

Before leaving, I take out my little BlackBerry and check my work e-mail—no messages—and follow Sallie upstairs.

"I found a bunch of old letters from you, from summer vacations and college. Do you want them?" Sallie asks.

"Definitely."

Sallie picks up the stack of letters, neatly tied with a blue gros-grain ribbon, resting on top of Lydia's jewelry box, then opens the box and takes out the antique pearl-and-gold earrings I gave Lydia on her thirtieth birthday. "Here, take these." Sallie shoves the earrings into my hands. "She loved them. She'd want you to have them."

"No, I couldn't. I'd feel funny wearing them. They were my gift to her."

"Then save them for Allison. God knows, Colin isn't going to need them," Sallie insists.

"You never know these days." This seems important to Sallie, so I take the earrings, along with the packet of letters, which feel sur-prisingly heavy. Oh, the good old days before e-mail.

I'll never wear the earrings. Lydia loved old jewelry, especially earrings. I collect, haphazardly, vintage clothing, mostly scarves and vests. On our birthdays, for years, I gave Lydia antique jewelry, and she gave me clothing. I loved the ritual of hunting for Lydia's gift, scouring estate sales and checking out funky stores on out-of-town trips. I found those earrings in a tiny shop in New Orleans.

Lydia, on the other hand, used to hate shopping. We would joke that if we traded husbands, she and Aaron would live in a tiny shack and have millions in the bank while Matthew and I would spend ourselves into bankruptcy.

It's petty, I know, and I was ashamed of myself, but seeing those earrings reminded me of the last birthday present Lydia gave me, and how she hurt my feelings. Lydia must have grabbed the first thing she saw in a store, an orange-and-gold tweed vest, two colors I detest. The style was okay, long, with interesting brass buttons, but Lydia had to know I would never wear it. I interpreted the hidden message: Lydia was just going through the motions of buying me a gift. She was too busy or preoccupied with her own life to shop and didn't even care if I liked the gift. I wasn't worth fussing over anymore. Now that I look back, that empty gesture was the beginning of Lydia's complete withdrawal from me. I made so many allowances and excuses for Lydia's moods that it took me weeks, maybe months, to understand the whole picture. The vest still hangs in the back of my closet, untouched and unworn. I couldn't bring myself to throw it out.

I kiss Sallie good-bye, promising to call in a few days, toss the letters in the backseat, and forget about them.

FOUR

"It just doesn't add up." I spear a forkful of lettuce and move it around my plate.

Val scans the crowded coffee shop, where we are one of many pairs of lunch companions crammed around tables so small that our knees touch. She chews thoughtfully on her club sandwich before speaking in a low voice, although privacy in these cramped quarters is a joke. "Okay, let's go over it again. Let's leave aside the big things for now, the incongruity of Lydia, the world's most responsible mother, committing suicide," she prompts.

As a photographer, Val Chandler has a gift for illuminating a person's character through the filtering eye of her camera, a trait I recognized years ago, after a few out-of-town reporting trips together. Since then, her talent for finding the unlit corners in a story has helped me countless times.

Despite my aversion to people who can eat anything, never exercise, and not gain an ounce, Val is my best friend in the office. We share a similar world view about most things, which is surprising, given that Val's African-American, the daughter of a highly decorated, politically conservative Army intelligence officer (whose political beliefs are to the right of Attila the Hun, Val likes to joke) and a former ballerina.

She grew up attending elite New England boarding schools and summering at the family compound on Martha's Vineyard. The only thing that saves her from being an insufferable WASP snob is the color of her skin, I often tease her, reminding her of my humble Polish and Russian peasant roots.

"And she was a Catholic, too, although a lapsed one," I mention again.

"Catholics are perfectly capable of committing suicide," Val reminds me, pushing her French fries in my direction.

I ignore her plate. "I know. It's the little details that bother me. No note. The messy kitchen, the unwashed dishes, the cheese wrappers strewn around, the half-empty Chianti bottle. The missing button on her nightgown. If Lydia had really planned to kill herself, she would have vacuumed, scoured the house, and left a freshly cooked pan of lasagna cooling on the counter. The only thing that makes sense is her method: no messy bloodstains on the sheets."

"You hadn't spoken to her in five years. She could have given up the happy homemaker routine," Val says.

"No way. Too ingrained. And why wasn't there a note?"

Val reaches over and puts her hand on mine. "Claire, listen to yourself. You found the body of someone you loved. Why you loved her so much is something I'll never understand. I hate to speak ill of the dead, but from everything you've told me, Lydia sounds like a selfish bitch. I know you used to be close as kids but, for the last several years, she caused you nothing but grief. Yet you've always made excuses for her, always assumed that somehow you were at fault. Can't you just accept that Lydia was a very unhappy person? It's not all that surprising that she killed herself."

My first impulse is to defend Lydia, but I try to stay calm and rational. "I know what you're saying has a lot of truth to it. In fact, it's one of Aaron's favorite tunes. But I can't just stop caring about her. Especially now."

Val smiles in sympathy. "Your loyalty is admirable, even though Lydia didn't deserve it. I know how hard this must be. Plus you're carrying the burden of an unresolved friendship. That's a lot of stress, even for Superwoman. Why don't you take a few days off, play with your kids, get a massage?"

"I've been home since Monday. I can't relax. You know I hate massages. Why did she call me? Why did she want my help, after all these years of freezing me out?"

"You'll never know. And that will be the hardest part for you to accept. Lydia's reason could have been completely mundane. Maybe she wanted to get a divorce and needed you to refer her to a lawyer or something. Maybe she wanted to use your connections."

"No, that doesn't sound like Lydia. She'd never admit that her marriage wasn't perfect or that Matthew had flaws. And she was perfectly capable of finding her own lawyer. Or whatever."

"Well, you said yourself she looked depressed that day in the bakery. We better pay the check. I have to be on Capitol Hill in twenty minutes."

After Val heads for the metro, I walk back to the office slowly, mentally planning my afternoon. My modest goal is to clear my desk of phone messages and piled-up mail. In my current state of befuddlement, there's no way I can focus on my current assignment, leading and coordinating with some reporters in the New York bureau an investigation of an on-line trading firm whose top executives may have been involved in an insider-trading scam. The story isn't as juicy as recent corporate scandals like Enron and WorldCom, or even Martha Stewart's case, but breaking it would still be a coup for the magazine.

I settle into my chair and sign on. The computer screen flashes "message pending." There are a few e-mails from colleagues expressing their condolences because they heard an old friend had died. The only thing that travels faster than news through this building filled with nosy people is gossip. Not in the mood for electronic chit-chat, I delete the messages without responding.

I dial in my voicemail code and listen to my phone messages, pausing only after the one from my boss, editor-in-chief Leslie Palmer. I dial her extension.

"Claire, sorry about canceling lunch at the last minute. Why don't you come up now? I have a little time before my two o'clock."

"Sure, I'll be up in about ten minutes."

From force of habit, I divide my mail into three stacks. The first stack contains only press releases, which go directly into the trashcan. Tackling the second pile, I come to an envelope I wasn't expecting, and I feel a chill. Ripping it open, I find a short note from Lydia, attached to a copy of a monthly brokerage account and a stock certificate for thousands of shares of Theragenic stock, dated last January. I feel chilled from the creepiness of receiving correspondence from beyond the grave.

"Claire," she scrawled. "Some backup, just in case."

Just in case? Just in case of what? Just in case I decide to kill myself before Monday morning? I look at it again, but the brokerage account looks pretty standard. All it tells me is that Lydia and Matthew have some bucks in their joint account, about $900,000. I look through the documents for a few minutes, bewildered. I wonder why she sent them, but nothing irregular leaps out at me. I give up and climb two flights of stairs to Leslie's palatial office, with its panoramic view of downtown.

Leslie ascended to the top job at *Nationweek* in the late 1980s, when British publishing magnate Calvin Flinterson bought it. Cal raided several prestigious publications for writers and editors, luring them with higher salaries and bigger promises. He snared Leslie away from the biweekly *Currency,* where she had built her reputation by breaking the Wall Street brokerage-house scandals in the late seventies. Though she had worked her way up from researcher to assistant managing editor, she wasn't going to rise any farther in *Currency*'s macho culture unless she grew a penis. So, she leapt at Calvin's offer at *Nationweek.*

With oversized glasses and preppy clothes ordered straight from L.L. Bean, twice-divorced, plain-spoken Leslie lavishes her nurturing skills on the staff, most of whom, like me, are devoted to her.

She rises from her chair to hug me. "Sorry I couldn't join you and Val. The Proprietor insisted on dragging me to his lunch with the Treasury Secretary." She rolls her eyes.

"Well, you didn't miss much. I'm lousy company."

Leslie looks appropriately solemn. She had called me at home a few nights ago to make sure I felt up to working, offering to give me as much time off as I needed. "This business with Lydia must be a shock. How are you coping?"

"I'm kind of numb." I take a deep breath. "Actually, Leslie, if it's okay with you, I'd like to take you up on your offer. I would love a week or two of vacation time to sort things out. I know it's short notice."

Leslie listens attentively as I mumble some stuff about Lydia's suicide, how it seems a bit suspicious to me, and the need for closure. She ignores her ringing phone a half-dozen times, the ultimate compliment from a journalist.

If she thinks I've veered off into the deep end of psychobabble, her manner doesn't betray it. "I understand, of course. It must have been such a shock to find her like that. So, what's on your plate now and who can we hand it off to?"

We talk logistics for a few minutes. I can finish my part of the reporting for the on-line trading scam cover within the next day or so and give the team some direction before taking off. "Then, there's the derivatives story. It needs lots more reporting, but I think it will pan out."

"Why don't you type a memo about what needs to be done and give it to Thomas? He's been trying to steal it anyway," she says.

"What else is new?" I ask. Thomas, twenty-seven years old, is the business section's aspiring Bob Woodward. After Leslie hired him last year, she asked me to "mentor him along," when I could find the time, although he acts as if the reverse is true.

"Anyone else on the trail?" Leslie asks.

"Not that I know of."

"I'd like you to return to that story when you come back, make sure Thomas has crossed all his *T*'s. I don't think we can wait more than two or three weeks to publish."

"Right. If I have to, I can always make a few calls in my spare time from home. Then I'm looking into that real-estate deal involving those Indian tribes in Arizona. I can give my notes and a memo to Debbie, if that's okay. She has better contacts than I do, anyway."

The prospect of some time off makes me feel calmer. I rise from the plush chair, conscious of Leslie's two o'clock meeting.

"You should be able to leave the office by Friday night, right?" Leslie says.

"Sure. But, I'll check in with you next week. And call me if you or Thomas need anything."

"Likewise. And, Claire, I hope you find what you're looking for," she says, one hand already reaching for her ringing phone.

I hate to exercise, but I force myself to speed walk a few miles, carrying three-pound weights, with a little jogging, three or four times a week. I still haven't lost the pregnancy pounds, as I had hoped, but the exercise gives me an energy boost and helps me fall asleep faster.

That's if I make it out of the front door without succumbing to maternal guilt. Tonight, I try to head that off before it starts, scooping the three kids together for a family hug. "Listen, you guys, Mommy's going out to exercise for a little while. As soon as I get back, we'll have dinner and then we'll do something special, like ride bikes in the park until it gets dark."

"No, Mommy. We miss you too much. We haven't seen you all

day. Stay here." Zach buries his head into my knees. Among my kids, he's the gold-medal winner in emotional manipulation.

"Just go. I'll take him," directs Trini, our baby-sitter–housekeeper, whom Aaron calls, with good reason, the most important person in my life. Born in the Bahamas, she speaks with a trace of an English accent, although she's lived in the United States for the last twenty of her forty-eight years.

Trini moved into our basement apartment shortly before the twins' birth. I met her after she answered an ad for a nanny-housekeeper that I had placed in the *Bethesda Gazette,* making the ad the best forty-three-dollar investment of my life. Better than buying AOL at two dollars per share in the early nineties, and I mean it. Trini lived with her last employers for twelve years, until their kids were in high school, and I'm hoping to break that longevity record.

It's not that Trini is perfect. She talks way too much, especially first thing in the morning, and lets the kids watch too much television when she doesn't feel like schlepping to the park. But she would place her slight, wiry body in front of a speeding four-ton truck if she thought it was going to harm one of my children. And, because we pay her slightly more than the going rate, she never minds if I have to work late unexpectedly or need to slip out of the house for an hour or two to run an errand in the evening.

I head out, knowing that Zach's wails will stop before I reach the corner. Screaming for dramatic effect is an old habit of his. I loop up and down the wide, tree-lined streets rather than taking the running path in the nearby park. Our Bethesda neighborhood is called Oakhill. Its proximity to downtown, seven miles away, the restored Victorian houses, and the first-rate elementary school help keep real-estate values up. This time of year, early spring, the neighborhood is at its prettiest, the green yards perfectly manicured, blooming with pink-and-white azalea bushes and yellow forsythia.

I try to clear my mind of thoughts of Lydia but, on my way back, slowing down to catch my breath, I anticipate what Aaron's arguments will be when I tell him my plan to poke around her suicide.

She's dead, and it's time to move on. I'm too stubborn to learn from my mistakes. I'm looking for answers that aren't here. My husband is unflappable—one of his strengths in the courtroom—but, over the years, Lydia had become a source of friction between us. He doesn't understand what he calls my "obsession" with our lost friendship. Aaron had grown weary of Lydia's unreliability with social plans, and didn't understand why I didn't confront her when she repeatedly disappointed me.

I can't exactly say it's a rare source of friction, although Aaron and I get along remarkably well for a couple defined by contrasts. I'm barely five feet two, with blue eyes and red hair, and a temperament to match: impulsive, combative, with a directness viewed either as refreshing or downright rude, depending on who's doing the viewing. My husband towers over me by a foot, his once jet-black hair speckled with gray, deep-set brown eyes usually hidden behind wire-rimmed glasses. I talk quickly, while Aaron chooses his words carefully and delivers them softly, a trait others sometimes mistake for slowness, often to their own undoing, especially in court.

I can handle Aaron's objections. The basic tenet of our marriage—the only way opposites can live together—is to give each other breathing room, to agree to disagree a few times a day. The real reason I dread tonight's discussion is that Aaron has a flawless track record in predicting the outcome of situations involving Lydia. I'm back at our front door, exercise time up, before I can dwell on that disconcerting thought.

I don't broach the subject of Lydia until later that night, after the kids are fed, bathed, read to, and tucked in, a routine that takes us to nine-thirty on a good night. I curl up next to Aaron on the couch in the study, wondering if the discussion we were about to have was worth disturbing the first quiet moment we shared all day.

"Honey, I want to talk. About Lydia."

Long sigh. "It's been five years since the two of you have really spoken. She's dead. Can't you give it up? Please?"

"No, not yet." I tell him how odd Lydia's suicide seems. About the financial statement Lydia mailed to my office with the scrawled note, "just in case." About my plans to explore Lydia's death.

I know what he's thinking, recalling past discussions I've drawn him into, replaying what might have gone wrong with my friendship with Lydia. He's remembering the bad dreams, the detours I used to take past Lydia's house, as if the cars parked in the driveway, or the new flowerbeds in the front yard would yield any clues. When Lydia wouldn't return my phone calls, when Aaron's appeals to Matthew for an explanation failed, I moped around like a spurned lover while Aaron simply accepted the situation. "People move on, make new friends, leave old ones behind. That's life," Aaron said.

Life according to a guy. Even guys like Aaron, who don't harbor a chauvinist thought in their politically correct brains, who spend their weekends coaching their daughters' baseball teams, and baking cookies with their sons. Even the most modern and sensitive males can't quite comprehend the close bonds of women's friendships. *Prying, interfering, meddling,* these are the words men use to describe closeness.

"Of course I can't leave it alone. You know that. She was my best friend for a very long time. There has to be some explanation."

"Look, I think you're making a mistake, but you're going to do this anyway. We both know that. I wish I could be here more in the next few weeks, to help you cope, but I can't. My trial is starting soon. I'll be in Cleveland for most of next month. Are you sure you're okay?"

"Of course. I just need more information."

Another sigh. "In the end, you won't know any more about Lydia's death than you do now. She was depressed and gave up. End of story. Why don't you ever listen to me?"

"I do, honey." Aaron isn't being callous. He truly believes I've already wasted far too much time brooding over Lydia. And that was when she was alive. I kiss him on the cheek and leave him to his law journal, reflecting on the irony. Aaron and Lydia used to be a mutual admiration society.

I remember years ago, sitting around Lydia and Matthew's apartment folding laundry while Colin napped. I was pairing Matthew's socks and rolling them in neat balls, per Lydia's explicit directions, wondering if I'd ever have my own husband for whom I'd perform cozy domestic chores. I used to throw my own socks in the drawer in a big heap, and fish out two that seemed to match whenever I needed a pair. However, hunting for socks as needed wasn't Lydia's style.

"Of course you should break up with Aaron," Lydia was saying, interrupting my monologue on how I could never marry someone so young, so unscathed, so seemingly normal. "He adores you, he has a steady job, and no needle tracks."

Aaron was younger than most of the men I dated (translation: He had no ex-wife, messed-up children, no huge therapy bills). My initial reaction to him was: sweet guy, uncomplicated, not my type. Spurred by my genuine disinterest, winning me became Aaron's personal quest. He was relentless, a quality I admire. It took three years for Claire Newman, rebel with a long history of unsuitable attachments to men who were commitment phobes, had no visible means of support, or both, to succumb to smart, kind, successful Aaron Willentz. My parents spent the weeks between our engagement and wedding praying that Aaron wouldn't back out.

Back in those days Aaron was relieved to discover I had close friends like the Finellis, whose traditional values mirrored his own. Maybe I wasn't the radical-hippie-flower-child I professed to be. Matthew and Lydia had the same last name, an aberration in our social set. They attended church on Sunday. They were raising a family—Colin was a toddler and we expected more children to follow at well-planned intervals. Despite Matthew's thriving practice they lived frugally.

41

The four of us spent many weekends together, cooking dinner—although Lydia rarely ate, she was an accomplished cook—discussing housing prices and the patent for an invention of Matthew's, a bicycle helmet with adjustable neck supports designed to reduce head injuries.

Once the novelty of Aaron wore off—I'd never brought other boyfriends around much—Lydia reverted to her old habits. Long silences, unreturned phone calls, plans scrubbed at the last minute in messages relayed via Matthew, whom I never had the heart to snap at.

Aaron used to think it was his fault—that Lydia and Matthew had soured on him—but I knew better. Classic Lydia behavior: warm advances followed by hasty retreats. Normally, I just waited her out, busy with work or other friends, knowing she'd eventually call with an invitation for dinner or to chat, making vague references to being busy or to Colin's latest cold.

Not the easiest friend, but Lydia's moods were familiar. She took me for granted for so many years that I came to accept her behavior as normal. And I've never shied from a challenge. I'd stopped noticing years ago that Lydia didn't behave like other people's best friends. I never called her on being unreliable or inconsiderate. She was the grown-up, after all, with more important obligations than mine. I didn't have children yet, so I didn't question Lydia's belief that you had to schedule social plans around your children's naps, or that hiring a babysitter on a Saturday night was a major big deal. Besides, Lydia and I were bound by a shared past; we were practically sisters. Relatives can get away with all kinds of behavior you'd never accept from someone outside the fold. It simply never occurred to me that someday she could disown me permanently.

FIVE

Later the next day, as I retrieve grocery bags from the backseat, I notice the stack of letters and put them in the study. I wonder again why Lydia kept them. She wasn't the sentimental type who hoarded girlhood letters—that's something I would do. Maybe Lydia remembered her childhood fondly as the happiest time of her life. Not me. My life has only gotten better as I get older. If only someone could figure out how to clone your age-twenty body and transfer your age-forty knowledge and experience to it, life would be ideal.

At around two in the morning, I realize sleep isn't coming and, if I toss around in the bed much longer, I'll wake Aaron. I go into the study, turn on the lamp, and pull out the letters.

I flip through them, something Sallie obviously neglected to do. In the middle of the stack from me are some other letters, bound with rubber bands. For one set, the postmarks start in 1981. I immediately recognize the handwriting—the distinctive loopy scrawl of my brother. It's news to me that Lydia and Rob were ever pen pals.

I don't recognize the handwriting on the second, smaller stack, but I do remember the return address: 5115 Crestwood Avenue. They must have been written by Jody Hoffman, a girl who went to high school with us, and tried many times to insert herself between me and Lydia. How odd that Lydia would save those letters, too. Jody was a twit, not a close friend of either of us.

Naturally, I'm far more interested in Lydia's correspondence with my brother. I realize it's nosy, plain wrong to read them. But under the circumstances, as well as being alone and awake at two-thirty in the morning, who besides Mother Teresa wouldn't have?

My punishment for snooping—the return of the sick, hollow feeling in the pit of my stomach—is almost instant. I read the letters twice, hoping that I've misunderstood, but the implication of certain excerpts is unmistakable:

From May 23, 1981:

"Lydia, I'm begging you to reconsider. Are you following your head or your heart? I know it's over between us, that we're not teenagers anymore. And Matthew sounds like a great guy with a great resume. But it's all been so fast. Are you sure this is the real thing? Please, for your own sake, not mine, don't commit unless you're really sure. Don't settle for anything less, now or ever."

From December 11, 1983:

"My only regret about that one wonderful night is that it was so fleeting—no matter how many times I replay it in my head. It was so special, so magical. I hope you're not being too hard on yourself, or wasting your energy on guilt. Not that I expect a nice Catholic girl like you to buy that argument."

The last one, dated March 3, 1989, was terser than the preceding letters:

"Are you okay? I go back and forth between being worried about you and being angry. Why won't you call me back? Please get in touch with me, any time of the day or night. I know you have all my phone numbers. I'm here for you, as always."

I must have been deaf, dumb, blind, and completely self-absorbed. How could it have escaped me that Lydia and Rob had a private history, independent of me? Of course, we were all living in different cities, in college and after, for many of those years.

It figures. Just as I'm struggling to come to terms with Lydia's final betrayal, she strikes again from beyond the grave. And this time my own brother is her accomplice.

My stomach churns at the discovery of yet another secret Lydia kept from me. And what was Rob thinking? These letters nailed him as a conspirator against me. I couldn't deal with any more in one night. I have to get some sleep, or I'll be wasted tomorrow. I climb into bed, careful not to jostle Aaron as I snuggle next to him. At least I can count on him. I put my arms around his back and snuggle against him. The clock turns to three-thirty, then four, before I doze off.

The sirens are getting louder and closer. Breathing heavily, I pull Max's limp body out of the deep end of the pool. He's heavy, dead weight, and I can barely lift him to safety. I'm screaming for help, but I can't make a sound. There are people around the pool, but I can't get anyone's attention. The shrieking sirens are getting closer.

I jolt upright in bed and shut off the alarm. 6:45. Aaron must have set it. At least it rescued me from another nightmare.

Aaron emerges from the bathroom dressed and shaved. "Good morning, hon. You look startled. Sorry, I meant to turn off the alarm before I went into the bathroom. You okay?"

"I'm fine. Just another bad dream." I start to describe it, but the twins run in, pouncing on my legs. "Mommy, wake up. It's a school day. Can you dress us?" asks Max, the morning spokesman. Zach doesn't say a word until he consumes his first bowl of Cheerios.

I throw the quilt off my legs and get up.

"Any chance you can meet me for lunch today?" I ask. "I can come downtown. We can make it real quick." I want to tell Aaron about my discovery last night and sometimes the only way we can conduct a private conversation or finish a sentence is to meet out of the house. If we wait until the kids are asleep, one or both of us often dozes off, too.

"Sorry, I can't do it this week. Trial preparation." Aaron is starting a huge trial next week, representing a soft-drink Goliath against a new-age beverage company over patent rights to a plastic bottle. He's beginning to get that distracted look, which means not to bother him with extraneous information, like routine family matters, until the case is over.

I know the drill. Aaron and I will never be one of those couples joined at the hip. Much of the time, I'm perfectly happy to be the only available parent of the household, as long as I'm cushioned by Aaron's income and the ability to pay Trini to help with the physical chores. Other times, I'm torn between missing Aaron, wishing he was home more often, and appreciating the solitude his absences give me.

Which is not to say that I don't experience moments, hours, days, of resentment and fatigue, of thinking that I never signed up for the deal that says my husband is free to pursue his career single-mindedly while mine takes a backseat to domesticity.

"Will you be home for dinner?" I ask, already knowing the answer.

"Don't know. I'll try. But I doubt it. Call you later." He kisses me and hugs the boys on his way out.

"Come on, guys. Let's get ready. Whose turn is it to wear the red sweatshirt?"

"Mine," they yell simultaneously. I chase them out of the bedroom. It occurs to me that I have another option for lunch that could yield more information about Lydia.

* * *

It's my morning for nursery-school car pool. The school is on the way downtown. Today I can relax a little, knowing I'm not, as usual, playing beat the clock to get to work. Before we leave, I call Jill Browner at her office. It's eight o'clock, but she's already at her desk. Lunch is a good idea, she says, but tomorrow works better for her.

In the car, I mull over what I want to ask Jill tomorrow, mentally tuning out the Beatles tape that the twins choose every morning over the protests of their fellow car poolers, Zoe and Greg. "Mommy, Paul sings the slow songs and John sings the fast ones, right?" Max asks.

"Sounds right, but you better check with Daddy. He's the expert."

"This song is so, so silly. Life is not very short. Life is very long," chimes in Zach.

"Actually, honey, it only seems long because you're a kid." He ignores me, but I'd feel remiss not pointing it out. "Hey, Greg, please stop touching Zoe's seat belt. You know it upsets her."

"I'm not touching *her,*" protests Greg, already an accomplished liar. Even Aaron, who rarely faults any child, no matter how devious, calls him, behind his back, Greg Harvey Oswald.

"Okay, we're here. Let's everybody look for a parking spot." I pull into a tight space and help the kids out of their cumbersome car seats and safety belts. Guiding the children through the crowded lot, I grab two of them in each hand while carrying the nutritious snacks, a bag of peanut-butter crackers and cheddar goldfish. I'm trying to redeem our good name. Last time it was our turn to bring snack, Aaron absentmindedly let the boys pick out chocolate milk-boxes and Oreos. We received a tactful but stern note from Mrs. Edson, informing us that the other parents didn't share our liberal view of "nutritious."

"It's a good thing the boys start kindergarten soon. We've

offended the rice-cake crowd," I told Aaron. "Don't you know chocolate is a major stimulant, worse than cocaine? Get ready to be snubbed at birthday parties."

As I hand Mrs. Edson the bag, I notice she checks the contents before thanking me. The boys are too engrossed with their trucks to look up as I wave good-bye.

Maybe a caffeine jolt will activate my brain. Leaving my car parked in the school parking lot, I cross the street to Quartermaine's. The commuter crowd has thinned, and the line's short, mostly mothers and babysitters with strollers and small children. I take my double-skim latte to the black-marble counter, rummaging around my leather backpack for a small notebook and a pen. *Jill,* I write, and underline it.

That's as far as I get. The letters between Lydia and Rob keep intruding into my thoughts. How could my best friend and my brother keep secrets from me and for so long? Why? My anger is bubbling up, but I'm not sure it's justified. After all, weren't Lydia and Rob entitled to have a relationship without sharing it with me? Except it seems so sneaky that they kept it from me. Am I oversensitive or were they duplicitous? I should sort out my own feelings before I confront Rob. I'm not ready to talk to him about it yet.

It's funny how I don't shy away from confrontations over insignificant things—the dry cleaner's failure to remove stains, a stranger cutting ahead of me on the movie line or lighting up in a no-smoking section. Yet, if someone I care about hurts or disappoints me, I brood in silence for days, sometimes weeks. I wonder if the hectic pace of my life these past several years has spun me into oblivion, where I no longer have a clue about most things going on around me—Lydia's depression; her long, secret romance with Rob; who knows what else.

No, that line of thinking is not going to help me figure out anything. I open my little notebook and compose a list. The very first item: Coach Roger McCaffrey.

* * *

The catty remarks about Lydia and the coach have been replaying in my head since I overheard them. If Roger and Lydia were close, she may have confided in him. For all I know, maybe Lydia was having an affair with him. Just another secret in a long list of them.

My game plan calls for paying Roger a visit, which happens to dovetail nicely with my intention of spending more time with Colin. After school, I call Colin and offer to pick him up after his next practice —Thursday at six he tells me—and bring him over for dinner.

"That sounds like a lot of trouble for you, Aunt Claire. I can make myself a sandwich."

"It's not any trouble. We'd love to see you. Please say yes."

"Sure, that would be fine. Dad already told me he couldn't pick me up after practice. He has some charity dinner and won't be home until eight-thirty."

"So how were you planning on getting home?" I hate the thought of him walking into an empty house, with no one to eat dinner with, unless the housekeeper happens to be working past her usual departure time.

"It's not too far to walk, less than a mile. And someone would have offered me a ride. Or Coach McCaffrey would have except . . ." His voice trails off.

"The coach would drive you home except for what?" I prompt.

"Oh, it's nothing."

"Okay, forget it. You don't have to tell me anything you don't want to." I'm curious, but if I don't respect Colin's privacy, he'll pull away.

"So, I'll see you Thursday. Want anything special for dinner?"

"Whatever you're making is fine. See you."

Am I imagining it, or was he in a hurry to hang up?

Later that night, washing dishes alone—it was nine-thirty, but Aaron wasn't home yet—I remember the stash of unread letters from Jody to Lydia in my room. Might as well read those, too, for a laugh. They weren't likely to contain any explosive secrets and, besides, I never liked Jody much. I didn't have the slightest twinge of guilt about reading her letters from long ago. I used to get the feeling that Jody was secretly plotting to turn Lydia into her best friend, but wasn't smart or interesting enough to attract Lydia's full attention.

The postmark on the first letter is July 3, 1978, the summer we were fifteen. I was away that summer, working at Camp Silver Birch in the Berkshires, the camp that I used to attend as a child.

Dear Lydia:

We just arrived at our cottage a few days ago. I tried to call you to say good-bye a few times, but there was no answer. I hope you're enjoying the summer so far. Is summer school boring? I bet I know the answer.

My cousins are already driving me NUTS. I'm not sure how I'm going to be able to tolerate spending the whole month in this dinky town, with nothing to do, except take care of the little brats in my family. Even if my aunts are paying me. Why my family has to keep having these family reunions in the Catskills is beyond me. At least my Dad and uncles only have to be here on weekends; they get to live at home during the workweek.

I'm taking my cousins—ages five, eight, and ten—swimming now. Please write. Miss you.

Love and XXXs,
Jody

I never corresponded with Jody, but it didn't surprise me that Lydia did. Lydia sometimes defended Jody when I called her a moron, or ridiculed her for being boy crazy. The only time Jody paid any attention to me was when Rob and his friends were around, then she really sucked up. I haven't thought about Jody for decades, and her letters remind me why.

The letter brings me back to that summer long ago. Up until a few weeks before I left, going back to Camp Silver Birch with a few of my childhood friends seemed like a great idea. We were all going to be counselors. Staying at home held little appeal. Rob was going to be gone practically all summer, anyway, working as a lifeguard in a beach resort on the Jersey shore owned by one of his friend's uncles.

No wonder my mother urged me to take the camp job. She and Dad had the house to themselves for two whole months. To sweeten the deal for me, probably because she was nervous I might change my mind and ruin her own plans for peace and quiet, Mom offered to bring Lydia along with us when we drove to Cape Cod after summer camp.

It sounded like an ideal summer. But then, in June, I started going out with dreamy Johnny Lucci, a tall, dark track star in Rob's class. I had a crush on him for months, and dropped a few not-so-subtle hints to Rob. Finally, Johnny asked me out. I adored him and didn't want to be in the Berkshires, out of his orbit.

It was too late by then to change my mind. I had made a commitment to Camp Silver Birch and to my camp friends. I also had pangs about leaving Lydia, who was going to summer school to take driver's ed, and helping her parents in the bakery.

Jody's next few letters are equally dull. Her ill-behaved cousins, the mosquitoes, the lack of a decent shopping area nearby. Then there's a gushy one about meeting a waiter from a nearby resort and driving around with him at night in his Mustang convertible, sharing a bottle of Mateus wine, and making out. I almost stopped reading out of boredom, but they were right in front of me.

July 20, 1978

Dear Lydia:

I don't think you should feel guilty about flirting with Johnny at the Rec Dance, especially since he asked you to dance so many times. Claire doesn't own him. And she's the one who went away.

Did you hear from Elizabeth? She wrote me that she's planning a pool party for the end of August, the week before Labor Day probably. Johnny is definitely coming, she says, and you're invited. Are you still going away with Claire's family for a few days of FUN AND SUN or did you think of a way to get out of it?

Remember I'll be home the first week of August. We can hang out and go shopping and to the movies. I want to see you as much as I can before your possessive best friend comes back.

Love and XXXXs,

Jody

Lydia flirting with my boyfriend while I was away? It doesn't seem possible. She would never do that to me. Oh, why bother about something that happened twenty-five years ago? Confused Jody probably misunderstood some third-hand gossip. If Lydia had been seeing Johnny on the sly, wouldn't she have confessed eventually? I would have thought so. Especially since Johnny never called me again once he went to Albany for college. But I'm discovering that a few of my assumptions about Lydia and our friendship are just plain wrong.

If Lydia had been fooling around with Johnny, I would have known. Right. Just like I knew what was going on between Lydia and my brother. I must have been really out of it during those teenage years—did I smoke a lot more pot than I remember?

Other hurtful phrases from the letter ring in my head. Why did Jody call me possessive? Was that her word or had Lydia used it in a previous letter about me?

Another thought occurs to me. At the last minute, Lydia did weasel out of going to Cape Cod with my parents and me. She wrote me that she had to stay and help her parents—they had expanded the bakery into the dry-cleaning store next door, and things were a big mess. She said she felt too guilty about going to the beach and leaving her parents with so much cleaning to do. The bakery's expansion wasn't a lie—I'd seen it with my own eyes. I remember how disappointed I was that she didn't come.

Was it all a big excuse just so she could go to Elizabeth's party and flirt with my boyfriend? I tell myself I'm being silly. Lydia was a loyal friend. I think back to all the times she tutored me in math, the time she boycotted Carolyn Schuster's sweet sixteen because I wasn't invited. How she drove me around because she got her license three months before I did and brought me my homework every day the year I had mononucleosis. We all used to flirt with everyone back then. It's not like she would have dated Johnny behind my back.

There's only one letter left. Maybe Lydia stuck up for me or told Jody to go to hell. I carefully unfold the yellow, lined paper decorated with smiley faces.

July 29, 1978

Dear Lydia:

I can't believe he tried to French kiss you after the movies. Maybe he thinks you're as fast as someone else whose name I won't mention. Of course we know that he's fast. The captain of the track team, ha ha.

I can't wait to come home in a few days. I've saved $75 of my babysitting money and want to buy some cool clothes. I'm so glad you'll be around to shop with me. Are you getting a new outfit for Elizabeth's party? Don't forget, he's leaving for college soon—you don't have much time left.

I'll call as soon as I get home. Until then, be good. And have fun, if it's possible to do both. If not, you know which one I'd choose. Gary says he may come to visit me over Thanksgiving. Can't wait to see you.

Love and XXXXs,
Jody

Was I really such a dolt that I never suspected Lydia was fooling around with Johnny, years before her secret romance with Rob? The Lydia of these letters didn't jibe with the teenage Lydia I remember, the loyal best friend.

I lean back on my pillows and close my eyes, thinking.

"Stop trying to know my every thought," Lydia had once yelled at me, slamming the door of my house as she left for home.

Was I overly possessive about our friendship? Or was Lydia just being moody? It wasn't as if we didn't hang out with other kids, or go to parties or have other friends. We just chose each other first, as best friends do.

Anyway, what difference did it make what Lydia did twenty-five years ago? Focus on now, the last five years, why she might have wanted to kill herself. Whatever Lydia's reasons were, they couldn't have anything to do with minor transgressions with my boyfriend, or my brother, when we were teens. Getting up, I take the letters and stuff them in the bottom of my file cabinet, where I'm not likely to come across them again any time soon.

Six

From Bethesda, Jill Browner's office in Gaithersburg, Maryland, is in the opposite direction from downtown Washington, but downtown is my first stop, to check the *Nationweek* library. On my way to my office, I stop to check if Val is in. Her cubicle is dark; she's either on assignment or not in yet. I scribble a note and leave it on her chair.

My hall is pretty quiet, although several people are sitting at their desks as I pass, newspapers spread in front of them. One of my favorite parts of working at a newsmagazine is getting paid for drinking coffee and reading four newspapers a day. I also love how the institution of lunch is sacred, even for the warped individuals who spend two hours working out at the health club across the street.

After checking for phone and e-mail messages, I walk the two flights up to the library. Most writers make research requests over the phone, but I find that I often get better results making a personal appearance. The *Nationweek* librarians, highly skilled at ferreting out information, can be selective about which reporters and editors merit their dedication.

Phoebe, the human speed bump, is stationed at the reference desk. I pretend to study a magazine until Lenny joins her. The three of us exchange pleasantries. I wait until Phoebe answers a phone call to approach Lenny with my request.

"Can you dig up anything on a company called Theragenics Inc.? It's a biotech company in Gaithersburg. *The Washington Post, Wall Street Journal, New York Times,* and *BusinessWeek* should be enough. The founder's name is Jill Browner. I remember reading a small blurb in the *Post* in the last month or two."

Lenny jots down notes. "When do you need this stuff?"

"Really quickly. Like within an hour. Is that okay?" Lenny doesn't know my request is personal since it's identical to hundreds of other requests I've made before.

"Sure, we're not busy now. I can sneak it in right away. I'll call you when it's ready."

"Thanks, Lenny."

I take the stairs to my office to wait. I stare at my telephone. Its silence seems accusing, as if I'm slacking off in my quest for answers about Lydia's death.

Generally, given a phone and enough time, I can find the answer to practically anything. It's simply a matter of trial and error, of plugging away, of tracking down the right experts.

Persistence, not genius, is what distinguishes the truly successful reporters from the rest. It's the daily commitment, the choice, repeated over and over again, to make that one extra phone call, to pursue the long-shot tip that, ninety-nine times out of a hundred, isn't going to pan out.

This persistence, to which I aspire, is not particularly endearing when carried over to my personal life. Aaron calls it old-fashioned stubbornness and extols the virtues of giving in gracefully once in awhile. But then, Aaron's never spent four hours on the phone tracking down the sold-out playhouse Allison desperately wanted for her fourth birthday; or invested eight hours, a full workday, in contacting china dealers to find the serving piece his mother hoped to add to her long-discontinued pattern.

If you ask me, other people give up way too easily. People sometimes tell me they couldn't call when they were in Washington because they lost my number. As if they couldn't dial 411 or look up my work number in a copy of *Nationweek*. Old friends act surprised when I call to announce I'll be in Tulsa or Detroit for a few days on a story, can we get together? "How did you find me?" they ask in disbelief, as if they work undercover for the CIA or belong to the Witness Protection Program. I love phone directories. They are so full of information. Sometimes, in idle moments, I thumb through them just for fun.

In fact, unlike *Nationweek*'s younger staff, the tech whizzes like Thomas, I'm still more at ease with old-fashioned digging than searching for information on the Internet. Thomas, I've noticed, would just as soon not talk to anyone if he could find some fact on the web. Not me, at least not yet.

I'm adapting, of course, to modernity and electronic reporting. I don't want to be one of those old-time reporters who wouldn't give up her manual typewriter for personal computers when her publication switched to new technology.

And, like practically everybody I know, I've fooled around with Internet directories to see if I can track down old acquaintances and lost loves. I can. Not that I ever followed up and actually contacted the person. It's one of the curses of the Internet—how quickly you can find most people. I have no wish to contact Jody Hoffman, but I bet I could find her within half an hour. Or less. She's probably signed up with one of those high-school-reunion web sites.

Lenny calls back almost immediately, interrupting my reverie. The clips are ready; I can leave. I shut the lights off in my office, wishing that I weren't on this particular quest.

The low, redbrick office-complex housing Theragenics Inc. is indistinguishable from dozens of other biotech companies with headquarters in the industrial parks off Route 270 in Gaithersburg. Proximity to the National Institutes of Health, government agencies like the Food and Drug Administration, and several universities, as well as affordable office space, makes Gaithersburg a mecca for low-budget startups.

Jill's directions are precise and I find the building so easily that I'm twenty minutes early. Rush hour is long over, but I usually overestimate the distance from Bethesda to Washington's outlying suburbs. It's a form of self-preservation: Why remind myself that a brand-new, bigger house with a dry basement would cost hundreds of thousands less if we lived another ten miles outside of Washington, D.C.?

The security guard eyes me suspiciously as I study the directory on the lobby wall. Jill Browner, Chief Executive Officer, is listed above a bunch of other names. I take the elevator to the second floor. The reception area is well lit but empty, except for a young lab assistant sporting a gold hoop in his left ear, his white coat covering jeans and a T-shirt. He leans over the front desk, retrieving keys to the men's room, and looks up as I enter. "Hello. May I help you?"

"I'm Claire Newman. I'm here for lunch with Jill Browner. But you don't look like the receptionist."

"Well, uh, we don't have one anymore. Self-service. But I'll call Jill." Apparently informality is part of the Theragenics culture. He picks up the phone and relays the message. It sounds as if he's speaking directly to Jill, not to an assistant. "She says to take a seat. She'll be out shortly."

I look through the magazines on the coffee table (no *Nationweek,* but no *Time* either, only a few worn issues of *Science Trends* and *Smithsonian*). The office is eerily quiet. Curious, I walk to the corridor behind the front desk and stand on my toes to peer through the entryway down the hall. Most of the offices in the corridor are dark. It's not a holiday week, so everyone couldn't be on vacation. Must have been a recent downsizing. The carpet under my feet is spotted with grime; apparently, no vacuum has touched its surface in weeks.

This is not the bustling company I envisioned from the newspaper clips I'd read; they hadn't mentioned any major cash problems. However, those articles were short, a few paragraphs announcing that, despite rumors to the contrary, Theragenics, Inc. was not going to be acquired by a huge, unnamed pharmaceutical company after all. No mention that the failed deal might have precipitated a financial crunch.

As soon as I sit down again, I hear footsteps. "Claire, hi, sorry to keep you waiting. I had to finish a conference call," Jill apologizes.

"No problem. I'm early anyway. Good to see you." I peck her cheek. "How are you?" It's a silly question. She looks terrible: eyes ringed by dark circles, pasty complexion, stringy hair. Dressed in a series of fashion don'ts: a shapeless sweater tucked into baggy olive corduroys, no belt, her brown loafers could stand some polish.

"I'm okay. I've been better."

I steer her through the door. "You can tell me about it at lunch. Where to?"

We take my car. Jill directs me to a dingy diner a couple of miles away. I pick at wilted iceberg lettuce salad topped with rubbery tomatoes, thankful that I didn't order coffee. Jill's looks as sludgy as her sweater.

"Jill, your office looks kind of deserted. What's going on?"

"It's a long story. I'll give you the abridged version." She rubs her eyes. "We're on the verge of a major breakthrough. A gene therapy for Alzheimer's disease. Two drug giants, one Swiss, one American, were recently very interested in acquiring the company. For big bucks." She sips her coffee.

"The money would be nice, of course. But what really counts is that either of those deals would bring a huge infusion of capital," Jill says.

For as long as I've known her, Jill has disregarded material comfort and possessions.

"Your grandmother died of Alzheimer's, right?" I remember Matthew telling me about it.

Jill nods. "Before she got sick, she was loving and sweet. She used to cook special food for me, bring me breakfast in bed, take me to the movies. By the time she died, she was a different person. Mean. I was her only granddaughter but she didn't know me from the night nurse."

Jill looks so downcast I change the subject. "So, which of these companies are you going to choose?"

"I'd be lucky now if either of them still wants it."

"What do you mean? What's happened?"

"Oh, Claire, everything is such a mess now. At first, everything was humming along," Jill says. "Morale was through the roof; everybody from lab assistants and secretaries were planning how to spend the bonuses they would get when the sale went through. While the rest of them were calling travel agents and car dealers, I started to study our lab data to prepare for meetings with the bankers. I mean really study it. I found something terrible." She pauses to swallow her food.

"My senior researcher had been slightly fudging his results for at least a year. I panicked. The only person I could turn to was Matthew. You know, he's helped me financially over the years. He owns a chunk of stock and he's on my board."

"Oh, he owns stock?" I ask, not mentioning the copy of the stock certificate Lydia had mailed me.

She gulps more coffee. "Not that I needed anyone to tell me what to do. I fired the researcher, and started redoing the data myself. I'm pretty sure I can replicate his results honestly. But it takes time. Lots of time. I barely eat or sleep anymore."

"What a mess. Did you have to tell both companies, and they pulled out?"

"No, that would have ruined everything. First I tried stalling, saying I needed more time to come up with a fair price. The Swiss company dropped out. The Americans agreed to push our negotiations back a few months. But then, someone, I can't figure out who, went to the company and said that the lab results couldn't be replicated. They said the results were false and I was orchestrating a cover-up."

"Wow. So they pulled out of the deal for good?"

"Within hours. Devastating. That company thinks I'm unethical. All kinds of rumors are flying. Some of my long-time investors pulled their money out. And reporters began sniffing around. Not you, of course. I know we're speaking as friends."

"Absolutely," I say. "This is completely off the record."

Her company nearly in ruins, Jill had been forced to lay off three-quarters of the staff. "Everyone's mad at me—the ones I had to let go and the ones who are still working. Money is really tight. I can't even afford paper clips."

"How long will it take you to redo the data?"

"Six months, maybe more. I'm pretty sure I can replicate the results. The problem is: Will anyone believe me?"

"What an incredible story," I say.

"Claire, it's not a story. It's my *life*. I let everyone down, my employees, Matthew, the rest of my investors. And, worst of all, Lydia."

"Lydia? What do you mean?"

"Well, I feel responsible for her suicide."

"How . . . ?"

"Don't you see? I kept going to Matthew with my problems. He spent a lot of time trying to help me. I think he was so preoccupied with Theragenics that he didn't notice that Lydia was getting worse. And Lydia was probably upset by the financial hit they would take if my company tanks. It all contributed to her precarious mental state."

"Did Matthew say that?" I ask.

"No, of course not. Matthew says I'm being ridiculous, that Lydia's death had nothing to do with me. But you never know what sends someone over the edge."

"Jill, Matthew is right. You're not responsible for Lydia's death. But I'm sorry to hear you're in such a bind with your company."

"Look, I didn't mean to bore you with this. I know you want to talk about Lydia. And I do, too. I'm racked with guilt. Sorry to dump this all on you. I thought we could help each other deal with our grief. Instead, I'm going on about my own problems. Please forgive me."

"No problem. Really. So, do you think it was the researcher, the guy that you fired, who blew the whistle? To get back at you?"

"He says he didn't. And I have no proof, but it had to have been him. Hardly anyone else knew what was going on. And he was pretty angry at me when he left."

"Why would he falsify the results? Especially if you can get the same results honestly?"

"He was overzealous, most likely. Couldn't wait. He's in his early thirties, impatient for fame and money. He likes to live it up, take girlfriends to fancy hotels in New York for weekends, that kind of stuff. He's immature, but I thought he was a good scientist. It's my own fault. I gave him too much freedom in the lab. I'm not a good manager."

"So, this big drug company, which one is it?"

"I can't tell you. I'm being lawyered to death, here and in New Jersey. They told me not to discuss it with anyone, including friends and family. I can be sued."

I pretend not to notice her mention of New Jersey. Obviously, the company is based there. That narrows it down, but not by much. I try another tack. "So, this guy—what did you say his name is—where is he now?"

"Chris? I hear he is trying to get a job at the National Institutes of Health. Good luck. I'm not about to give him a glowing reference."

"Chris what?"

"Chris Klarman," Jill says.

"With a *C* or a *K*?" I ask.

"*K*. Claire, why are you asking for these details? You're not writing a story. We're just talking. Aren't we?"

"I know. I'm just curious. Asking questions is force of habit." I take a few more bites of soggy salad. "You know, Jill, I wanted to call you so many times. I'm really sorry I didn't. Maybe together we could have helped Lydia."

"What happened between you two, anyway? Lydia wouldn't talk about it. All Matthew ever said was that you guys had some kind of falling out. I missed you at their parties. Not many people there I could relate to. Eventually, I stopped going so much myself."

"There was no falling out; Lydia withdrew from our friendship. And now that she's dead, I'm trying to find out why she would kill herself. It just doesn't make sense to me."

"I know. I used to talk to her a lot. She was depressed, but I had no idea it was so bad, so hopeless. Such a shock." Getting the normally reserved Jill to talk today is like turning on a tap. She rambles on about Lydia, Colin, and Matthew.

"Jill, besides you, Chris Klarman, and Matthew, who else at Theragenics knew about the problems with the data?"

"No one."

"Any chance Matthew went to the drug company?" I say, thinking out loud. Maybe Jill and Matthew were closer than I thought, or were fooling around. The thought is almost absurd. Jill is such a straight arrow, she's practically asexual. And it's hard to imagine Matthew being more attracted to disheveled Jill than to sensuous Lydia. He was crazy about Lydia.

"Matthew? That's ridiculous. Aside from being my best friend, he's highly invested in the company. Financially and psychologically. I couldn't have formed the company without him. He owns 30 percent of the stock outright. He stood to make a million, maybe more, on the deal. And, without the deal going through, I probably won't be able to pay him back now for years."

"Pay him back? What do you mean? I thought he got stock in return for investing in your company."

"He made some personal loans over the years, too. Plus he brought in a few outside investors. This sorry episode doesn't exactly make him look like a hero."

"Outside investors? Like who?"

"A few of his rich doctor friends. You know how doctors like to dabble in investments. But they trusted Matthew. And he trusted me."

"Jill, did Lydia know what was going on at your company?" I ask.

"Not much. Matthew might have mentioned they were about to get a windfall or something. But she wasn't interested in the details of their investments. She left it to him. He was pretty worried more recently about her mental state. I thought he was exaggerating about how bad she had gotten." Jill looks stricken. "You know, she was really the only woman friend I had. I really miss her."

Jill looks so forlorn that my heart goes out to her. Lydia could be a great friend, when she felt like it, with a gift for empathy. I, on the other hand, love to dispense advice, but am impatient when people don't act rationally or fail to follow my advice. Still, the concept of girl talk between Jill and Lydia seems like a stretch. What in the world did they talk about, if not science or Jill's company? Surely not clothes or decorating or pop culture. Sex? Somehow, I can't picture it.

"How about some pie? I feel like I haven't eaten in days." Jill seems in no hurry to get back to the office.

"Go ahead. You could use the calories. I'll get some tea."

I wait until the waitress slaps a slice of gluey apple pie and a pot of tepid water on the table. "Jill, I want to ask you something. I hope you don't think I'm gossiping. I'm trying to get a fix on Lydia's state of mind, on what could have driven her to suicide."

"Go ahead. I know how tight you guys used to be."

"I always thought Lydia and Matthew had the perfect marriage. Had things changed?"

Jill concentrates on her pie, avoiding eye contact with me. "It's funny. Matthew and I talk a lot, but mostly about business or health care. He loved her. And he'd sooner jump from the Washington Monument than hurt Colin. But, yes, I guess, he did spend a lot of time away from home, working, playing golf, that sort of thing."

"One more thing. I know you need to get back. When was the last time you saw Lydia?"

"That Sunday afternoon, hours before she died. We had a tennis date at her club. She called that morning to cancel. She was tired from the medication and thought she might be coming down with a migraine. I stopped over to check on her that afternoon. Matthew had taken Colin to Little League, and then he was leaving for his meeting on the Eastern Shore."

"Was she depressed?"

"Claire, I can't tell you how many times I've thought about this. She seemed a bit down, but nothing out of the ordinary. She was tired, sure, and complaining of dizziness. But those are common side effects of the antidepressants she was taking, those MAO inhibitors. And in the few hours between our phone conversation and my visit, she had baked a lemon pound cake. My favorite. Does that sound like one of the last acts of a suicidal person?"

"It sounds like Lydia." I feel a pang, remembering the home-baked chocolate-chip cookies Lydia once bestowed upon me.

"You know, I never got to tell her something very important. I'll always regret that."

"Do you want to tell me? Maybe it will help?"

"Why not? I've already poured my heart out about everything else." She pauses for a few seconds.

"About three years ago, I was thinking about adopting. Marriage didn't appear to be in the picture and I wanted a child. I was scared that I couldn't raise one alone, though, especially with my career. When I talked it over with Lydia, though, she was great, really supportive. She said I could do it, that she'd help me. She offered to babysit, teach me how to cook, whatever it would take."

"I can see her saying that," I say.

"You know, Claire, she said something that has stuck with me. Something I think you already know. That no matter how important your work is, no matter how much you love it, it's nothing compared to how you love your child."

"So what happened? You didn't adopt."

"I changed my mind. Work got crazy for a few months, and then I decided I wasn't cut out for motherhood. I didn't want to jeopardize my progress on the gene therapy. Now I'm forty-two and my career is coming apart. I have no life to speak of. I wish I had taken Lydia's advice."

"It's not too late. You're only forty-two. Plenty of women our age give birth or adopt children."

"You're kind to say that. But it's too late," Jill says. "We better get going."

She looks desolate, but she manages a small smile. "Claire, thanks for calling me for lunch. We should do it again soon."

I pull into the parking lot of Allison's school. She's standing near the wooden bench talking to friends, but she picks up her backpack, a private signal that she sees me. I'm under strict orders that bar honking.

"It's three-fifty. You're five minutes late," she scolds, slamming the door.

"What happened to hi, Mom, thanks for picking me up? How was your day?" I pat her head lest any spies are lurking nearby. "We have plenty of time. Your appointment isn't until four-fifteen." We're headed to the hair salon.

"My day was okay. The usual boring stuff. Aerobics was good. Can I sleep at Eleanor's Friday night?"

"I think it's our turn to have her. But either way is fine. Whatever her mom prefers."

"Now remember, this is a trim. If they cut off too much, I'm going to be very, very mad. At *you*." Allison hates to disturb one strand of her thick auburn hair for purposes of cutting or combing.

"I'll stand over Lauren and watch. Like last time. I promise."

She clicks on a Patsy Cline tape, conversation over. When no one is looking, she's an affectionate child. At night when I tuck her in, she puts her arms around me and whispers that she loves me.

This particular hair salon in northwest Washington caters to kids. It has a juice bar in the back and a small television screen installed near each chair. As Allison is whisked away for a shampoo, I sit in a chair, trying not to be overwhelmed by the fumes of hairspray and fruity smelling products. I don't open the old, dog-eared copy of *People* that's in my lap. Instead, I think about Jill and Lydia and the choices we make. Lydia's dead. Jill's on the verge of financial ruin, but she may wind up discovering a cure for Alzheimer's, and winning a Nobel for Medicine. For the moment, anyway, I'm glad to be sitting in an overpriced hair salon for overindulged children, waiting for my daughter.

SEVEN

Cradling my coffee mug, I stare out the kitchen window, enjoying the rare moment of quiet. The kids are in school; Trini's in the basement tackling laundry; Aaron's in Cleveland. Aaron. I grab the phone on the fourth ring, seconds before the machine picks up.

I can tell from his hello that he's tired and cranky. I attempt to humor him. "Hi, honey. What's wrong? Trial not going well?"

"I was up until three last night. And we're going to lose."

"You always say that. And you never do. Well, hardly ever." He has lost two cases in the last year, which to him constitutes a streak.

"I can't really talk now, but I wanted to check in. Everything okay?"

"We're fine. Aaron, I've been thinking. I'm starting to get a funny feeling about Lydia's death."

"What you mean a funny feeling?" Aaron asks in a tone I don't like.

"Aaron, I'm your wife, remember? Not a witness on the stand. There's something I found out before you left that I meant to tell you about. And it may be significant." I summarize the contents of the letters between Lydia and Rob.

His voice becomes gentler. "Wow. That's quite a secret, all right. Have you talked to your brother yet?"

"Not yet."

"Claire, I don't know what you're thinking, but those letters have nothing to do with her suicide. I'm sure she didn't kill herself because she has secretly been in love with Rob for most of her life. Matthew's a pretty good catch, you have to admit, for a non-Newman."

"No, I don't think the letters explain anything more about her suicide. Really, Aaron. If every forty-year-old woman who had second thoughts about choosing her husband as her life's mate killed herself, there wouldn't be enough moms in Bethesda to start a book club or drive a car pool. The letters are just an aside. I'm thinking maybe Lydia's death wasn't suicide at all." Then, I drop the bomb. "Maybe Lydia was murdered."

You'd think I'd said I was communing with Lydia's spirit via Ouija board. "Claire, honey, get a grip. The strain is getting to you. Stop obsessing about Lydia's suicide. It's making you crazy. Go back to work. Do something. Maybe you should find a therapist to help you through this. I'm sorry I'm out of town now. I thought you were okay, but obviously you're not."

"Aaron, don't patronize me. Please. I know it sounds nutty. I'm just poking around a little. I'm not doing any harm. I'm just asking a few questions, following a few leads. Really, I'm fine."

"Is your theory based on anything solid, any evidence you saw at the house that morning, something the police might have missed?"

"No, it's more like intuition."

"Claire, you're not making sense. Lydia killed herself. End of story. Why would anyone murder a nice suburban housewife? She wasn't turning tricks or running a cocaine-smuggling ring. Or do you think Matthew knocked her off for insurance money like in the movies?"

"I'm not suggesting Matthew murdered her. Anyway, he has an

alibi. We both know he was out of town that night, on the Eastern Shore." Matthew had stayed at an inn in scenic Port Chatham, Maryland, on the Chesapeake Bay, where he was participating in a medical conference the next morning.

We had covered this ground before. Lydia died sometime during the early-morning hours. Colin didn't know that when he had left for school. Their household custom was for Matthew to wake up Colin and give him breakfast, allowing Lydia to sleep in, because she often had insomnia. Although she told Colin repeatedly that it was fine to wake her in the mornings, Colin preferred to get his own breakfast and let his mother sleep.

Thank God he was so considerate. The thought of Colin finding Lydia's body is too painful to contemplate.

"Claire, gotta go. My client's buzzing me. Call you later. Listen, I know you must feel betrayed by what you found in those letters. How about waiting a few days to call Rob, until you've had a chance to think things over?"

"I'm fine. Don't worry about me. Just focus on your trial," I reassure him, careful not to react to Aaron's parting reminder that I know as much about investigating a murder as I do about astrophysics.

"One last thing. Maybe we could bribe Trini to work this weekend. We could go to that inn in West Virginia for one night. I'll be finished here Friday afternoon," Aaron says. If he's offering to whisk me away for a weekend, after five days away from his kids, he must really be worried about my mental health.

"I'm fine, Aaron. Really. We don't have to go away. The kids will want to be with you this weekend."

For a minute or two after hanging up, I consider Aaron's logic. The medical explanation for Lydia's death is sound: She died from ingesting large quantities of wine, cheese, and other foods that interact harmfully with her antidepressant, Nardil, a monoamine oxidase inhibitor. This class of drugs works by blocking the action of a chemical substance known as monoamine oxidase (MAO) in the nervous system. Lydia knew that certain aged or fermented food or drink with a high tyramine content, like cheddar cheese, Stilton, Chianti, or other red wines, are poison when mixed with MAO inhibitors. Tyramine can cause sudden and severe high blood pressure, which can lead, as it did for Lydia, to a fatal stroke.

Lydia knew what she was doing when she ate those foods, especially in such large amounts. The morning I found her, the list of foods containing tyramine was taped to her refrigerator door, in plain sight. From all reports, she was vigilant about what she ate and drank. Eating those foods was no accident.

No, what puzzles me, what makes me suspect that it wasn't a simple suicide are other things. Lydia not leaving a suicide note. Lydia mailing me the brokerage statement and stock certificate with a cryptic note. Why would she wait until Matthew was out of town to kill herself? She had to figure Colin might come in her room before school and find her. This fact set off the loudest alarm. A mother's first instinct, especially a devoted mother like Lydia, is to protect her child, not inflict severe, lifelong trauma on him.

So, Lydia didn't perfect every detail of her plan. Maybe Aaron's right about me losing my grip. Aaron's firmly grounded, I have to admit, even if he is a little quick to criticize. He's a good mate precisely because he's good at pointing out my shortcomings. I wouldn't want us to be one of those gushing couples that praise each other in public. It's unseemly, like bragging about your children. And it's tempting fate—practically begging the supreme being, if she exists, to wipe that smug smile off your face.

I love my husband. I adore my kids. Naturally I know my kids are smarter, funnier, kinder, and better-looking than anyone else's. I'm their mother. However, if anyone asks, outside of the grandparents, I say that Allison acts like a teenager with PMS, and I worry about the twins' habit of dismembering Barbie dolls—didn't Jeffrey Dahmer do that as a child? Why call attention to what the rest of the world already thinks, that despite occasional setbacks, like stumbling upon the body of my former best friend, my life is pretty damned privileged?

Still, I wish my husband, of all people, expressed more faith in my abilities once in awhile. True, I'm not a detective, but I've been investigating stories for nearly twenty years. Doesn't that count? Sure, what I know about murder comes from reading books, but that's also true about other things I'm good at, like cooking, decorating, and fixing toilets. Reading, then applying that knowledge to experience, is how people learn.

Suppose Lydia was murdered? It sounds crazy, but it could have happened. I've read plenty of mysteries. Toward the end of my pregnancy with the twins I was confined to bed for a few weeks. Watching movies got old pretty quickly, and made me crave popcorn loaded with melted butter and salt, both forbidden by my nervous obstetrician. Val saved me by bringing over an armload of mysteries. I read one a day. Solving a murder boils down to finding who has the means, motive, and opportunity. In other words, who wanted Lydia dead? Who would benefit most from her death? And who would be clever enough to make the murder look like a suicide, without raising the suspicions of the police or getting caught?

What harm will it do if I ask a few questions? If my hunch about murder is wrong—the likeliest scenario—I've lost nothing except time. And, if I'm right? The possibility seems so remote that I fail to think the implications through.

I've brought headphones along on my power walk, but the thoughts in my head are overpowering the Blink 182 tape that Allison had left in the player. I wish I had checked it before I left the house.

If Lydia's death was so suspicious, why am I the only person who thinks so? Except for Sallie, a devout Catholic, but she's not exactly an objective bystander when it comes to her daughter. Silly as it sounds, even before Aaron sarcastically dismissed the idea of

Lydia being murdered, the thought of Matthew as the potential murderer had occurred to me. In these post-O.J. times, who *doesn't* first suspect the spouse when someone dies in a suspicious manner? And spouses are always considered prime suspects by the police. Obviously, Matthew isn't under a cloud of suspicion. He was a hundred miles away at the time of Lydia's death, preparing for his morning meeting. Matthew had mentioned to Aaron, in response to his lawyerly concern about a police investigation, that he had joined two colleagues for a late dinner at the inn, and then shared an after-dinner brandy before going up to bed.

Still, even without his whereabouts that night confirmed by others, I have to agree with Aaron's assessment: Matthew is no murderer. He wouldn't hurt a fly, much less his own wife, the mother of his child. So, if not Matthew, who could it be? Lydia must have had an enemy. Someone she'd pissed off even more than me.

As I walked, I tried to focus on good memories of Lydia, to wipe the distracting thoughts of murder out of my mind. She was such a gracious hostess. I loved the barbecues she used to throw. Although she kept the guest list under a dozen, she cooked for a crowd: grilled chicken or steak, platters of cold salads, blueberry pies. The guest list usually included someone I knew: Jill Browner or Sallie or neighbors. The crowd was more low-key than the lawyers, journalists, and political types I encounter during the week—more doctors, midlevel government managers, and homewives, as Allison likes to refer to them.

For me, the best part of the evening came when everyone else left and I helped Lydia and Matthew clean up. Matthew and I were usually tipsy from polishing off the margaritas or the last dregs of wine. We'd gossip about the guests, discuss political rumors, or critique my latest boyfriend. Until Aaron came into my life, Matthew thought no one was good enough for me.

One summer Lydia and Matthew were house hunting for a vacation place on North Carolina's Outer Banks. Much of our cleanup conversation revolved around the characteristics of the ideal beach house. "Oceanfront, with a big deck for reading and watching the sunset, an outdoor shower, close to a good restaurant or two, and a bookstore. Can't you guys hold out for East Hampton?" I asked.

"Too expensive. And too far to commute on weekends. Or does your fantasy include a private plane?" Matthew had joked.

"Hey, *you're* the rich doctor. I'm just a struggling reporter with a crummy one-bedroom in Dupont Circle."

"Your memories of Long Island summers must be hazier than mine. I remember East Hampton as too many people, too expensive. I like North Carolina better," Lydia said. "Why don't you come with us next weekend to look? Colin would love it. Anyway, we can't buy anything without your stamp of approval."

"Can't. Big plans. Wolf Trap tickets. After the Judy Collins concert, I'm going to break up with Jonathan."

"That's an excuse I can live with." Lydia had met Jonathan once for a drink, long enough for her to conclude that he was hung up on his ex-wife. I didn't agree about the ex, but he was too much work out of bed, and not so great in it. He was annoying, calling to cancel on the dinner party at the last minute, claiming he was too exhausted to be social. No reason to tolerate the Washington one-upmanship game of complaining how weary your important job makes you. As for that important job—chief of staff for the Democratic senator from Louisiana—big deal. The republic would survive even if Jonathan were social once in awhile.

That night, Lydia looked the way I like to remember her, tanned and fit, in white jeans and a red silk sweater, sun streaks highlighting her blond curls, striding purposefully around the kitchen in her red espadrilles, as if a stack of dirty dishes was her biggest worry. I can't conjure her in my mind anymore without thinking of that awful morning, her body as still as a slab of marble, face whiter than her eyelet sheets.

* * *

I arrive at Colin's practice a little before six, and sit in the car until I see the boys leave the field and cluster around the water jugs and sliced oranges. Coach McCaffrey is leaning against a shady elm tree, looking as gorgeous as ever in his sweats and T-shirt, talking to a few players.

Careful not to embarrass Colin by hugging him or talking to him in front of his friends, I walk over to the coach. A few boys are lingering near by.

"Hello, Coach. I'm Claire Newman. We met at the Finellis'. After the funeral." He grasps my extended hand and squeezes it tightly.

"Sure, I remember. You're Lydia's old friend, right?"

"Right." No need to bore him with the full explanation. "Listen, can I talk to you a minute? In private?" I nod at the boys a few inches away.

He leads me a few feet away, almost on the edge of the track. "I was just wondering how you think Colin is doing. He seems almost back to normal already. I'm afraid he's repressing all his grief."

There's an awkward silence before he answers me.

"Boys his age aren't known for expressing their feelings. Especially in front of their friends. He seems pretty good, though, considering what he's been through. I've been cutting him a little slack on the field, but not enough that he'd notice. I don't want him to think that I pity him, or that the rest of the team does either."

"I'm sure that's wise. I guess you know him pretty well. And Lydia, too, I understand." His face is flushed from running, so I can't tell whether he's blushing.

"Lydia was a big help, like many of the other moms. You know, bringing snacks to the games, driving car pools to the away matches, that kind of thing." He starts walking back to where the boys are.

I follow him, taking large strides to keep up. "Oh, I thought you two were good friends." My tone is light, nonjudgmental.

"Sure, we talked sometimes about stuff. But I hadn't spent much time with her lately. I'm not sure why."

"The reason I ask, Roger, is that I was so shocked that she committed suicide. I wanted to know if you noticed any unusual behavior in those last few weeks?"

"I didn't really see her except at games, so I wouldn't know. I guess she seemed depressed, now that I think back. But . . ." He stops. "I hope you don't mind, but I have to give the boys some instructions for Saturday before they run off." I wonder why he seems so ill at ease in my presence. I'm not hitting on him or flirting or anything, like some middle-aged soccer moms probably do.

"Of course. But what?" I tug on his elbow as I walk faster to keep up with him.

He hesitates before answering. "Well, you know, I used to hear the mothers talking a lot on the sidelines. Some of them made comments, a few times, about, uh . . ."

"About what?"

"Well, she was sort of moody. You must have noticed, being old friends and all."

I'm disappointed. Not much of a revelation. Roger looks pained, probably because he said anything negative at all about Lydia. No one likes to speak ill of the dead. Suddenly, I feel guilty, too. "You seem to have such a good rapport with all the boys. Been coaching them long?"

"No, just a couple of years."

"Oh, I thought you were here longer. Where did you come from?"

He mumbles something about Connecticut. Enough small talk, he must be thinking. "It was nice talking to you. Hope you'll come back to watch Colin play."

"Of course I will. See you soon."

A look of relief crosses his face as soon as he's put some distance between us. Talking to the boys, his body relaxes, as if he's taken a few cleansing yogic breaths. The boys are attentive as he gives them pointers for Saturday's game, and answers their questions. Discreetly, I wait by the tree until Colin comes to get me.

"Anyone need a ride?" I hear Roger yell as we walk back to my car.

"It's nice of him to drive the boys home," I comment, fishing for more information about the coach. "Beyond the call of duty."

"Sometimes he takes us to 7-Eleven for Slurpees."

"Your mom must have loved that. Right at dinnertime. Did she ever stop being the food police?" I hope Colin doesn't think I'm poking fun at Lydia. By mentioning her name, I'm hoping Colin takes the cue that he can discuss her with me, if he feels like it.

"She let up on it a little. But she didn't want me to go home with Roger, the last month or two. Mostly she'd come get me or arrange a ride with someone else."

Was that significant? Maybe a pretense for seeing Roger? Or was there some other reason she didn't want him driving Colin home? I know I may be digging too deep.

"Hey, Colin, do you remember when you were little? Whenever I took you to the park I used to buy you ice cream from the Good Humor truck? Chocolate éclair pops, right?"

"Sure I remember." Colin reaches over to turn on the radio. I can take a hint. We drive the rest of the way in silence.

EIGHT

Once the kids leave for school, I pull out the brokerage records and the stock certificate to study them again. Why did Lydia send these? I stare at the same sketchy facts: As of January 1, the account had a balance of $947,038; as of January 30, the balance was $948,112. I scan the pages again, noticing something for the first time. This must be it. Some business reporter I am. On January 14, six hundred thousand dollars had been withdrawn from the account. By January 19, that sum had returned, which is why I hadn't noticed it before. Perhaps Lydia was more observant. Where did that money go for such a brief time?

Maybe nowhere suspicious. Maybe Matthew had temporarily borrowed funds to cover business expenses. I've heard doctors at cocktail parties grumbling about the delays in reimbursements from insurance companies that wreak havoc on their cash flow. Yet there had to be a reason why Lydia had sent me these records, as "backup."

The money only went missing from Matthew's account for a few days. I can think of one way to find out where the money had gone, but it brings me smack up against a moral dilemma.

I probably have the means to break into Matthew's brokerage

records, if I choose to go that route. Now, it's not much to brag about but, in my seventeen years as a reporter, I've never lied, cheated, or broken any laws to obtain information. Some people, my husband the Eagle Scout, for instance, might say I'm making meaningless distinctions here. The distinction is clear to me: I'm about to take a detour previously outlawed by my moral compass.

Don't get me wrong. I'm no Pollyanna. I never met a good reporter who didn't engage in some shading of the truth. For instance, describing a story in the vaguest, most general terms: "I'm looking into the changing dynamics of the labor market," I might say to a source, who'd hang up immediately if I said I'm working on an exposé of sweatshop conditions in Korean garment factories.

Sometimes, the shading comes from not correcting erroneous assumptions made by someone I'm interviewing. In other instances, as a litmus test of a source's veracity, I ask questions to which I already know the answers. At interviews, I charm and flatter people to elicit telling anecdotes that I later use against them. We all do it.

Breaking into Matthew's private financial records is different, and I know it. Sure I can rationalize: It was Lydia's account, too, and she sent me the records for a reason. Obviously, she invited me to snoop. What choice do I have?

I'm not fooling myself, though. I can opt to mind my own business. I doubt these records are going to shed any light on her death—how could they? Yet Lydia must have sent them to me for a reason. I keep coming back to this fact and it's one that nags at me persistently.

Reluctant to cross an ethical line, I check Theragenics' stock price. I'm curious to see how the stock is doing. Within seconds, I'm on the Theragenics web page. It confirms exactly what Jill told me: The stock price had tanked from a few months ago, down to a mere fraction of its all-time high price six months earlier.

That precipitous drop should have put a dent in Matthew's holdings. Casting aside any pangs of conscience, in I plunge.

First I type in www.KingStrawnInc.com, which takes me to the brokerage's web page. To access Matthew's account, I have to pretend I'm him and answer a few prompts. Birth date, no problem. Social Security number I copy from the front of Lydia's pages and type it in. Password? Hmmmm. I try Matthew's birth date, but no go. Nor Lydia's either. Probably I am only going to get one more guess before the computer signs me off. That's what happens when I mix up my ATM and computer passwords. Two wrong answers and the ATM eats my card. I type in Colin's birth date. Open sesame. The machine whirs and beeps.

I expect Matthew's balance to be down drastically from January, which is the monthly statement Lydia sent. That's logical. Between the Theragenics slide and last month's falling Dow, he's got to be hurting. Aaron has been grumbling that our savings and retirement accounts are low, and we don't have most of our eggs in the risky Theragenics basket, like Matthew. So, I'm shocked to see that Matthew has an extremely healthy balance indeed—nearly 1.6 million dollars. Where did the cash infusion come from?

No clues in the monthly statement I'm looking at. I have to go back and check the records month by month. I pull up the April statement, but it doesn't tell me much. I close it and pull up March.

It's thick, fifteen pages long, and hard to decipher. Without an advanced degree in accounting I'm not sure what to make of it. Hoping to discern a pattern, I'm relieved to see that Matthew owns only four stocks. That should simplify matters. But he appears to end the month with the exact same stocks he started with—so what are these fifteen pages of transactions?

There is a flurry of activity midmonth, when Matthew sold shares of a company called HCC Inc. HCC's price fluctuated wildly that month, from a high of forty dollars per share to a low of twenty dollars per share, taking a nosedive right after Matthew sold fifty thousand shares. At least that's what it looks like.

Something else catches my eye as I scan the statement. Matthew owns one hundred thousand shares of Theragenics, which confirms what the stock certificate already told me. I trace the transactions relating to Theragenics for the month of March. Unfortunately, there are none. Zip. In fifteen pages of trades, not one share of Theragenics bought or sold. The price of Theragenics plummeted in March—from ten dollars per share on March 1 to five dollars per share on March 31. It appears that Matthew lost a bundle on Theragenics in just one month.

That's odd. Matthew's no fool. He had to have seen what was coming. Why wasn't he smart enough to unload Theragenics before its descent?

I study the other stocks in the account. They sound high tech: BioVest, T3Cell Partners, and HCC Inc. Matthew owned a thousand shares of HCC at the beginning of the month. Then he started selling heavily, at ten thousand shares a clip. Wait a minute, now I get it. He owned one thousand shares and sold five lots of ten thousand. Obviously, he was selling HCC short.

Am I reading the statement wrong? Oh, who cares? None of this stuff has anything to do with Lydia's death. I'm positive. Why waste my time? I'm about to sign off in frustration when years of ingrained, conscientious recordkeeping kick in. Before I give up, I print out Matthew's monthly statements from February through May and stuff them in a file in my desk drawer.

On the premise that, when one door slams shut, another one opens, I remove the *Montgomery County White Pages* from the cabinet. I'm really at a loss about what to do next, but my reflexes tell me to do what a reporter always does: Follow up on what I have until I get enough information to go down another path. Also, when I reflect on my lunch with Jill, it occurs to me that perhaps she was so nervous and overly chatty because she was hiding something. I'm grasping at straws again and I know it.

Only one Christopher Klarman, at a Rockville address. My map is in the car. No point calling first, he'd probably tell me not to come.

Chris Klarman lives in the kind of townhouse community favored by affluent singles. Located a few miles off Rockville Pike, a congested but convenient strip of shopping malls and restaurants, the development appears to have been built during the 1980s real-estate boom. The row houses are attractive and well kept, with standard amenities such as a swimming pool and tennis court adjacent to a central courtyard. I park next to a shiny black Saab.

I knock on 6A and the door opens immediately. "Oh, I'm expecting a pizza," says a man with blond hair and a babyish face. He wears gray sweats that accentuate his compact, muscular build. Probably a wrestler in high school.

I hold out my hand. "My name is Claire Newman and I'm looking for Chris Klarman. Sorry I don't have any food."

"Can I ask why?" His voice is soft. He opens the door wider, but doesn't ask me in.

"Look, I'm not a kook who goes around knocking on strangers' doors. I'm on a personal mission. Matthew Finelli's wife, Lydia, was my best friend. You may not have heard, but she committed suicide a few weeks ago."

"Yeah, I heard. Sorry. But I can't help you. I've met Matthew a few times, but I didn't know her." The door is six inches from my face and moving closer. "Where did you get my name, anyway?"

"Jill Browner mentioned you. Chris, please let me come in for five minutes and explain. I'll leave as soon as your pizza comes. I promise. I'm sure your parents didn't raise you to slam doors on women. Even women reporters." I flash a smile.

He's sizing me up. My petite, unthreatening appearance is an asset in this line of work. Otherwise intelligent people often believe that red hair and freckles on a grown-up are outward signs of naiveté. "Okay. Five minutes. But, like I said, I didn't know Mrs. Finelli. Though I have met her son. Colin. Matthew brought him to the lab a few times on the weekends. We played video games on my computer."

"Well, I'm Colin's godmother. Lydia and I grew up together."

He leads me into the living room, removing a stack of newspapers, three empty Heineken bottles, and dirty gym socks from the black leather sofa. "Have a seat."

"I know this sounds farfetched, Chris, but I have reason to believe that Lydia's suicide may have been connected, in an obscure way, to the failed acquisition of Theragenics. So, I have a few questions." This explanation sounds incredibly lame. I wonder if he knows I'm bluffing, that I have no idea what I'm looking for, or how he can help me. I put on my most confident smile. Some women reporters subscribe to the belief that looking the part of a damsel in distress elicits sympathy from male sources, but I've always rejected that as sexist and demeaning.

He winces. "Hey, don't lay that on my head. I feel bad enough already. I screwed up. And I said some dumb things to Jill, things I didn't mean. But this lady's death, it's not fair to blame me."

"Listen, I'm not saying what happened to Lydia was your fault. Not at all."

"She was upset about the money, right? The Finellis would have made a bundle." He looks pained. "So, what do you want?"

"Just this one thing. Did you go to the drug company and tell them about the data?"

"Look, I don't see what any of this has to do with Mrs. Finelli." I wait him out. "I know Jill thinks I did. But I didn't. Like I said, I respect Jill. She's a supportive boss. None of the bullshit games and power plays that go on in other labs."

He sounds sincere. "Chris, if it wasn't you, do you have any idea who might have done it?"

"Beats me. None of us wanted the deal to evaporate. Some of us had already spent our bonuses." On leather couches and brand-new Saabs, no doubt.

The doorbell chimes. "That's my cue. I promised to leave when the pizza came." I walk to the foyer with him and wait while he pays the deliveryman.

"Chris, thanks. I'm not suggesting Lydia's death was in any way your fault." Which is true. I'm not sure myself whether Lydia's death was even a suicide. "Really. I think the reasons people kill themselves are complicated, and based on years of suffering, and rarely have to do with money. Enjoy your lunch."

He puts down the pizza box. "I'll walk you to your car. My mom taught me manners." He's offering me three more minutes to extract information.

"Chris, how well do you know Matthew?"

"Not very well. He hangs around the office, but mostly with Jill, not us flunkies. We've talked, had some beers, bounced ideas around."

"So, he knows a lot about Theragenics?"

"Uh-huh. He really understands what the gene therapy will mean for the commercial market. You know, until his wife died, I thought he was a very lucky guy: the private practice, the Porsche, the country club."

"Lucky. Yeah, me, too." We're at my car.

"Look, when you see Jill, tell her how sorry I am. Not that I expect her to forgive me in this lifetime." He looks me straight in the eye. "I didn't tell anyone about the data. Why would I? It only makes me look even worse."

"I'll give her your message. I promise." I adjust my seat belt and drive off. My visit with Chris has surprised me. He's not what I expected. He's likable. I understand why Jill trusted him. If I had to guess, I'd say he's telling me the truth. But, if he didn't tell the pharmaceutical company about the cooked data, who did?

NINE

The kids won't let Aaron out of their sight all weekend, which is standard behavior after he's been gone all week. And he's planning to leave again on Monday. In an entirely accidental display of cooperation, the three of them collapse early Sunday night, worn out from our two-hour bike ride in Glen Echo Park.

Aaron finishes tucking them in and joins me in the kitchen, where I'm cleaning up the remains of Chinese takeout and starting to pack tomorrow's lunches. "You know, hon, it would be more efficient if you made fifteen sandwiches every Sunday night and froze them. Then you could pull three out every morning. They would defrost in their lunch boxes."

"Thank you, Mr. Efficiency Expert, but your children wouldn't eat previously frozen peanut butter and jelly. And I wouldn't either. Besides, this only takes a few minutes. And it spares me the worry that twenty years from now they'll be telling their therapists that I was so preoccupied with my career that they had to eat soggy sandwiches."

The truth is, I enjoy the mundane domestic chores of motherhood—packing lunches, shampooing hair, reading bedtime stories.

Aaron wraps his arms around me. "That's why I love you. That overdeveloped sense of responsibility."

I hug him back. "This knife is sticky, but it's sharp. Watch it."

Aaron brings a cognac bottle and two glasses to the couch and we curl up, my feet in his lap so he'll take the hint and rub them. "Wait. I can't relax yet. I'll get the snifters. I hate drinking good brandy out of juice glasses," I say.

"Picky, picky. But sit. I'll get them. You relax."

It's so cozy. For all of five minutes. Then, I bring up the ever-so-sore subject. "Aaron, I want to talk to you. About Lydia's death."

"Claire, listen to me. I've been thinking about this. You've got to accept that Lydia was troubled. That's all. There's nothing mysterious about her death. This other stuff you say you've discovered—her secret relationship with Rob; her flirtation with a young, handsome coach; no suicide note—they don't mean anything. All they prove is that Lydia was dissatisfied with her life. Her very comfortable life."

"Well, why did she send me those financial documents then? Do you think she suspected that Matthew and Jill were having an affair?"

"She probably had an investment question. That's all. You're a business reporter, a good one, and she knew it." Aaron's tone is patient, but I can tell it's taking some effort. "Who knows? Maybe she and Matthew were having marital problems and she wanted to know how much they could afford if one of them moved out. It could have been anything or nothing."

Aaron's calm reasoning makes me feel a tad foolish. Maybe he's right and I've become unhinged from the shock of finding Lydia's body, from realizing that our friendship is, finally, irrevocably, over. I could drop the whole thing, my entire silly investigation. The lure of putting Lydia's death behind me, of taking a week or two off work to read novels, play with the kids, or plant tomatoes in the garden, is almost irresistible.

Almost. I just can't ignore my intuition that there's more to Lydia's death than everyone thinks. Something only I'm capable of finding out.

"Look, you're probably right, but I'm going to spend a few more days poking around anyway. Just to satisfy my curiosity. I admit I'm thrown by her death. If you want me to, I'll talk to a therapist, too. It couldn't hurt."

Aaron looks relieved. "Good. I'll worry less if I know you're getting some professional help." I'm glad peace has been restored. We stay downstairs cuddling before we go to bed. Impending business trips have a way of focusing the libido.

I dress carefully to achieve a casual look for my appointment with Karen Kline, caterer to the high and mighty with undeveloped taste buds. Linen pants and jacket, sleeveless cotton T-shirt, low-heeled sandals. Tall, skinny Karen, with her artfully highlighted shoulder-length blond hair and the cheekbones of a runway model, makes me feel as squat as a fire hydrant, and every bit as glamorous.

Yesterday, desperate for a pretense to visit Karen—another thread to follow that may not lead anywhere—I hired her to cater a dinner party for five couples next month. She has no idea I normally wouldn't dream of hiring her. On the rare occasions that we entertain, I like to be the chef. Also, from what I've sampled of her catering, frankly, I'm a better cook.

I had explained: "I've been so upset about Lydia, I just don't have the energy to plan and prepare a dinner and cook, but I don't want to cancel, either. I owe everybody who's coming."

"Claire, believe me, I understand. I usually need more notice, but under the circumstances, we can fit you in."

"What circumstances?" I ask.

"I mean as a fellow friend of Lydia's," Karen said warmly. I can't remember why I never liked her much, and thought she was cold. Maybe she's been a nice person all along, and I was too jealous of her closeness to Lydia to notice. Karen offered to discuss menus and prices with me over the phone but I asked to come over. If I'm going to shell out hundreds of dollars for a mediocre meal, I want to increase my odds of obtaining a few choice crumbs of information.

Karen runs Capital Cuisine from her house, a white-brick colonial that looks larger than the Finelli's modified ranch across the street. I follow Karen down the carpeted stairs to her home office. Her long legs are encased in slim, black stretch pants. A pearl-gray cotton sweater, low-heeled black mules, and a thick silver bangle complete her elegant outfit.

Her basement kitchen has been upgraded with restaurant-quality equipment, with an eight-burner Viking stove, dual Sub-Zero refrigerators, and yards of pink-flecked granite counters. We perch on leather bar stools at the counter, a stack of menus between us.

"How about a cold drink?" she offers. "It's so hot and humid I can't believe it's only April."

"I know. I'd love a drink, thanks. It seems like we missed spring altogether this year. From snow days to summer."

She pours Pellegrino water into tall iced glasses and expertly slices a lime into paper-thin circles. "I saw you and Aaron at the funeral, but Randy and I left without talking to anyone," Karen says. "I hope you didn't think we were rude."

"No, of course not. It was an emotional day. We left quickly, too."

"I heard you found the body. I was kind of surprised." She hesitates. "I thought you and Lydia weren't friends anymore."

"We hadn't seen each other for awhile, but she had called me recently. What about you guys? I guess the four of you were pretty tight."

"We were. Our husbands became friends first and, for years, Lydia and I tolerated each other because we were neighbors and our husbands had a lot in common. Eventually, we discovered we actually liked each other. We had been talking about her working with

me, part-time, helping with the cooking, but it never happened."
Karen looks downcast.

"Lydia was a good cook. Not that she ate," I say.

"I know. Her eating was getting worse. There were so many
things she couldn't touch because of her medication. She was
scrupulous about it." I feel a sudden bond with Karen, who, like me,
is choking up. We sip our water.

"Karen, you know how she died, right?" She nods. "Does it strike
you as strange?"

"It did at first. But not Randy. He says that sometimes patients
who take MAOs—that was her type of medication—try to test the
limits by eating some forbidden foods. Sometimes they go too far."

"That doesn't sound like Lydia, does it? She obeyed the rules."

Karen nodded. "I know. It's strange." She reaches for the menus.
"Have you looked at these?"

We discuss appetizers and desserts. I keep the selections simple—less room for error—and brace for the total price. It won't
occur to Aaron to ask how much a catered dinner party costs, and
I'm not a proponent of full disclosure of household expenses. My
paycheck allows me to discreetly pay for luxury items (like clothes
for me and the kids) with price tags that would send Aaron into
orbit. Karen names a figure.

"Are you sure that's right? It sounds low." It's almost a bargain,
hardly more than I would have spent on raw ingredients.

"I give discounts to friends," she explains. "Twenty-five percent."

I find myself liking Karen more and more every minute. "That's
really nice of you, Karen. Thanks." I put down my glass. "Do you
mind if I ask you something? About Lydia?"

"Go ahead."

"The last few years I didn't see her much, as you know, but I
don't understand why I hardly ever ran into her by accident."

"You mean at Whole Foods or Blockbuster?"

"Exactly." With a population of about a hundred and forty thousand, Bethesda is still essentially a small town: a series of neighborhoods, loosely bound by elementary schools, soccer leagues, karate and dance studios, churches and synagogues. Residents fancy themselves as unique individuals with discerning tastes, but nothing could be further from the truth. We're a bunch of lemmings, shopping at the same stores, eating at the same restaurants, seeing the same movies, and ferrying our kids to the same allergists, orthodontists, and swimming coaches. As a result, we meet each other coming and going.

For instance, my most common errand route is a five-block strip that includes a supermarket, drug store, bagel shop, Thai restaurant, coffee bar, and dry cleaner. This strip is the modern equivalent of the general store: Everybody passes through, taking a few moments out of busy routines to chat, arrange play dates and tennis games. There are people I know by sight, simply from years of standing behind them at the checkout line or taking showers in the stall beside them in the pool club's locker room. Yet, in five years, I ran into Lydia only a handful of times. I couldn't understand it, unless Lydia had become a complete recluse and resorted to having her groceries and dry cleaning delivered. She was such a tightwad that I doubt that was the case.

"Lydia was becoming more and more isolated. She and Matthew hardly ever ate out, or invited people over. Once in awhile, I'd talk her into going walking with me. Sometimes Matthew and Colin went to a movie or out to eat. You know how she was. She'd rather go without than enter a store." Karen smiles. "Not me. I run errands ten times a day. With three kids and a business, who can avoid it?"

I ask about her daughters, eight, twelve, and fourteen.

"They're pretty freaked out about Lydia's death. Especially Julia. Although she hardly ever talks to Colin anymore. The boy–girl thing, you know."

Karen jots a few notes about my order in a leatherbound notebook. "I'll call the week before to finalize the details. In the meantime, call me if you have any questions or if you change your mind about anything."

"Thanks again. Karen, just one more thing. Would Randy mind if I call him? Aaron thinks I should talk to a therapist, to help me over the trauma. Do you think he can refer me to someone?"

"Are you kidding? He knows every shrink in town. He'll be glad to. I'll mention it." She clasps my hand. "Thanks for coming by. It's nice to see you again." She walks me upstairs to the door. "I understand how you must feel. I miss Lydia, too."

Has Karen undergone a personality transplant or did I have her pegged completely wrong? She's not the least bit cold or snippy. I'm ashamed of the many times I've made snide comments about her catering. If the food for my party is halfway edible, I resolve to hire her again to make up for my badmouthing.

I decide I like Karen, even if she is one of the women Lydia must have turned to as a replacement for me. I can imagine them together, walking or shopping. My mind drifts to a particular excursion with Lydia. At the time, that Saturday-morning outing seemed no different from hundreds of other times Lydia and I had gone shopping. I didn't know then that it would be one of our last shopping trips.

Lydia was looking for a formal dress for a black-tie charity ball. My role, as usual, was to convince her it was okay to spend money on herself.

"I can't buy anything for at least a month. I need to lose another seven pounds first," I said, imagining that she was rolling her eyes. Skinny by sheer force of will, she lacked compassion about my constant dieting. She just didn't get how my best intentions could be derailed by a box of Mallomars.

In the second or third store we tried, Lydia found what she had in mind. A short black chiffon dress with a low neck. I persuaded her to spend a wad on spike-heeled silk sandals, overriding her objections that they made her look like a French hooker.

"You'll be the sexiest doctor's wife at the party. It will take everyone's mind off colitis." The event she was going to was a fundraiser.

"Do you get dressed up for any event that isn't tied into a disease?" I asked her. "But then why shouldn't doctors worship diseases? Without them, they'd be living in a split-level in Beltsville, worrying about the payments on the Ford Explorer. Like the rest of the world."

As we walked to the car, Lydia smiled, but I could tell her mind was already somewhere else. She looked at her watch. "We should be getting back soon. I'm not sure we have time to stop for lunch. What do you think?"

"I think we need lunch. You'll be home by one-thirty." Is it only in retrospect that it seems I had to cajole Lydia into spending time with me?

Now that we've established a tentative rapport, I'm eager to delicately feel out Karen to see if she knows anything about Lydia and Roger. I decide to wait a few days, until I can call her with some party detail without seeming like a pest. Then, I can sneak a question or two into the conversation. Luckily, I don't have to wait that long. The next morning, as I walk out of Starbucks with my tall iced latte, Karen walks in.

"Claire! It's good to see you," she says, pecking my cheek. "I was going to call you in a few days for a final head count."

"I'm still waiting for the last two couples to call back. I'll let you know by the end of the week. Hey, want to sit down for a few minutes after you get your coffee?"

She glances at her watch. "Sure, I have about fifteen minutes before my haircut."

"I'll save us a table outside."

Once she sits down, I know there's no time to waste. "Karen, something has been bothering me for awhile. When I was at the Finellis', after the funeral, I overheard two skinny blond women gossiping. They were talking about Lydia and Coach McCaffrey having a 'very close' relationship."

"Streaked hair, lots of jewelry?"

I nodded.

"That would be Pauline Taylor and Carol Stewart-Taylor. They're sisters-in-law. Not my favorite people, nor were they Lydia's."

"Do they have sons on Colin's team?"

"Yes, but don't pay any attention to what you heard. I think they were vying for some of the coach's attention and didn't like any competition." She leans over and whispers. "I'm being as bad as they are, I know, but I've heard rumors about Pauline and her personal trainer. I think she goes for young, hard bodies."

"Did Lydia ever say much to you about her friendship with Roger?"

Karen dismisses my question. "Nothing romantic was going on between Lydia and the coach. If they were engaged in the slightest flirtation, I'm sure Lydia would have mentioned it to me."

Don't be so sure, I think to myself. Lydia had a few secrets. "Roger says Lydia hadn't talked to him much lately, and she seemed depressed."

Karen consults her watch, and sighs. "You're full of questions all the time, aren't you, Claire? I really have to run. Talk to you soon." Grabbing her paper cup, she walks quickly down the street.

As I throw my empty cup in the trash, I wonder briefly what sent Karen on her way so quickly.

There's a phone message from Karen the next morning, when I get back from walking. Another detail about the dinner, no doubt. I call her back.

"Claire, I'm sorry if I seemed rude yesterday at Starbucks." She pauses. "Listen, there's something I know, about the coach and Lydia. I didn't think I should tell you. It didn't seem right. But, after tossing and turning all night, I'm going to trust you."

I weigh the risks of having her change her mind again. "Karen, I'll be over in ten minutes." I grab my keys. I'm a mess, but a shower and fresh clothes will have to wait.

Karen looks a little pale when she opens the door. "I'm really glad you called me," I say softly. I follow her into the den and we sit opposite each other in the plush, velvet club chairs.

"Claire, you have to promise me that this will go no further than this room. It's the kind of talk that destroys people's lives if it's put in the wrong hands."

"Of course. You can trust me." I lean toward Karen. In an instant, the words spill out.

"It happened about six or eight weeks ago. Lydia came over one evening, extremely agitated. She said she had to talk something over with me but, first, I had to swear I wouldn't tell anyone. We went out to the deck, because I didn't want the girls to overhear or interrupt. From the way Lydia looked, I knew it was serious."

"Something happened with the coach that afternoon?" I prompt.

Karen nods. "Lydia had gone to Colin's school for some PTA planning thing, and on the way out remembered that Colin had forgotten to bring home directions for that Saturday's game in Poolesville. She was driving a whole bunch of boys there. It was almost six, but she thought maybe she could catch him. He stayed late a lot, catching up on paperwork and stuff."

Patience is not my best trait. I wish Karen would leave out some of the extraneous details.

"Roger's office door was closed, but Lydia thought she heard him talking inside. She figured he was on the phone. So she waited, and after a few minutes, she knocked again. No answer. So, she opened the door." Karen leans back and shuts her eyes for a few seconds, as if summoning strength to continue.

"And saw what?"

Karen hesitates. "Lydia said she saw Roger embracing a boy. The boy had evidently been crying. As soon as Lydia opened the door, they pulled away, startled. The boy mumbled something and ran off."

"You mean something sexual was going on, and Lydia interrupted?" I can hardly believe the level of sexual activity that must be going on under my nose.

"Hold on, Claire. I didn't say that. Lydia wasn't sure. Roger started to run after the boy, then decided to give him some space for awhile. Roger asked Lydia to sit down, that he'd explain."

"And his explanation was?"

"He said the boy was talking to him about his parents' divorce, and broke down. Roger said he was comforting him; he put his arm around him, and that it turned into a hug when the boy started sobbing. Roger insisted it was all completely innocent. That Lydia shouldn't jump to any conclusions. And, the thing was, she didn't know exactly what she had seen. Or what to do about it."

"Did she know the boy?"

"Yes, she recognized him. He's an eighth grader."

"What's his name?" I hope Karen doesn't insist on keeping it confidential. I can't help wondering if Karen is telling me everything she knows or is withholding information.

"I may as well tell you. His name is Russell Wilkinson. I know his mother, Alicia Wilkinson, a little bit. She's a friend of a friend in my book club."

Sometimes I think I'm the only woman in Bethesda, if not the United States, who isn't in a book club. I remember Aaron's rejoinder to my lament: "Middle-aged men have affairs. Women join book clubs." He may actually be on to something.

"So, what did Lydia do?" A tough call, I had to admit. If she reported what she saw, and even if it was innocent, she'd get Roger fired and permanently ruin his reputation, not to mention his life. On the other hand, keeping quiet about potential sexual abuse, from a middle-school gym teacher, no less, is an equally horrifying situation.

Karen sighs. "We went over it again and again. Lydia felt pretty sure it had been innocent. The boy's parents are having a bitter divorce—we knew Roger wasn't lying about that. And Lydia said she couldn't fathom the other possibility, not about Roger. He was so concerned and caring about the boys, she couldn't imagine him acting inappropriately or hurting them. And she believed Roger wasn't gay or in the closet, or she would have picked up on it."

"He sure seems hetero to me. I would bet on it," I say.

"Me, too," Karen says. "But that wasn't the point. The thing we kept going back to was: What if we were wrong? What if he really was touching Russell? What if there had been past incidents, or would be future ones?"

"So, what did you tell her to do?"

"What I would have done. Call the boy's mother, tell her what I had seen, and leave it up to her to decide whether to take it further."

"Did Lydia listen to you?"

"Finally, after agonizing for a few days. She said she would watch Roger like a hawk, even though she believed him. The whole thing made her very nervous."

It would make me nervous too. "That sounds fair. What did Alicia think?"

"She thought Lydia was overreacting to what she saw. Alicia said Russell confided in Roger, and that they trusted him completely. Russell was going through a rough time and she was grateful for Roger's help. Then she called Lydia back and said she mentioned it to Russ. He went ballistic. He said Lydia was a nosy busybody and if Lydia or Alicia said anything bad about Roger to the principal, he'd run away. And never come back. The other boys would tease him, he said, and the coach would get in trouble and be mad at him."

"So, it ended there? Lydia must have been relieved."

"Not quite." Karen frowned. "Roger got really mad at Lydia for telling Alicia. He said Lydia knew him well enough to trust him, and how could she think the very worst of him and not expect him to be hurt? They had words over it a few times. He called her on the phone, too, to check whether she was going to call the principal or had told anyone else. Lydia thought he should have understood her position better. I agreed with her. She did the right thing, what any responsible mother would do."

"Did they ever make up?"

"Not really. Although they were in touch because Roger kept calling her, checking on whether she had told anyone." Karen looks guilty. "Of course, Lydia denied telling anyone else about it. Besides Alicia, I mean. And I'm the only one she told. And now you know."

"Do you think Alicia discussed it with anyone?"

"I doubt it. She's completely preoccupied with fighting her husband and talking to her lawyer. That kind of nasty divorce really saps time and energy."

"In the end Lydia believed Roger. Why?"

"He convinced her and in the end she believed him absolutely. She really couldn't imagine him as a bad guy, despite her initial doubts. That's why I hesitated to tell you about it."

Maybe Lydia *didn't* trust Roger absolutely. Maybe that was why she wouldn't let Colin ride home with him after practice, and why she went to all those practices and games herself, to keep an eye out.

"Karen, do you think this incident could possibly have had anything to do with Lydia's death?" I'm thinking aloud.

"No, of course not. Sure, it bothered Lydia a lot that Roger was mad at her, but I don't see how that could have made her depressed or led to her suicide," she went on. "You know, Claire, thanks. I feel better unloading to you."

I get up to leave. "Don't worry. I won't tell anyone. Thanks for telling me. I agree it probably had nothing to do with Lydia's death."

Yet, despite my assurances to Karen, I'm not so sure at all.

The more I thought about what Karen said, the less I trusted my ability to sort it out. I had to discuss it with someone. Around ten, I finally call Val.

"Sorry to call you so late. Are your kids asleep?"

"Just barely. What's up?"

Without using any names, I repeat what I've learned from Karen.

"Wow. It's really more exciting in the 'burbs than I thought. So, what do you make of it?"

"Oh, Val, I'm so confused. What if Roger really is a child molester? Maybe he killed Lydia as a way to shut her up."

"Does he strike you as that kind of guy?" Val asks.

"No, not really. He seems like a nice jock-y sort of guy. Not really smart enough to plot a murder and make it look like a suicide."

"Well, if Lydia believed he was innocent, don't you think he probably is?" I'm not sure what to think. I wonder if Val secretly thinks I'm losing it, but is too loyal to say so. "Maybe. Thanks for listening."

I promise Val that I'm going to relax, stop thinking about Lydia's death for the rest of the night, and try to get some sleep. It's not as easy as it sounds.

TEN

here's a message for you near the phone," Trini says.

It's from Sallie. I dial, amused that she left her phone number in Holly Dale, as if I could ever forget it. I must have dialed it at least a thousand times.

"Hello, Claire. Hoped this was you. I just mailed you a copy of the autopsy report. Nothing in it looks unusual, not to an old lady, anyway. Maybe you'll find something." Sallie sounds more like her old self. "I was in Washington for a day last week. I meant to call, but I had to rush to catch the last shuttle." She lowers her voice. "Something else has come up. Did you know you were still Colin's legal guardian?"

"I am? Are you sure? I assumed they changed that years ago."

"I asked Matthew. He says Lydia was adamant, refused to name anyone else. By the way, Matthew wants to give you some of her jewelry. So, what's up? Find anything yet?" Her tone is light.

"Nope. Not yet. But I'm working on it." I hope she can't tell I'm holding out on her. Lydia always claimed that Sallie was a witch, with supernatural mind-reading powers. "You know, I still have trouble accepting that her death was a suicide."

"Tell me about it. It's all I think about," Sallie says.

I don't want to hang up too abruptly, so we chat about Colin and Matthew, their new housekeeper, my plans to spend more time with Colin. "Claire, with a little effort on your part, I think he'll open up to you. He still feels close to you on some level. He keeps a lot to himself, but he feels everything acutely. Like his mother."

"I'll try my best, Sallie. I promise. Call you in a few days. Take care."

It's curious that Lydia trusted me as Colin's guardian long after she stopped speaking to me. I dial Matthew's office, surprised that he comes to the phone so quickly.

"Claire, I've been meaning to call. Thanks for giving Colin dinner the other night. He enjoyed it. What's up?"

"Can you and Colin come to dinner tomorrow night? Nothing fancy. Trini's a very basic cook." That's putting it mildly. We eat lots of rice and beans and stewed chicken. On work nights, given a choice between an overcooked meal already prepared and a good meal I have to cook myself, Trini wins every time.

"I'd love to, but not tomorrow. I have a late surgery."

"If you're not going to be home, can I pick Colin up? Around four? Then he won't have to eat alone."

"Sounds great. I worry about him rattling around the house by himself when the housekeeper leaves. She's great, but she can't stay past six or seven because she has her own kids. I'll call you back if there's a problem. Claire, next week, why don't you and Aaron join me for dinner, without the kids? It will give us a chance to have a good talk."

"Sounds fine to me. Aaron's out of town, but he'll be back for a few days next week. How about Wednesday? You can bring Colin to our house to stay with Trini and the kids while we're out. If he wants to, that is."

Our conversation is natural, as if we never stopped speaking, as if the five-year gap never occurred.

"Claire, one more thing," Matthew says, as if it's an afterthought. "I don't want to make a big deal out of this, but I understand you've been going around asking people questions about Lydia. Why?"

I try not to sound defensive, wondering if he means Sallie, Jill, Karen, or all three. "I'm pretty thrown by Lydia's death, Matthew. I guess I'm trying to come to terms with it, in my own way. And my way generally involves asking people questions."

"Brenda Starr, girl reporter," he teases. "I get it, but I certainly wouldn't want you to subject Colin to any unpleasant memories, if you know what I mean."

I keep my resentment in check. Obviously, Matthew is far too bereaved to be thinking straight. "No, of course not, Matthew. You know I'd never do anything to hurt Colin."

"Right. I do know that. Well, I've said my piece. Look forward to seeing you. I'll stop by to pick Colin up on my way home tomorrow night. Around eight, okay? Oh, I have some of Lydia's jewelry to give you. I'm sure she'd want you to have it."

I'm not sure at all, but I hold my tongue. "Eight's fine. Take your time. See you tomorrow."

Colin was just a toddler when Lydia and Matthew asked me to be his guardian. I was flattered and surprised. For years, Lydia had teased me about my adolescent lifestyle—my nocturnal schedule, messy apartment, and makeshift meals.

"We want to ask you something serious," Matthew said during a Sunday-night dinner, bringing in the brownies and coffee. I'd just put Colin to sleep by reading *Goodnight Moon* four times while Lydia and Matthew cooked.

"No, you can't fix me up with another nerdy resident. I don't care how many brownies you ply me with. Forget it."

"Fixing you up with Stuart was Matthew's idea. My hands are clean," Lydia reminded me. "And Matthew swore on a stack of Bibles that he was good-looking."

"If I were you, Matthew, I'd look both ways before crossing, and avoid dark alleys. God may have something planned." Actually, Stuart wasn't hideous looking, if you could get past his body odor, which I couldn't. Someone with years of medical training ought to know enough about personal hygiene to take a shower once in awhile.

"Anyway, this is something else," Lydia said. She explained that they were drawing up wills because they were going to a medical convention in Los Angeles, then on to Palm Springs next month. It was going to be their first real vacation since Colin was born; Sallie was coming to babysit.

Of course, they didn't have many options in the guardian department. Neither one of them had siblings. Sallie was in her fifties; Matthew's parents, based in Arizona, were pushing seventy; and Matthew and his father barely spoke. Lydia and Matthew had other close friends with children, but none to whom Colin was as attached. "What it comes down to, Claire, is that you're the only suitable guardian as far as all three of us are concerned," Lydia said, bestowing a hug upon me.

"I'm honored. I gladly accept. That is, if you're sure my lifestyle is appropriate for raising a child. Some of your married friends might make better parents," I teased, trying to deflect emotion. "I assume your house and cars come with the deal? And a trust fund for Colin's education?"

"You won't have to worry about money. But, before you run up your credit cards, remember we're young and healthy. We plan to be around for a long time. Unless the plane crashes," Lydia said.

Lydia and I were barely thirty; Matthew was thirty-two. None of us believed in our own mortality. That night, in a gesture of my maternal responsibility, I scrubbed Lydia's pots and pans until they were shining, instead of leaving them to soak overnight in her sink, my usual practice. Until the following year, when Colin was hospitalized after a severe asthma attack, I didn't give a thought to being his mom on deck.

* * *

Lydia called me from Georgetown University Hospital one morning, her voice hoarse from crying. Colin had a virus, nothing major, or so she and Matthew thought, until he woke up wheezing and retching in the middle of the night. He couldn't catch his breath. They had wrapped him in a blanket and sped to the emergency room, where doctors gave him a shot of steroids to open his bronchial tubes, and medicated him with a nebulizer until his breathing stabilized. He was out of danger now, but the doctors wanted to monitor his reactions to various medicines. I had never heard Lydia sound so rattled. Sallie was already on her way from New York. I offered to leave the office right away to come to the hospital, but Lydia urged me to stay at work. "Okay, I'll leave around four, and bring dinner for us."

When I had arrived, armed with sandwiches and sodas, Lydia's clothes were disheveled, and her eyes red and swollen. Colin was hooked to an IV, pale but sleeping. Sallie was looking ragged, too, sitting on a chair, staring at her grandson.

"He looks fine, thank God," I say in my most reassuring voice. He did look fine, except for the raccoon circles under his eyes, accentuating his skin's whiteness.

"He just crashed for a nap. The medication was making him bounce off the walls. And he goes nuts any time a nurse comes near him with a needle. The doctor says not to expect him to sleep too much, so he'll probably wake up soon." Lydia shuddered. "Actually, it was such a relief to see him running around."

Sallie got up, smoothing the sheets, arranging flowers in a vase, refilling the water pitcher.

"Where's Matthew?" I asked.

"He's tracking down the pediatric pulmonologist for lab results," Sallie answered.

I hugged them both. Then I led Lydia to a chair and handed her a turkey sandwich. "First eat, then tell me about it." I gave Sallie the bag. "Help yourself, turkey or roast beef."

"You're so thoughtful," Sallie says. "Always there in a pinch."

"Hey, I love this kid, too." I'm not as calm as I look. Merely walking into a hospital and seeing sick people makes me queasy, not because of any traumatic childhood event. I'm just a sickness wimp. "Lydia, why don't you let Sallie drive you home for a shower? I'll stay here in case Colin wakes up."

"No, I can't leave him."

"You're not leaving him for long. I'm here. And Matthew is somewhere in the hospital, right? I'll page him the second Colin wakes up."

"Come on, Lydia. Claire's right. You'll feel better after a shower. We can be back in an hour," Sallie said firmly.

When they left, I pulled the chair next to Colin's bed and held his little hand. "Don't worry, little man. Aunt Claire is here," I told the sleeping boy.

Poor Lydia, I remembered thinking. He was so fragile. So vulnerable. How in the world do you keep your kids safe? I didn't have a clue then about the depths of parental terror. I was so smug, so proud of myself merely for showing up with a few bags of food. That was just one of the many things I never got to tell Lydia once I had my own kids. By the next day, Colin was almost back to normal.

I don't have any nieces or nephews yet, although I hope that someday Rob or Aaron's younger brother, Allan, might come through with one or two. Colin is the only child, outside my own, to whom I've ever felt a powerful connection. Generally, I prefer the company of adults. They're quieter, neater, and they can read their own menus. Poor Colin. I've failed him miserably. For the last five years, I've been a stranger to him. Repairing my relationship with Colin is the only part of this mess that is in my power to fix.

I let myself into the Finelli house, and find Colin and his friend Nathan huddled over the computer screen. As soon as they see me, they sign off, and Nathan leaves. Colin gets up, too.

"How about a snack? We can stop at the yogurt store."

"Okay. I remember how you used to take me for treats when I was little. When Mom wouldn't take me to McDonald's and I wanted those junky Happy Meal toys that all my friends had."

Colin looks sad and I feel a twinge of disloyalty for the implicit criticism of Lydia. Long before anyone knew about hereditary fat genes, Lydia had fretted about every morsel Colin ate, as if, at any moment, he would morph into a fat kid, like all her overweight cousins. As soon as Colin had teeth, I began subverting her excessive concern by sneaking him cookies and candy. "Kids need sugar," I would admonish Lydia if she caught me. "He's not going to get fat. Look at him. He's a stick. And look how active he is."

Lydia would tell me that I'd understand when I had my own kids, which didn't turn out to be true. Aaron and I are not too strict about what our kids eat, but Lydia was probably overreacting to Sallie pushing food and sweets on her during childhood.

Colin towers over me now by a couple of inches, Lydia's face on Matthew's tall, skinny frame. His thick blond hair is side-parted, long on top and shaved underneath, with a wedge of bangs drooping over his brown eyes. The little-boy sweetness is gone, but the acne and bad posture, hallmarks of puberty, haven't kicked in yet. The haircut, baggy jeans, and droopy T-shirt can't disguise his natural good looks. Before long, the girls will be lining up, if they aren't already.

"Colin, before we leave I want to tell you something." We're in the car, but I haven't started to drive away. "I'm sorry, terribly sorry, about the circumstances that brought us together after all this time. But I want you to know the reason I dropped out of your life in the first place. It is not because I ever stopped loving or caring about you."

"Then why?" he asks flatly. "You used to be here all the time."

"For reasons I really don't understand, your mom thought it would be better if we stopped hanging around together. That's why you didn't see me for a long time."

"How do I know you won't disappear again?" he asks. "You must not have tried very hard with Mom." His expression is calm, but I can read signs of anger.

Abandonment issues, as the shrinks would say. Who could blame him? "You know, Colin, I did try with your mom. Very hard, but I felt hurt and angry. Maybe you're right that I didn't try hard enough. I'm sorry about that now. Especially if it hurt you."

"Are you still mad at her?"

I take his hand for a few seconds. "Absolutely not. And, you know, she called me a few days before she died. I think she wanted to patch up our friendship. I would have liked that. I promise you, I will never leave your life again. You have my word, okay?"

"Okay." He doesn't sound convinced.

"Let's go," I say. "We can talk more on the way." It might take awhile, but I will prove my staying power to him. No one can fault me for lack of persistence.

In the car, Colin barely responds to my questions about school. "How are your grades?"

"Pretty good. Mostly As." His cheeks flush. He's embarrassed to admit he's a good student. I let him lead the conversation, careful not to push too many questions on him. You can do this, Claire, I tell myself.

We sit on a wooden bench outside the yogurt store, licking our cones in companionable silence. I dive into the second part of my prepared speech. "Colin, it's important to me that you understand how I feel about you. I want you to know that I love you and I am here for you. If you need anything, if you want to talk about your mom, or anything else. Even though we stopped seeing each other, your mom was my best friend for a long time and I loved her very much. We were like sisters. And, a long time ago, I promised both of your parents that if anything ever happened to them, I would be there for you."

Poor word choice. "I don't mean that anything bad is going to happen to your dad. But sometimes it's easier to talk to adults who aren't your parents. So, I'm here. Unless it's about math homework. Then, I'm useless. Aaron could help you with that. Okay?"

He nods. I feel an urge to buy him something. "Do you need school supplies or anything at the drugstore before we go to my house?" Allison asks me to take her to CVS at least five times a week.

"No, thanks." We get into the car again. "Aunt Claire, there is one thing. I don't want to bother Dad about it. Mom had a cool camera and Dad says I can have it. But it's broken, jammed or something, and I don't know where to get it fixed."

"You're in luck. One of my closest friends is a terrific photographer. I'll ask her the best place to bring it. In fact, let's go pick the camera up at your house now, so I can take care of it right away."

"Thanks, Aunt Claire, but there's no rush. It can wait. I just like to fool around with the camera."

"No, let's get it now while we're thinking about it. We're only five minutes away. And, if you're interested in lessons, we can ask my friend Val. She really knows what she's doing. Pick out a tape. They're in the glove compartment."

"All I see are these dumb kiddy tapes and folk songs. Oh, here's some Beatles. Are they yours?"

"They used to be. Now the twins own them." His house is only three songs away. Hardly enough time to contemplate the vast difference between Colin's life and that of my own coddled offspring.

Aaron and I often worry that we try so hard to protect our children that they'll grow up lacking resilience, and will be unfit to cope with any setbacks. In our household, running out of cream cheese for your bagel is considered a major catastrophe. Allison has been known to fall apart over such heartbreaking situations as our family vacation in Disney World conflicting with the date of a friend's birthday party.

"Life is full of tough choices," I tell her. "Get used to it."

Glancing at Colin, the baggy shirt dwarfing his narrow shoulders, all I see is his vulnerability. Reaching adulthood with a better perspective than my children on what's worth crying about seems a small consolation for his loss.

Colin runs inside and re-emerges with the camera. When he climbs into the front seat again, he removes something from his jean pocket. "Aunt Claire, here's the credit card Dad gave me to use when he's not around. To pay for the repair."

"Don't worry about the money. I'll take care of it."

Colin looks downcast. I've hurt his pride, treated him like a baby. "Colin, I'll tell you what. Keep the credit card in case you need it for an emergency, which is what your Dad intended. I'll copy down the number. If the camera store will charge the repair to the credit card, we'll be even. Otherwise, you can pay me back." He brightens as I copy down Matthew's American Express number and expiration date in the small leather notepad I keep in my purse.

We drive in silence, listening to the Beatles. From the driveway, we can hear the boys yelling in the backyard. Trini is watching them climb the jungle gym. I tell her she can stay outside with the kids, I feel like cooking tonight. Allison is down the street at Eleanor's, which is just as well. No need to overwhelm Colin. While Colin and the boys play tag, I start dinner. Aaron will be late again and I'm planning to eat with the kids. Trini's in the yard, but I can't help looking out of the bay window, watching them play.

The boys are lying on the grass resting when Allison gets home, flinging her leaden backpack on the kitchen table. "Please bring that upstairs, honey. Then, go outside and say hello. Rescue Colin from the boys."

She's hanging back, suddenly awkward. "Or, if you don't want to go outside, set the table." It works. She joins the boys.

Allison's quiet at dinner, but not Zach and Max, who are revved up from their argument over who gets to sit beside the honored and very cool guest.

"Here, I'll move my plate between you guys, okay?" Colin suggests.

Zach dominates the conversation, asking Colin questions about baseball, another of his passions. I clear the table.

"Colin, I have a good idea. We can play Junior Monopoly until your Dad comes to get you," Max suggests.

"Sure, we can play for awhile," Colin says kindly. He's grown to be such a nice, gentle kid. He seems to be exerting a positive influence on my children; for once, Allison participates instead of mocking her brothers and their "baby" games.

"Colin, I'm going to sit on the porch and wait for your dad. Come out when you feel like it," I say, grabbing my wineglass and heading for the wicker chairs.

A little while later, Colin joins me. The twins are engrossed in a video game; Allison's instant messaging her fourteen closest friends. "Thanks for being such a good sport, Colin. The boys just worship you. It's no wonder. Allison ignores them as much as possible."

"It's fun. I like being here. The noise and everything."

His comment reminds me of something Lydia used to say. "When your mom was a kid, she liked my house better, too. For the same reasons. My brother and his friends were pretty loud. There were always people around, and music blaring on the stereo. I spent half of my childhood looking for a quiet corner to read in. I thought Lydia was lucky to be an only child."

"It's not all it's cracked up to be."

"I think I knew that even then." I restrain myself from clasping his hand, hearing Allison's voice in my head: "Why do you have to be so huggy and kissy? Give me some personal space."

As I hear the crunch of Matthew's tires against the gravel in the driveway, I make another date with Colin. "How about coming over for the afternoon a week from Saturday? Do you have time to help Allison practice before her big soccer match?"

Colin watches Matthew walk around his sports car toward the house. "Sure, Aunt Claire, that's fine. I already told Allison I'd help her."

ELEVEN

Dr. Randall Kline has a cordial yet efficient phone manner. Yes, he can fit me in for a few minutes between patients this morning. "Karen briefed me and I have some names of therapists who specialize in bereavement issues," he says.

Bereavement issues. That's what makes me edgy around shrinks, all their jargon. Randy's office is on Massachusetts Avenue near the Dupont Circle metro. Following his precise directions, I take the elevator to the eighth floor and wait in the small reception area. Not a bad magazine selection. No *Nationweek,* but plenty of glossy shelter magazines. A few minutes later, a woman in sunglasses emerges from the office, looking down as she passes me to avoid eye contact. Seconds later, Randy emerges.

"Claire, please come in. Nice to see you again. Sorry, of course, about the circumstances," he says, extending his hand. Do psychiatrists learn how to make their voices soothing during medical school? Or is a reassuring voice a form of self-selection, driving doctors with nasal, whiny voices into specialties like anesthesiology or radiology?

Making observations, such as how voices determine careers, was the kind of game Lydia and I used to play on long drives, or when we were just hanging out. One of our classics, hatched in college, was the correlation between a guy's sexual style and his living-room couch. Lydia's initial observation was that a brand-new or flashy couch indicated an indifference to foreplay. Within a few years, we expanded this singular pearl into an exhaustive study of furniture and male sexual habits. The night she met Matthew, she called to tell me he had the rattiest looking plaid sofa she had ever seen, which she took as a good omen. Aaron topped that: The living room of his bachelor apartment contained a coffee table, a stool, and a loveseat. In fact, he inspired our subcategory of "men without sofas."

With his well-appointed office, Randy clearly doesn't fall into that category. The place looks like a professor's study. A professor, that is, with fine taste and family money. The sofa is plush blue chenille, the wing chairs are covered in soft stripes of blue, celadon green, and rose. A watercolor of the ocean dominates one wall. On the opposite wall, behind a Chippendale cherry desk, hangs a row of gold-framed diplomas. The Chinese rug, which covers most of the wood floor in pale hues of blue and green probably costs more than I earn in a year. Apparently, Randy's practice does very well, or he's gone to significant expense to make his patients think so.

Unlike his beautiful wife, Randy is just plain old good-looking: tall and fit with thick, wavy brown hair and a neatly trimmed goatee. His nose has a definite hook, but it's the kind of imperfection I find appealing. Men who are too pretty, too smooth, too interested in their wardrobes, turn me off. Although I wouldn't complain if Aaron expanded his clothing color palette beyond navy and gray.

By the looks of it, Randy's golf games with Matthew are supplemented by more strenuous workouts. His chests and arms are muscular under his woven cotton sweater. His gray flannels hang neatly from his toned frame. He projects healthy self-esteem, but also understatement. Nothing ostentatious that might make his patients feel they're being overcharged to support his comfortable lifestyle.

"You really do have a couch. Are your patients supposed to lie down?" When I'm nervous, I tend to make inane comments.

"I'm not a Freudian. But it is comfortable for my afternoon naps," he says. "Please, sit down." The chair he selects faces a wall clock. Must be force of habit.

"Thanks. My husband thinks I'm taking Lydia's death hard, maybe a little too hard. I have to admit that finding her body was a shock, and I can't get the scene out of my head. I'm having some trouble sleeping. Anyway, my husband thinks I should talk to someone about it. Professionally, that is. I think so, too, of course," I add, realizing I sound like a subservient wife here on my husband's instructions. Which is better than Randy guessing the truth, which is that I'm here to see if I can squeeze some information out of him.

"You seem somewhat reluctant about asking for help," Randy observes.

"You're right. I'm not entirely comfortable about pouring my heart out to a therapist. It seems kind of self-indulgent," I blurt out, without thinking. "No offense, of course. You know, I'm a reporter. I guess I like to control the situation by asking questions, not answering them."

"Why don't I give you a few names and you can think it over? In this instance, going to a therapist is like elective surgery. Nothing bad will happen if you decide against it. You're in charge, which I gather is important to you," he says. I detect no trace of sarcasm in his tone. He hands me a card from his desk with three names and phone numbers neatly handwritten on it.

"Randy, do you mind if I ask you a few questions about Nardil? Reporter-type questions, not anything confidential about your patients or about Lydia." I did some hasty Internet reporting on Nardil before I came.

"Claire, Lydia was not my patient. She was my friend and my neighbor. I never discussed her case with her psychiatrist. Or with anyone else, for that matter."

Lydia's psychiatrist. There's an idea, one avenue I haven't explored with Sallie. "No, of course not. It's just that Karen told me patients taking Nardil sometimes commit suicide by eating forbidden foods high in tyramine. They don't really mean to kill themselves, they're just testing limits or something. Do you think that's what happened to Lydia? An accident, not suicide?"

"I don't know. Unfortunately, what you describe does happen sometimes. But in Lydia's case, she had to ingest so much of those foods to cause a stroke, that I don't think it was accidental. Look, I'm not comfortable discussing this." He glances discreetly at the clock.

I can take a hint. "I better get going." Time is money—in his case, probably two hundred dollars per fifty minutes. "Thanks again for the names. By the way, do you have any general information about Nardil and other MAO inhibitors and food reactions, stuff you give to patients? I'd like to learn more."

He opens a file drawer. "I can give you some handouts. And, Claire, do think about those doctors."

"I know. High control needs, right?" I smile to show I'm joking.

"Claire, I'm not making a diagnosis. You seem to be coping admirably. As I'm sure you always do. Good luck." He shakes my hand good-bye. Again, I'm tempted to give up my investigation. Randy's a psychiatrist and Lydia's friend and he's not doubting it was suicide. Who am I to think I know better?

Later that night, once the children are tucked in, I crawl into bed early, hoping to catch up on some sleep, or some rest, even if sleep doesn't come. At least I'm prone. And I love being in my bed, propped up on my down pillows, with the feather-light, dark-green silk comforter pulled up around me. I turn out the lights and stare out the large windows into the dark backyard. When Aaron's not home, I don't pull down the blinds because I love waking up bathed in sunlight.

After twenty minutes, it's obvious that sleep isn't going to happen. I keep mulling over what Karen told me about Roger and Russell. I don't know what I should do with this information. Is nice-guy Roger a child molester? Lydia must have felt the same way I do about it. Yet, I can't help thinking how in all the cheesy television movies I've ever seen, the lovable coach, the kindly neighbor, actually do turn out to be the perverts.

I'm also stymied because I don't want to betray Karen's confidence, or make a fool of myself. As Karen pointed out, these are the kinds of accusations that ruin innocent people's lives. I can't confront the coach yet. I need more facts, some solid evidence, but where am I going to get it?

Maybe from Roger's old school. Luckily, Connecticut is a small state. I get out of my cozy bed and head for my Rolodex in the study. My friend Abby, my former classmate from graduate school at Columbia, is the editor of the *Hartford Ledger*'s Sunday magazine, and mother of three. It's 10:40, which is too late to call someone with children on a school night. I settle for leaving her a message to call me back on her work voicemail.

The next morning, she calls me almost as soon as I'm back from car pool. We only talk a few times a year, so we spend a few minutes catching up. As soon as she mentions Joel, her youngest, I latch on to an opening.

"Joel's the son who's the soccer star, right?"

"His team made the state championships three years in a row." Her pride is evident.

"Abby, the reason I'm calling involves soccer." I consider telling her the truth, but decide it will be simpler to pretend it's for a story. "We're looking into doing a big cover story on the suburban soccer craze and whether it's getting too competitive."

Abby laughs. "Want to interview me? It's completely nuts. One of the fathers had to be physically restrained at a game last week; he actually got suspended. The coach told him he couldn't come back the rest of the season."

"Yes, that kind of thing, exactly. And how that stuff affects kids. Anyway, we may do a box on the dark side of soccer. Someone mentioned an incident in Connecticut a couple of years ago. Something about a coach who molested a student, or something like that. Does that ring any bells?"

"Not that I can think of. That's definitely a story I would remember. You say it was in Hartford?"

"That's what he said, but you know how people's memories are. It could be anywhere in Connecticut. Or Massachusetts or Rhode Island for that matter. That's why I wanted to ask you. It would have been a couple of years ago."

"Let me ask around the office and see if anyone remembers. I'll call or e-mail you later."

I feel guilty sending her on a wild goose chase for nonjournalistic purposes. "Okay, I'll be working at home today. And, Abby, don't spend more than ten or fifteen minutes on this. It may not pan out."

"Don't worry. I don't even have ten minutes this whole week. Good to hear from you. Catch you later."

"Good to talk to you, too. Thanks." I know Abby will ask around. She's superefficient. All I can do now is wait.

Several hours later, I check my e-mail. Good old reliable Abby.

Claire:

Nobody here seems to remember anything. With one exception. A guy we recently hired from Stamford thinks there might have been something like that in Westport in the fall of 1999 or 2000. Sorry I couldn't find out more.

Abby

At least it's a start. Suddenly, I'm overcome by curiosity. This is the kind of reporting the Internet was made for. I settle in at my desk, knowing the kids will be home soon.

I call up a few basic search engines. Within minutes, I have the name of a community newspaper, the *Westport Weekly*. Not much luck there, as there's no on-line index for 1999. I check the *Hartford Ledger* on-line index again, but come up empty. I try the *New Haven Record*. Maybe they had a good stringer from Westport. I try soccer, but nothing comes up on the screen. I type in Roger McCaffrey and hold my breath. Bingo. Within seconds, I have several citations from April, May, and June of 1999.

The headline from April 11, 1999: NINTH GRADER ALLEGES FONDLING BY SOCCER COACH. The story is only a few paragraphs, stating that coach Roger McCaffrey, of private high school Westport Country Academy, was under investigation for allegedly fondling a freshman named Jason Turnbull. The story doesn't contain any quotes from Roger, who, according to the article, had been suspended with pay, pending the investigation.

The following three stories report on the tumult that followed Turnbull's accusation. Parents and students held a rally in support of Roger, who maintained that Jason made up the story. One of Turnbull's classmates was quoted saying that "Jason has always had a problem distinguishing truth and fiction." Another classmate suggested that Jason had a vendetta against the coach after being suspended from the team for showing up at practice with alcohol on his breath.

In a story a few days later, some outraged parents and students accuse Roger's defenders of making up lies about Jason Turnbull. They compared the boy to a rape victim who gets skewered for speaking the truth, and held a counter-rally with placards: DON'T KILL THE MESSENGER and TURNBULL TELLING TRUTH.

The next story details how the two sides—Roger's defenders versus Jason's—continue to skirmish. Next, a story dated May 15 released the findings of the investigation. The Academy Committee found no evidence to support Jason's allegations. Roger was cleared of the charges and immediately reinstated. The Turnbulls say they'll transfer Jason to another school at the year's end. A few other outraged parents threaten to do the same.

The final story, dated June 10, was brief. It announced Roger's resignation and quoted from the letter he submitted to the headmaster: "I will leave at the end of the school year on June 25, to accept another job offer in another state. . . . I'm grateful for the community for standing by me in recent days. However, in light of recent events, I believe my departure is the best course of action. I hope it hastens the healing process in our community. It has been an honor and a pleasure to teach at the Academy for the past three years . . ."

The twins are running upstairs to find me within seconds of being dropped off, begging me to take them to the park, as promised at breakfast.

"Guys, you have to give me a little more time. Something important has come up, and I can't leave yet."

Trini offers to take them. "That's a great idea. I'll meet you there as soon as I finish."

"But, Mommy, a promise is a promise," Max intones.

"I've been looking forward to it all day," says Zach, piling on the guilt.

"I'm not breaking my promise. I'm just going to be a little late. How about if I give you money to buy something at the Good Humor truck?" I'm not proud of it, but I'm not above resorting to bribery.

That seems to placate them. "I'll meet you there by four, I promise," I say, flashing Trini a grateful look.

I go back to the computer, feeling energized. I try the Connecticut edition of *The New York Times* and some local newspapers in neighboring towns, but there are no other stories.

As with many news accounts, there's plenty of room here to read between the lines. Did innocent, falsely accused Roger resign out of pride? Or was there some under-the-table deal, like the school would clear his name as long as he left? Innocent or guilty in Connecticut, Roger's teaching career would be over if he was accused of a similar incident a few years later.

I wonder about the odds of being falsely accused twice—too much of a coincidence, or an indication that, these days, everyone is too quick to accuse?

My mind won't stop turning over the new information. Was Roger's secret a big enough motive for murder? If he would go that far to permanently silence Lydia, what will he do when I confront him? I look at the clock and realize that I have to leave for the park or risk losing all credibility with the boys. I sign off, wishing the next step in my investigation was as clearcut as the twins' demands.

TWELVE

ommy, why are you putting makeup on?" asks Max.

"It's a school night. You're not going out, are you?" chimes in Zach.

"What's this, the guilt patrol? Daddy and I are going out to dinner with Matthew, Colin's dad."

"Can we come?" asks Zach, ever the optimist.

"Sorry, honey. It's a grown-up restaurant. But Colin is coming over to keep you guys company."

"Colin is coming here. Yippee! Let's find some hard puzzles. Come on, Zach." They are not too hard to appease. Allison never minds if we leave because Trini is far more indulgent than we are about watching television and talking on the phone for hours. Aaron should have been home by now. The doorbell and telephone ring within seconds of each other. "Trini, can you get the door?" I yell.

I'm not surprised to hear Aaron's voice on the phone. "Claire, don't kill me but I just got out of a meeting. I'm not going to be able to break free for another few hours. I'm really sorry."

"That's okay. You warned me this wasn't a good night to make plans. Matthew just got here. I guess we'll go ahead without you.

See you at home later. Sorry it turned out this way." Actually I'm relieved, although it might prove awkward to be alone with Matthew. Aaron might have noticed me pumping Matthew for information and gotten mad. Anyway, there's no point upsetting Aaron when he's under extreme pressure from work. Although my superconscientious husband is *always* under extreme pressure from work.

Trini is preparing a large plate of macaroni and cheese, the house specialty, for Colin. Matthew is sitting at the table talking to the kids. He rises to hug me.

"Matthew, hi. That was Aaron. Sorry, but he's tied up at the office."

"Do you want to reschedule when it's convenient for Aaron?" Matthew never fails to make the polite gesture.

"No, that's silly. You're already here. Let's go anyway. The kids will be fine. I've been looking forward to a grown-up dinner all day."

"Me, too," Matthew says, squeezing my hand slightly.

"'Bye, everybody. I left the number of the restaurant on the counter in case my cell phone dies. It's been on all day. Don't call unless it's an emergency." The kids barely look up as we leave.

Just like old times. Except Lydia is dead. Neither of us say it, but we both have to be thinking it. When Colin was small, I often ate dinner with the Finellis on Sunday nights, the only day of the week we were on similar schedules. Sometimes I would drag Lydia to a movie after dinner. "Come on. Colin is asleep. You need to spend some time out of the house, with an adult. Let's go," I would insist. Once in awhile, Lydia would beg off, protesting that she'd rather take a bath or read a book. She'd encourage Matthew and me to go instead. Matthew loves violent, mindless, action movies and occasionally I would relent. "What a sport," he used to say when I gave in. "The popcorn is on me."

"So are the tickets. I'm not wasting my hard-earned money on blood and guts." That was our deal. Any movie with subtitles was

121

my treat. "You're a great date," I told him many times. "How come the good ones are always taken?"

Tonight, I gladly accept his offer to drive. "A girl could get used to this," I say, crouching into his Porsche. "Aren't you afraid we'll pull our backs out?"

"Come on, Claire. We're not that ancient."

I suggest Café Jack, a new place tucked on a street behind Old Georgetown Road. As I give directions, I study Matthew. He hasn't changed out of his work clothes. He looks thin, haggard, and in need of a haircut.

I've always adored Matthew. He embraced me as his friend as soon as we met, never feeling threatened by my closeness with Lydia, the way some men might. Even in my most bitter moments I could never really blame Matthew for Lydia's silence. That was between Lydia and me. The others—Matthew, Colin, Sallie, Aaron—were merely supporting actors in the drama Lydia had scripted.

My relationship with Matthew had always been simpler than the emotional dance Lydia and I shared. We were all so young when they married—in our midtwenties—that I had no idea how rare it is to actually like the spouse of a close friend. I assumed it was the natural order of things: A friend you love chooses someone else whom you grow to love. Now I know that marriage seldom adds another friend to the equation; a subtraction of affection is far more likely. Matthew was different, though, the only friend's husband who consciously set out to win me over, who valued my friendship himself. We were a threesome until Aaron came along and evened things out. Now it is my turn to include Matthew and Colin.

"We have lots to talk about," I say, as soon as we settle into the red leather booth and order wine. "Sallie tells me that I'm still Colin's guardian."

"Look, Claire, I know things were terribly strained between you and Lydia for the last several years, but I can tell you this. She never wavered on that point. Never."

"Why not?" I ask. "It doesn't add up. If she trusted me with her child, then why wouldn't she even speak to me?"

"As much as Lydia wanted you out of her life, she still wanted you in Colin's life. At least in the unlikely event that we weren't going to be around." He shrugs his shoulders. "I didn't press her on it because I agreed with her."

"Matthew, I never called you during those years because I didn't want to put you in an awkward spot. I knew your loyalty was to your wife. But now, well, the situation has changed. So, if there's anything you can tell me about why Lydia froze me out, I'd like to know."

"Oh, Claire, how you hate being out of the loop," he teases. "Okay, there are a few things I can say now. But, in return, you have to promise you'll quit asking other people about Lydia. Deal?"

If I didn't know better, I'd think he was flirting with me tonight. The way he's looking at me now, the way his hand had lingered on my back a few seconds too long when he helped me out of the low-slung car. My perceptions must be off, maybe I'm gulping my wine too fast. "Matthew, if you know anything, please tell me."

"Claire, you're a smart person. Why don't we start with the obvious. Lydia was jealous of you."

"Jealous? Of what?" I protest, even though he seems to be confirming one of my pet theories. "She had everything that I have—a family, a nice home, a good life, a career if she wanted to work. In fact, she had all those things first."

"But you had *more* — more family, and a successful, high-profile career. Let's not pretend that there wasn't a strong streak of competitiveness between you two."

"There was. That didn't mean that we didn't wish each other the best. You mean she was jealous because I have three kids?"

"That was part of it. We wanted more kids. It was a disappointment, more to Lydia than to me."

"Really. Why?"

"I have the son I always wanted. Colin's terrific. I can't imagine loving another kid nearly as much. He's enough. I like giving him my undivided attention. We're very close, which is important to me. I never had that. My father loves me in his own way, but he hasn't expressed it in all my forty-three years.

"Don't get me wrong," he continues. "I would have welcomed another kid or two into our family, if things had worked out that way, but I have no regrets in that department. I thank God every day for Colin. Especially now."

"So, Lydia did have regrets?"

"Obviously, Lydia adored Colin, but her identity was wrapped up in being the perfect mom. Perfect moms usually have larger families."

"No, there has to be more. Lydia and I were close too long to let a little jealousy get in the way." Or was this just another example of me not really understanding the depths of Lydia's troubled mind? How could I have been so far off the mark about my own best friend? Surely, no one changes that much in five years.

"Those reporter's instincts. I guess they never take a dinner break. Okay, there is one more thing. Please, let's keep it between us. It's a little embarrassing." Matthew lowers his voice. "Lydia thought I was attracted to you. It became something of an obsession with her. Ultimately, that's why she stopped being friends with you."

"That's ridiculous. You know that. Why didn't you reason with her? Was she that irrational?"

He looks me in the eyes. "Because she was right. At least on some level. She sensed I've always been attracted to you. It didn't matter how many times I told her that there was nothing sexual between us. That you were a loyal friend. In her mind, you were a threat. So, you had to go."

The room is spinning and it isn't from the wine I've been steadily gulping during his explanation. "Matthew, I know she was depressed but she wasn't crazy. How could you let her believe something so outrageous? I wasn't a threat to your marriage. Ever. That's absurd. We're all responsible adults. So what if you were slightly attracted to me? You never would have acted on it, any more than I would have."

"Claire, you're thinking of the Lydia you used to know. The sensible, reasonable person. The last few years, she wasn't like that. She wasn't easy to talk to. Or live with."

I steer the conversation back to more neutral territory. "If I was such a threat, then why am I still Colin's guardian?"

"Simple. She didn't trust anyone else with him the way she trusted you. Except for Sallie. And Sallie was getting too old to raise him. Why do you keep bringing up this guardian thing? Do you or Aaron have a problem with it?"

"Of course not. Anyway, you're in perfect health. I don't want to discuss your possible death, or my legal obligations. I just want to have a closer relationship with Colin. Especially now. My kids are fond of him. Is that okay with you?"

"Definitely. And I hope that includes me, too. Colin and I don't have any family around here. And I've missed you," he says, pouring more wine and patting my hand. "Claire, I want you to know how many times I tried to straighten Lydia out, to get her to call you." He sounds sincere. Years ago, I used to be puzzled by Lydia's physical attraction to Matthew: He's so boyish, blond, and skinny. Must be like sleeping with your kid brother, I used to think. But Matthew has a relentless charm, for instance, the way he used to seek my opinion about everything from politics and books to his latest wine discovery.

"Oh, by the way, Matthew, do you mind if I bring Colin to my house next Saturday? I want to encourage a relationship between the kids. None of them have first cousins, you know."

Matthew agrees, complimenting me on the charm and physical beauty of my offspring, with whom he had talked to for all of ten minutes that evening. "Of course, they're beautiful children. Look at you."

I ignore the flattery, which I think he's laying on a little too thick. Maybe the wine has gone to his head, too. Maybe grieving people should lay off the alcohol, even in small amounts. "So, tell me, Matthew, how are you managing? It must be hard to keep dealing with your patients' problems at a time like this."

He's silent for a few seconds, then speaks in a near whisper. "Something will happen during the day—a patient will say something funny, or I'll read something in the *Post,* and I automatically think, I have to tell that to Lydia. Then I remember." He traces a pattern on the tablecloth with his fingertips. "We had our ups and downs, like all marriages, but we were together for seventeen years. I can't believe she's gone."

Matthew talks about his grief as I pick at my food. "It's so good to be with you again, Claire, so comfortable, that I'm talking too much. Tell me how you're doing. I'm so sorry you found her. Like I said, I had no idea she called you. It should have been me."

"Well, better me than Colin."

"I was supposed to get home early that day, before Colin got back from school. It would have been me." We'd discussed this before. Although both of us were haunted by the idea that Colin could have easily walked into Lydia's room that morning before school.

"Matthew, can you think of any reason why Lydia might have called? The timing doesn't make sense."

"No, not really, but you have no idea how badly Lydia was doing. She just wasn't herself. I blame myself, of course. I should have been more attentive to her, worked less, spent more time at home. Truth is, I buried myself in work when things got rough at home. It was a big mistake, but I'm a single parent now. I'm going to be there for my boy."

"Matthew, you can't blame yourself. Depression is a serious illness. I'm sure you did everything you could." I pat his hand, and he places his other hand over mine, an uncomfortably intimate gesture.

I pull my hand away to stir cream into my coffee. "Jill told me she saw Lydia that Sunday."

"You've really made the rounds, haven't you?" He sounds amused.

"We had lunch the other day. To try and console each other. She mentioned she came over that Sunday, before you left for the Eastern Shore." I'm surprised Jill hasn't mentioned our lunch to Matthew. Of course, she's so distracted with work she probably forgot.

"That damn meeting. If only I hadn't left the night before, but I wanted to go over my notes, and the other presenters wanted to meet at seven to prepare for an eight-thirty session. I couldn't face the drive that early in the morning." Matthew and I had once shared an aversion to waking up early. My kids cured me of it long ago.

"If only I had slept at home that night, maybe . . ."

I cut him off. "You can't go through the rest of life saying what if. It's not fair. To Colin or to yourself."

"I know. You're right, as usual." He sips his coffee. "So, tell me what you've been up to."

I'm not sure what he means. "At the magazine? Same old stuff. I'm working on a few stories, but I haven't been in the office much lately. I'm spending more time at home with the kids. When something like this happens, you realize how precious every day is. And Aaron's been out of town a lot on this trial."

"Still Superwoman, doing it all. You're incredible." He reaches for my hand again. "Claire, I hope this is the first of many dinners."

"Of course it is, Matthew. I want our families to be close again. A fresh start. At least something positive can come from this tragedy." I'm starting to sound like a Hallmark card.

"There's my beeper." Matthew stands. "Excuse me, I have to call the hospital. Could you ask the waiter to bring the check? We may have to leave."

I gesture to the waiter, relieved to call it a night. Too much intensity, too many revelations for one evening.

Matthew's back at the table shortly. "We have to go. Sorry." A patient whose brain tumor he removed yesterday is hemorrhaging. On the way home, he drives way too fast. "I'm not sure how long I'll be. I'll pick Colin up as soon as I'm finished, probably in a couple of hours."

We're nearly at my street. "Don't be silly. I'll run him home. It's almost nine-thirty. He's probably tired and ready for bed."

"If you don't mind, that's a better plan. I want him to get a good night's sleep. Thanks a lot, Claire."

"Thanks again for dinner. Speak to you soon." Aaron's car isn't in the driveway yet. I turn the key in the lock on the front door, wondering who left the television on. Colin and Allison are engrossed in *Nick at Nite.* "Hi, guys. I'm back. Colin, your dad had an emergency at the hospital. Did you bring your keys? Where are the boys?"

"I have the keys," he says, patting his jeans pocket.

"The boys are asleep. Trini's downstairs. Dad called. He'll be home around eleven. Can we watch the last five minutes of this show?" Allison asks.

"Sure. I want to make a phone call."

I go upstairs, check on the boys, and call Val. "Hi. It's me. I know it's late for a visit, but is there any chance I can drop over for a few minutes?"

"Of course. You know we're night owls. Alex just finished reading to the kids and they're asleep. But what's wrong? You sound upset."

"I'm fine. I just feel like talking to you. See you in twenty minutes. I have to drive Colin home first." The camera is in my closet. I sling it over my shoulder, explaining to Trini that I'll be back in an hour but she doesn't have to wait up.

"Colin, I'm going to bring the camera to Val's after I drop you off so we can get it fixed."

"Thanks, Aunt Claire." We walk to the car. It's dark and I can't help putting my arm around his shoulder. To my surprise, he doesn't flinch the way Allison does.

Val's neighborhood in northwest Washington, off Connecticut Avenue near Chevy Chase Circle, is similar to mine, only it's within city boundaries. I park in her driveway and walk through the unlocked side door. Val is sitting at the kitchen table, drinking a cup of tea out of a delicate bone-china cup and leafing through the *New Yorker*.

"Haven't you heard that D.C. is the crime capital of the world? You should keep this door locked."

"You suburbanites. This isn't Beirut, you know. And I was expecting you. Tea?"

"No, thanks. I just ate. Where's Alex?"

"Upstairs, glued to one of the sports channels. Want me to call him?"

"No, let him watch. This is girl talk." I make myself comfortable on the oak chair. There's not a dish in the sink, or a piece of paper out of place on the long white counter.

"It's good to see you, even at ten at night. What's up?" Val asks.

"I just had dinner. With Matthew."

"I'm listening," Val says.

"It was weird. I think he was flirting. And he told me Lydia was jealous of me and that's why she dropped me."

"You mean the infertility thing? She was jealous of your three kids?" Val is well-versed in my various Lydia theories, as she should be after listening to them for hours and hours over the years.

"Partly that. Partly my career. And she thought Matthew was attracted to me."

Val raises an eyebrow. "I don't know, Claire. Don't you find that explanation a bit self-serving? On Matthew's part, I mean, not yours. The idea that you and Lydia were such good friends that only a man could come between you?"

"He claims he's always been attracted to me."

"Isn't that an odd thing to say? He hasn't seen you in five years. His wife's only been dead a few weeks, you're happily married, and he's supposed to be an old friend."

"Look, we can't blame him for being confused these days." I feel defensive on Matthew's behalf, although I do mention how he touched my hand and my back, perhaps in a suggestive manner. I couldn't be sure. "Look, maybe I'm being too hard on him. He's completely distraught over Lydia's death. No wonder he's acting strangely."

"So are *you* attracted to *him*?" Now we're on Val's favorite subject—sex.

"Of course not. He's still Lydia's husband. Anyway, lanky blonds don't do it for me, as you know. I'm holding out for Antonio Banderas. It's just so weird to be with Matthew again. We're not sure how to act around each other. Especially without Lydia and Aaron. You know, I've learned so many secrets about Lydia that I'm starting to mistrust my perceptions."

"Where is Aaron? Cleveland again?"

"No, downtown in his office. He should be making a guest appearance at home tonight. I better go. You really helped me, Val. Thanks."

"This visit is too quick. Any reason you brought that camera?" Val asks. "Present for me?"

I explain that it's broken and I need her to tell me where to take it for repair. Val turns it over and pushes a few buttons, but it's jammed shut.

"Look, Claire, I know how mechanical you are. I'm going to the camera store anyway on Friday. I'll bring it in and talk to Billy, my guy there, about fixing it. He wouldn't dare rip me off."

"That would be great. Thanks. Tell Alex hi and bye. I don't want to go upstairs and wake the kids." I kiss her on the cheek. "Thanks again. You're a pal."

"Glad you could drop by, however briefly," Val says. "Let me know when you have another ten minutes cleared on your busy schedule." She watches from behind her door until I'm safely buckled in my car.

I only got close to Val in the last five years at work, so she never met Lydia or Matthew. Not that I can picture them as pals. Tonight isn't the first time I've reflected on how much easier it is to be Val's friend than it was to be Lydia's.

THIRTEEN

By leaning over Aaron's pillow and squinting I can read the digital clock: 9:30. No wonder the house is quiet. I'm alone, except for Trini, who must be cleaning or doing laundry downstairs. A few hours earlier, Aaron encouraged me to go back to sleep, promising to get the kids ready for school. He hadn't gotten home until after midnight last night. I was already half-asleep, so we didn't get to talk.

After a long, hot shower and two mugs of strong coffee, I resolve to call Rob this morning, as soon as it's a decent hour on the West Coast. No point putting it off any longer.

Not fifteen minutes later, as if operating on some mysterious sibling telepathy, Rob calls. "You could feel my mental vibes, right? I was waiting to call you. What are you doing up so early?"

"I'm on East Coast time. I'm in New York, at the Royalton. Having breakfast in bed. Thought I'd check in. Sorry I missed Lydia's funeral. Thanks for trying so hard to reach me. How you doing? I know she wasn't in your life anymore, but still, this must be very hard for you. Is there anything I can do?"

I can tell from his voice that he's tired. "I'm fine, really. You're in New York? What's up?"

"Three days here, then back to L.A. for a screening. No time to stop in D.C., but I should be back east in a week or two."

"Rob, I want to talk to you about something important. Maybe it could wait until I see you, but I'd rather not. How about if I take the shuttle to New York to see you today or tomorrow? Can you clear your schedule for a few hours? For real. No interruptions, faxes, phone calls, bringing clients along for a drink."

"You're going to come to New York to see me? That would be great." His tone shifts. "Uh, oh. Are Mom and Dad okay? I know I should call them more." Rob, too, has inherited the Newman worry gene.

"They're fine. And so are my kids and Aaron. I promise. This is about Lydia."

"Lydia," he repeats. "Hold on a minute. Let me check my Palm Pilot. How about tonight? I can cancel my drink thing and dinner thing and be free around five. We can have an early dinner, and then my driver can get you to the airport for the last shuttle."

"Your driver?" I try to sound amused, not judgmental.

"Getting around the city is such a hassle." He sounds defensive so I don't give him a hard time.

"Okay, hold on a sec while I talk to Trini. I'm sure she won't mind if I desert her." Now that I hear his voice, my excitement to see him outweighs my anger over the letters.

"No problem," Trini says. "Have a good trip."

"Rob, we're on. Meet you at your hotel at five. Leave a key for me at the desk, just in case you're late for a change."

"Can't wait to see you. I'm so glad I called. Later."

Suddenly feeling guilty about abandoning the kids and Aaron, I call Aaron for reassurance. "Of course, you should go. You need a break. And it's only for a day. You and Rob don't see each other enough. I'm fine with the kids. Tell Trini not to bother with dinner. I'll take them out for pizza. Claire, why don't you leave right away? Go to a museum or shopping."

As annoyed as I am by Aaron's attempt to distract me, I decide to view it as husbandly concern, not condescension.

"Another thing, Claire. Go easy on Rob about those letters. Give him a chance before you jump on him. And, remember, even your brother is entitled to some privacy. He doesn't have to clear everything with you first."

"Yeah, right. Presumption of innocence and all that." The letters. If only I'd never come across them. Then I could be looking forward to a relaxing dinner with my brother, not a confrontation.

Aaron is right, though. There's no reason not to take an earlier shuttle and spend a few hours in New York.

Notwithstanding his success as a Hollywood agent, and his resulting wealth, Rob is the person in the world most like myself. Physically, that is. Sure, he's taller and skinnier, but he has the same curly red hair and blue eyes, almost the exact same bump in his nose. Sometimes, sitting across a table from him, I'm startled by his face. It's as if I'm looking in a gender-bending mirror reflecting back the masculine version of myself. Temperamentally, we're not so identical. After twenty-two years on the opposite coast, Rob is more laid back than I'd be after taking six Valiums.

During takeoff my stomach flutters, but not from any fear of flying. The thought of a showdown with Rob over those letters fills me with dread. We rarely fight. In fact, we hardly ever disagree. Yet, I feel so betrayed over the contents of the letters that I have to confront him. I'm not about to start keeping secrets from my own brother.

The summer between sixth and seventh grade, Lydia and her parents moved from Queens into the white rambler with red shutters, across the street and four houses down from our split-level. After Lydia's distinguished performance at Our Lady of Blessed Sacrament, Sallie and Vince were acquiescing to her fervent wish to enter public junior high, despite the distracting presence of pubescent boys.

Then, and now, Holly Dale was one of the less fashionable suburbs on Long Island's south shore, populated by middle-class families who fled New York City's outlying boroughs so that their children could play kickball and ride bikes on safer, greener streets. The town was ethnically mixed, to a point. Families were either Jewish or Catholic. I didn't meet a WASP until I was fifteen, when I went to France on a summer exchange program.

The neighborhood was solidly middle class. Nobody was rich or hugely successful except for the occasional father—never the mother—who was a doctor or a lawyer. Mostly the mothers stayed home and took care of the children, and the fathers were policemen, firemen, teachers, owners of small businesses, or middle-level managers who commuted on the Long Island Railroad to offices in Manhattan.

My father was a high-school principal, and my mother, a high-school history teacher, was one of the few mothers who held a paying job. That suited Rob and me just fine. Thanks to our mostly absent parents, our friends tended to congregate in our basement playroom—family rooms hadn't been invented yet. We blasted the stereo, smoked pot, and cleaned out the pantry and refrigerator with our cases of acute munchies. My unsuspecting parents, who possessed a basic and misplaced trust in us, attributed the food raids to normal teenage appetites and stocked up often at the A&P.

My parents were casual about meals, curfews, and other routines. Lydia was fascinated by the looseness of our household. Sallie professed admiration for my mother —"so smart and well-educated" was how she put it—code, I later understood, for her opinion that my mother should spend less time in the classroom and at conferences and more in our kitchen. To compensate for the maternal neglect we suffered, Sallie was always stuffing Rob and me with homemade baked ziti and pastries. I could eat anything then, including cheesecake for breakfast, without gaining an ounce.

* * *

No matter how old we get or how many miles separate us, Rob tries to be my protector. For instance, when the twins were born, Rob sent me the nicest gift money could buy: sleep. After several days of round-the-clock feedings, Aaron and I were in sorry shape. The babies cried constantly, and Allison, understandably spooked by the new arrivals, would cling to my arms or legs for hours at a time. Trini had been living with us only a few months, and we were all tentatively feeling our way around.

In the midst of this confusion, the doorbell rang early one morning, hours before the daily UPS delivery of matching onesies. I'd opened the door to find Fiona Campbell, a silver-haired woman in her late fifties, wearing a starched white uniform and carrying a Burberry raincoat, standing on my porch. At first, I thought she was an apparition.

"May I help you?" I asked

"I'm looking for the Willentz household. You must be Claire Newman. I see you favor your brother Rob," she said in a British accent.

"You know Rob?" I stammered.

"Oh yes. As a matter of fact, he sent me here, as a sort of gift. I'll be with you for a month. Not to worry, dear. I'm a trained nanny, and I'm here to help you with your new twins."

Thinking that I must be hallucinating from sleep deprivation, I invited her in anyway. It was daylight, and she didn't look dangerous. Besides, I'd have turned the house over to armed bandits by then if it meant I could catch a ten-minute nap.

Aaron came downstairs, looking bedraggled. I explained the situation to him as I called Rob.

"This is how you thank me? By waking me at five A.M.?" Rob said in mock indignation. He filled in the blanks. A few weeks ago, at a dinner party, he bragged about his newborn twin nephews and someone mentioned Fiona. He tracked her down and hired her.

"Of course, she was booked solid for the next year or two. Half of Hollywood plans their babies around Fiona's availability. But I can be very persuasive, as you know. And she was curious about Washington. She's worked in Los Angeles and New York for the past twenty years. You'd never know it from her proper demeanor, but she's a heavy metal fan. And I'm pretty well connected there."

"You mean Trash Heap got involved?" Rob's client list had grown more established over the years, but he still had his knack for signing tomorrow's hit bands.

"Nigel and the boys were happy to help. I wanted to make it up to you for missing the bris. I mean the double bris. Anyway, Fiona is yours for four weeks. Sorry I couldn't get her longer. But, believe it or not, there are limits to my charm."

I tried not to think how much this gift was costing, although I knew Rob couldn't care less. He has way more money than he can spend in this lifetime, or the next. I was grateful beyond words, or maybe just too tired to form them.

I hoped Aaron would accept the gift in the appropriate spirit. He could be a tad critical of how Rob flung cash around. I had to agree with Aaron that the electric Barbie car Rob had sent Allison a few days ago was over the top. Rob, anticipating my disapproval, sent along a charming note saying he remembered how it felt to be displaced by a brand-new baby—and poor Allison had to contend with two. Allison barely left her Barbie car to eat or sleep.

This morning, to my relief, Aaron wasn't protesting a bit. Apparently, when it came to his own precious sleep, his moral standards were looser. Aaron grabbed the phone from me.

"Rob, my man, thanks. I was considering taking a second mortgage to hire more help. You've saved us."

I took the phone back. "Rob, forget that stupid bris. You know I only did it for Daddy. I stayed upstairs the whole time. I couldn't bear to see those babies butchered, and probably scarred for life, by that barbaric custom. But you know how Dad is, his first grandsons and all. Come visit soon. We all miss you."

By the time I'd hung up, Fiona, evidently immune to jet lag, was changing Max's diaper. She turned out to be a godsend. Between Fiona and Trini, we all got a little sleep. Aaron took refuge at his relatively peaceful office. Allison turned back into her sweet self as soon as Aaron and I stopped looking and acting like zombies.

I look at my watch again. Fifteen minutes until landing. I take the packet of letters out of my backpack and reread them. As the wheels of the shuttle scrape the pavement, I try to square my mental image of Rob as my knight in shining armor with the brother who kept me in the dark for years.

Spending a few hours by myself in New York doesn't hold its usual appeal. I'm too restless for a museum. I walk around SoHo for awhile, but the shops, with their stacks of perfect merchandise, don't interest me today. There aren't any shoes I want to try on. Finally, I give up and hop a cab to the Royalton, retrieving the envelope with the key card to Rob's room from the front desk. His palatial suite is decorated in stark black and white, but the angular couch I sink into is surprisingly comfortable.

I grab a mineral water from the minibar and pluck the strawberries and raspberries out of the untouched fruit platter on the table. Mindlessly, I channel surf on the huge stereo TV. I smile in anticipation at seeing Rob, no longer the problem child of our family.

"Now I understand why he was such a problem growing up," my father jokes now. "Who knew he was a genius?"

"All that money and look what he wears," my mother sighs. "The ponytailed tycoon." After years of being the "good" one, with dean's list grades and degrees from Brown and Columbia School of Journalism, I find it a relief to be overshadowed. Not that my parents consider me a slouch. "The house, the pool, the private jet, big deal. He doesn't have what you do, a wonderful marriage and three beautiful, healthy kids," my mother reminds me as often as possible. "And he's not getting any younger."

"He's forty-three. And loaded. He can attract beautiful young women for a long time. And he'll never lose the financial resources to hire multiple nannies." Like my mother, I wish he would settle down with someone, but every time I mention it, Rob accuses me of being jealous of his freedom. Looking around the suite convinces me to not waste any pity on my brother. I'm almost sorry when Rob appears at five-thirty, spewing apologies.

"I know, I know. You came all the way from Washington and I was just crosstown. And I'm the one who's late. Sorry, rush-hour traffic." He bends to kiss me on the cheek, removing his eight-hundred-dollar sunglasses.

"I'm not mad at all. I'm having a great time without you. You look great." Very California chic: long hair pulled into the usual ponytail, black T-shirt, and a silky tweed jacket that looks ultraexpensive even before he flings it on the bed, exposing the Carlos Peretti label.

"I'm so happy you're here, I'm going to order some champagne. We can order room service tonight, if that's okay with you. So we can be together without any distractions."

I love being with Rob. It gives me the warm, cozy feeling that someone is taking care of *me* for a change. Today, however, I don't feel like being charmed out of my anger. For ammunition I take the letters from my backpack and hand them over.

He studies them. "What do you know? They're all here. Looks like she kept every single one. I had the feeling since this morning that somehow you got your hands on them. Don't be mad, Claire. I can explain everything."

I shoot him a skeptical glance. "Sallie gave them to me by accident. She had no idea. They were with a bunch of my old letters to Lydia. I know it was wrong, but I read them. Sorry. I couldn't help myself, but my snooping doesn't get you off the hook. How could you keep such a big secret from me? And for so long?" My voice breaks.

"Claire, I don't blame you for reading them. I would have, too. And I'm not nearly as nosy as you are. Let me get the door and I'll explain."

I compose myself while Rob signs for the champagne. It's my favorite kind, I notice, but I couldn't feel less festive.

"Look, I know how you hate to be left out. So, I'll start at the beginning—your junior year of high school." Rob pours as he speaks, then hands me a crystal flute. "Remember that time I came home a few days early for Thanksgiving break? You had plans with that jerk Jerry Solomon. My other friends weren't home yet, either. Lydia was over at our house before your date and we decided to go to a movie. That night was the beginning."

He takes a few small sips. "After the movie, we wound up driving around and talking for hours."

"*Just* talking?" I interject.

He ignores my comment. "You know, Lydia spent so much time at our house that it was years before I realized I was attracted to her. I didn't want to make it weird between you two, so I never acted on it. And I knew Vince and Sallie would have gone crazy if we started dating. That night, we wound up at Long Beach. We smoked a joint and started talking about our feelings for each other. Somehow, me being in college, living hundreds of miles away, made it safer for us to admit the truth."

"So, it all began the night I was making out with Jerry Solomon in the backseat of his father's Lincoln?"

"Jerry was such an arrogant ass," Rob reminds me.

"True. But he was a great kisser. And I only dated him for a month. Go on."

"That night, we stayed at the beach, kissing and talking until we were freezing. Then we went to the car and fooled around some more. Lydia swore me to secrecy. I agreed. You know, Vince and Sallie liked me fine as long as I was your harmless hippie older brother, but they would have freaked if Lydia started dating a Jewish guy. And Lydia didn't want you to feel weird or left out. At least that's what she said. And I didn't want to rock the boat with Lydia by telling you," Rob says. My glass of champagne is untouched. "Besides, she had a point that it was our business, not yours."

I say nothing, trying to make him feel guilty about keeping secrets.

Rob continues. "We had a great time together. We talked about everything. We were always laughing. I saw a new side of Lydia, lighter and more spontaneous. Yet, she never took me seriously as a boyfriend. I was a diversion for her, that's all."

"Funny how things turn out," I interject.

"I accepted our relationship for what it was. Fun. No pressure. We went our separate ways, and connected whenever we could. Whenever we could manage it, we'd visit each other on the sly. I'm not going to kid you. Keeping it a secret from you and everyone else heightened the excitement. Then, once I dropped out of college and moved to California, things pretty much ended. We both got busy with what we called our real lives."

"How could you stand being at her wedding?" I ask, remembering how many vodka martinis he downed that night.

"You know, I tried to talk her out of getting married. I didn't think she and Matthew were deeply in love."

"Lydia always wanted to marry young. She wanted to be an adult. Partly to be able to escape from Sallie and Vince. But you're wrong about their love. Once she met Matthew, she fell hard. She told me she was going to marry him after their third date."

"Sure, she insisted that Matthew was the one, but I always had my doubts," Rob says.

"Why didn't you tell me about your relationship before? Especially if it was over? You could have told me when she and Matthew got married."

"Believe me, I wanted to. I don't like secrets. But Lydia wouldn't hear of it. And by the time you married Aaron, we had a bigger secret."

"A bigger secret?" I'm almost too shell-shocked to react.

Rob is sprawled in a club chair, but he moves to the sofa where I'm stretched out, and sits near my feet. "Remember that night in Washington, years ago, when you, me, Lydia, and Matthew were supposed to get together for dinner? It must have been about fifteen years ago, before you knew Aaron. I was in town for a day or two."

"Sure, I remember. It was more like thirteen years ago."

I remember perfectly. Lydia and Matthew were living in Washington for a few months. It was before they moved back permanently. Matthew was on a fellowship at Washington Hospital Center. Rob was in town for a few days and we made plans. Late in the afternoon, though, stuck reporting and writing a breaking story about a corporate takeover, I had to cancel. The three of them went ahead without me. During the appetizers, Matthew got beeped back to the hospital. He'd sped off, and Rob promised to take Lydia home after dinner. Lydia told me that much.

Turns out, Lydia omitted some crucial details in her version. "There we were, me and Lydia, alone, after so much time apart. Lydia looked beautiful, so sexy. She hadn't had wine for months because she was trying to get pregnant. After a glass or two, she confessed how fed up she was with their mechanical, baby-making—oriented sex.

"She drank more wine and got a little drunk. We were flirting like crazy. We wound up back in my hotel room."

I say nothing, waiting for more explanation.

"Claire, I swear to you, it was her idea. I was weak, I admit it. I knew she was married. But we were so attracted to each other. Our feelings were so powerful. In retrospect it sounds stupid, but we thought it was a way to put the past behind us, once and for all."

"The next morning, I met you for breakfast, right?" I say, for once not wanting to hear any more details. "You were in a good mood, but distracted. You said you were nervous about your meeting in New York, that you were trying to keep a difficult client.

When I asked Lydia about that dinner, she was pretty dismissive. I thought she was mad at me for canceling. I knew she was taking fertility hormones, which made her more moody than usual." I drop my voice, not wanting to sound critical. "So, that night didn't help you put things behind you, did it?"

"No, of course not. With the exception of your wedding, that was the last time I ever saw Lydia. She wouldn't call me back or answer my letters. Then, after you told me about her pregnancy, I kept my distance. It seemed like the gentlemanly thing to do, especially because of her paranoia that Matthew would find out about that night."

"You really loved her, didn't you?"

"Always," he says. "That night at the hotel she said I was the love of her life."

I make a few mental calculations. "Rob, ever think the baby might be yours?"

"I'm embarrassed to admit it. But, yeah, I did at first. We had one brief phone conversation about it. Lydia said absolutely not. She told me her due date and I counted on my fingers. Colin was due ten months after I was with her."

Ten months.

"Rob, Colin was born on August twenty-third, a month before the official due date. I happen to remember because Lydia went into labor at her shower. They told everybody he was a month premature, and that's why he only weighed six pounds." Lydia tried to talk me out of throwing the shower, saying the fuss embarrassed her, but I insisted.

Rob looks stricken. "Lydia made it clear that we were a closed chapter, but she wouldn't deceive me about something that important. Would she? What if he really is my son? Who does Colin look like anyway?"

"Colin looks like Lydia. Exactly like her, but Lydia kept a few secrets from me." I glance meaningfully at the letters. An alternate theory about the end of our friendship pops into my head. Maybe Lydia ended our friendship out of fear that I would discover that Colin was really Rob's son. Maybe as Colin got older, the secret weighed too heavily on her. Maybe she never expected that we would wind up in the same city. Or am I jumping to wild conclusions again?

"You know, Rob, I know it sounds crazy, but I'm starting to think Lydia's death might not have been a suicide. I think she called me to help her find out a few things." I tell him about the financial statements she mailed to me, and what I've learned about Coach McCaffrey.

Rob doesn't make fun of me for leaping to conclusions, the way Aaron has been doing. "Some of this stuff does sound funny. Probably only a few coincidences, though. You really don't have anything concrete. I don't suppose you're going to give up until you get to the bottom of this, right?"

If only Aaron was as accepting of my little quirks. "Aaron thinks I'm completely off the wall."

"Aaron may be right, but you never know. Claire, promise me you'll be careful. If you need any help, or anything, call me."

He hesitates. "Claire, do you think there's any chance Colin could be my son?"

"I don't know. Let me see what I can find out. Your blood type is A, like mine, right?"

"Uh-huh. What about Lydia and Matthew? And Colin?"

"Lydia's blood type was A. It was in the autopsy report. I'll ask Sallie about Matthew and Colin." I check the time again. "We better hustle to the airport." We'd talked through the champagne, dinner, and cognac from the minibar.

"Okay. I want to splash some cold water on my face. I'll be right back."

I take a last peek at the letters Rob has placed on the desk. Although the letters rightfully belong to him, I'm reluctant to leave them all behind. "Rob, do you mind if I take these letters back for awhile?"

"Sure. I don't need them," he says.

"I'll give them back to you soon." Carefully, I place them in my purse. Rob looks drained. "Hey, why don't you stay here and get some rest. I'm sure I can make it to the airport safely."

"No, I want to keep you company. We can rest in the car."

We walk through the lobby to the waiting car. I could get used to this kind of service. As the car zips through traffic, I lean back and close my eyes.

"Rob, don't forget. Next time you're in Washington, I want to arrange a dinner so you can meet Val."

"Your friend the photographer, right?"

"Right. I want you to help her get some high-paying freelance assignments—like publicity photos and album covers."

"I could do that. I'll be in Washington later this month." He pats my hand. "I'm talked out. Let's just close our eyes. We'll be there soon. Claire, are you still mad at me?"

"No, not really." It feels like the truth. I'm relieved to have their relationship out in the open. What was I thinking doubting Rob's loyalty? Sometimes life turns out to be more complicated than the history we write for ourselves.

My mind wanders back to a crisp Sunday afternoon, early in my pregnancy with the twins, before I knew I was carrying two babies. Lydia and I were in the park with Colin and Allison, who were six and three. All I knew was that I was more than twice as nauseous and sluggish than I'd felt with Allison, which I attributed to my advanced age of thirty-six.

Lydia was pushing Allison on the swings as I sat with Colin on the picnic blanket while he drank a juice box. He played imaginary drums on some twigs he'd collected from the ground. Lydia and Allison joined us on the blanket.

I point to Colin, busy with the twigs. "You know, Lyddie, one of my earliest memories is of Rob, playing with my dolls, using their legs as drumsticks. It must be a universal boy thing." I whisper so Allison won't hear. "Maybe this one will be a boy."

"Using dolls and sticks as weapons or musical instruments is *definitely* a boy thing. No doubt about it." Lydia rummages through the food bag. "Who wants graham crackers?"

At the time, I considered the conversation, indeed the entire afternoon at the park, inconsequential. We continued to see the Finellis a few more times, as always, and shared our news about the twins. When Lydia stopped returning my calls soon thereafter, I had connected her disappearance with our news about the babies.

However, now I see that Sunday afternoon in the park in a different light, and another explanation for Lydia's puzzling behavior occurs to me. Maybe Lydia felt she had to sacrifice our friendship, not because she wanted to, or because she suddenly hated me, but for a more noble reason. Maybe she was trying to protect her child, her family, the only way she knew how.

FOURTEEN

Another morning starts with the familiar sight of Aaron throwing a stack of clean shirts into a suitcase. The clock on the bedside table reads 5:36; the first flight to Cleveland leaves at 6:40. Rubbing my eyes, I sit up. "You know, honey, this traveling is getting old. We haven't seen you in weeks." Aaron reacts like I called him a criminal.

"It's my job, Claire. What am I supposed to do? Why are you hassling me in the middle of a trial?" His voice is tight.

"I wasn't hassling you. You don't have to pick a fight on your way out the door," I reply.

"If you want to see me so much, then why didn't you come back earlier from New York?" he accuses. "You're not even working this week, so what's the big deal if I'm out of town?"

"What do you think, that I'm sitting around eating bonbons?"

I glare at him, silently daring him to escalate matters. Instead, I see his features soften. "Claire, sorry I snapped. I know you're upset about Lydia. The trial will end soon and everything will be back to normal again."

I'm stung by his previous tone, but decide to let it go. "Good luck today. Don't worry about us. Everything is fine here."

"My cab will be here in a few minutes. I wish you had woken me when you got home. I was waiting to talk to you. How did it go? What happened?"

"You were snoring over Court TV, so I turned it off and was very careful not to wake you. It's kind of complicated. It will take awhile to explain. The headline is I'm not mad at Rob anymore. Call when you have time and we can talk about the whole thing."

"I will. Sorry I've been gone so much lately. Things should slow down soon."

"Right. I've been hearing that for ten years. Oh, my head. Why did I drink that champagne?"

"Lie down, I'll bring you aspirin," Aaron offers.

"No, you better finish packing." I hear the zip of the suitcase while I am in the bathroom. Then he's gone. I reset the alarm for seven-thirty and go back to sleep.

By nine I'm exhausted, as if I had worked a full day, and all I've done is get the kids to school. Lacking the energy to leave the house, I bring a mug of coffee into the study and pull the phone onto my lap.

There's no chance I'm going to wake Sallie. First, we exchange small talk, then I get to the point. "Sallie, do you remember the name of Lydia's psychiatrist? I'd like to call him and ask about her medications."

"That doesn't sound like such a good idea. I'm sure he won't tell you anything."

"It can't hurt to try."

She sighs. "You're right. Let me think. Dr. Davidson or Davison, something like that."

"In Bethesda or Washington?"

"Washington. Once when Lydia had an appointment I went along with her. She sent me on an errand to a gourmet store next door. There were some little shops there, too. The prices were astounding."

The computer is on the desk right in front of me. Idly, I switch it on to check my e-mail. I hope the whirs and clicks won't distract Sallie. "Sutton Place Gourmet? In Foxhall Square?"

"I think so. Do you want me to ask Matthew for the phone number?"

No messages on my screen. "No, let's not bother Matthew about this. He has so much on his mind. I can look it up. Sallie, one more thing. I noticed on the autopsy report that Lydia's blood type is A. Is Colin's the same type?"

"Yes, it's A, too."

"Then Matthew must also be A, right?"

"No, actually he's Type O. We all donated blood to the hospital blood bank when Vince needed transfusions. Why do you ask?"

"No special reason. I was just wondering. My kids are all A, too."

"Claire, are you okay?" Sallie sounds suspicious, as if she knows I'm fishing for something. Anything.

"Yeah, just tired. I have to run. Speak to you soon. Call me if you need anything."

"You take care, Claire. And call me when you find something out. Anything."

I pull the *Washington White Pages* from the shelf. Five Dr. Davisons, but none in Foxhall Square. I scroll down the Davidsons. Dr. Brian Davidson. The address checks out, New Mexico Avenue, which is the street of Foxhall Square. I copy the doctor's phone number on my pad, and dial before I lose my nerve.

"Dr. Davidson is with a patient. Can he call you back?" asks the secretary.

"Why don't you tell me a good time to call back?" I don't want to be stuck waiting by the phone.

"You can try again in twenty minutes. He should have a few minutes then. Are you a new patient?"

"My name is Claire Newman. I'm calling about a former patient of Dr. Davidson's, a close friend of mine. Lydia Finelli."

"I see." Am I imagining it or has the secretary's tone suddenly turned frosty? "Mrs. Newman, why don't you leave your phone number, in case you don't connect with Dr. Davidson today?"

"Fine." I also give her my cell number, carefully including the 301 area code.

Within ten minutes, the phone rings. It's the secretary again. "Mrs. Newman. This is Lisa, from Dr. Davidson's office. I gave him your message. He says he's sorry but he can't help you. He doesn't disclose information about former patients."

"Could I at least speak to him for a few minutes?"

"Sorry, that's our policy."

Before I can persist, I hear a click. Obviously, Dr. Davidson doesn't want to discuss Lydia's case. How rude, as the twins like to say.

I'm early for the annual spring parent-teacher conferences at nursery school. Zach and Max are in the same class and their evaluations could easily be discussed in one conference. Mrs. Edson, however, gave me a double time slot: 11:30 and 11:45.

I am entitled, after all, to two conferences. We pay two tuitions. As I wait, I station myself near the communal hot water urn, ignoring the herbal tea bags. I try to avoid ingesting any ingredients printed on the back of my shampoo bottle. I read the sign-up sheets posted on the door of the classroom, a subtle reminder to parents to stick to the allotted time.

I let Mrs. Edson effuse about the twins and the wonderful progress they are making, thanks to her sensitivity to their individual needs. The guiding philosophy of this pricey preschool is that anything good the kids do is a result of the school's nurturing environment; anything bad is the fault of their neurotic parents.

I can't fault the school's emphasis on building self-esteem, for students and teachers, but it's difficult not to mock its adherence to political correctness. Is it really necessary to tell impressionable three-, four-, and five-year-olds that the poor animals don't like being cooped up at the National Zoo? Must all art projects consist of ugly, recyclable materials? Mrs. Edson, at least, is not a vegetarian proselytizer, like last year's Ms. Bartlett, whom I haven't forgiven for the twins' boycott of the Thanksgiving turkey two years in a row.

With her frizzy brown curls, granny glasses, and a loose Indian-print shift that looks as if it were sewn from the bedspreads that used to decorate my college dorm, Mrs. Edson looks positively youthful, although she's actually pushing fifty. Her three children are grown, which allows her the illusion that she's infinitely wiser and more experienced than us beginner parents. It amuses her that many of us are her age, yet have children barely out of diapers.

I'm usually in a big hurry to get to work, and Mrs. Edson seems gratified by my unusual patience, beaming as I linger over the finger paintings and carefully study each flyer posted on the bulletin board. As if I am seriously considering volunteering for next week's field trip: a hike around the school grounds, armed with shovels and surgical gloves to pick up old cans and litter. Let the moms with the weekly manicure appointments get their hands dirty.

On my way out, I stop in the bathroom. The toilets are six inches from the ground, which makes them great for potty training, but not middle-aged backs. From inside the stall I hear two mothers at the sink, discussing their children's upcoming soccer practice. There's a reminder I don't need.

There's only one way to tell if Roger's in his office, which is why I'm knocking on his door at 5:45. The lights are on behind the shut door, and he appears quickly. Unless I'm imagining it, his face falls when he sees me.

"Oh, it's you. I couldn't imagine who'd be looking for me now. I'm just on my way out."

"Don't worry, Roger. This will only take a minute. I want to ask you something."

"Sure. Is everything okay with Colin? I assume that's why you're here." His expression has shifted to one of concern.

"Sort of." The only choice of seating is opposite him in an uncomfortable folding chair. I sit, acutely aware that my stomach feels like I swallowed a pound of lead. If I was convinced that Roger was capable of murder, I'm not sure I'd have risked coming here alone. I'm hoping to prod him into talking. To my surprise, my voice sounds steady.

"Roger, let me get to the point. I know what happened in your office that day with Russell Wilkinson."

To his credit, he doesn't try to deny it. "Lydia told you about that?"

I ignore his question. "I'm wondering if what Lydia saw—or thought she saw—has something to do with her death."

"Something to do with her suicide? I don't see how there could possibly be a connection. I don't understand."

"Maybe she didn't kill herself. Maybe she was murdered." I monitor his expression, which looks startled.

"Murdered? Claire, you've lost me. Why would anyone want to kill Lydia? And are the police saying this, or is this your theory?" My crazy theory is his implication.

Wouldn't he like to know what the police think? They think it was a suicide and are happy to let it rest. And unless I bring them some solid, new information, something strong enough to make them reopen the case and investigate, they will write me off as a lunatic. I have one chance to go to the police and make a credible case. I'm not going to blow it until I'm sure I have something. "It's my theory. At least for now. And I don't know why someone would want to murder her. That's why I'm here. I thought you might have some ideas."

He looks genuinely baffled, but that could be an act. "I'm not following. Claire, this sounds like nonsense to me. Anyway, what does this have to do with Russell? Lydia knew that what she saw that day was completely innocent. That's what she told me. I assume that's what she told you. So, why are you bringing this up? What does it have to do with you? Isn't there enough gossip at your own children's schools?"

"Look, Roger, this is serious. Not gossip."

He's standing up. "I'm not going to discuss Russell with you. I did nothing wrong. Russell knows that, his parents know that, and Lydia knew that. As for what you think, I really don't care. I've had it up to here with busybody mothers. I have to leave now. I have dinner plans." Angrily, he shoves papers into his canvas briefcase.

"Well, if you don't want to talk about Russell, that's okay. How about Jason Turnbull?" As a shock device, Jason's name works. Roger sits down again, composed but pale.

"Jason," he repeats, stunned. "Did Lydia know about Jason? I never told her about that. What did she tell you?"

"Lydia didn't know about Jason. At least, as far as I know. But I do. So why don't we discuss it. Or, if you prefer, I can show some newspaper clips to the principal. I'm sure he'd be very interested."

"How did you find out?" His voice is barely a whisper. Maybe now he'll talk.

"I'm a reporter. I've got my sources." I sound like a pretentious jerk, but at least I can leave Karen Kline's name out of it.

"Listen, Claire, I don't have to answer to you. But, for your information, I didn't touch Jason. The little sociopath made the whole thing up and his stupid socialite parents believed him. As for Russell, all I did was hug him. The way any adult would comfort a child in pain." He rises again and strides to the door with his briefcase.

"Claire, we're through here. I don't have to explain myself to you. You can ruin my reputation, and my life, if you want to, by dragging up this old mud. I don't know why you'd want to hurt me, but if you want to spread this malicious gossip, I can't stop you, but it's not going to bring your friend back to life. She was depressed and she took her life. You can tell the police whatever you want. I'm sure they have more experience than me dealing with rich, neurotic, suburban mothers with too much time on their hands."

Talk about hitting where it hurts. My first thought is to remind him I'm not a rich, neurotic housewife, that I actually have a job. A responsible job. I realize that's not the point. Without saying good-bye, I walk quickly down the hall as Roger fumbles with the lock on his door.

Back in my car, on reflection, I feel the slightest stir of sympathy for Roger. What right do I have to barge in on him and drag up his past? Then, I harden my heart. How do I know he didn't kill Lydia? Maybe he would have done anything to make the incident with Russell go away

It's not much but, at the moment, it's the only theory I have.

FIFTEEN

I arrive at the Japanese restaurant first. As soon as I'm seated and drinking my green tea, I see Val striding toward the table, dressed in a narrow, black pants suit and a crisp, white-cotton shirt tucked into her thin waist.

"Without you, work is unbearably boring," she says, "especially at lunchtime." She bends to kiss me on the cheek.

"I know. I miss you, too. I can barely think straight. I need to talk to you."

"Fine. Let's order first. I'm starving and I have to be at the White House by three."

We don't even look at the menu. Val calls my decisiveness with menus my single defining characteristic, a symbol of how sure I am, most of the time, of my own mind. She may be overinterpreting, although it's true that I don't sweat the small details. Life is too short to waste agonizing over tuna salad versus grilled cheese. Funny, though, how lately many of my deepest-held convictions about people's character, especially Lydia's, don't seem to be holding up.

In this particular sushi place we always order the same thing. Sushi and a green tea for me, sashimi and a Kirin for Val. Val can drink a beer or a glass of wine at lunch and then go shoot a few prizewinning photos. If I drink at lunch, I'm good for a nap.

"Before I forget, the camera store called. The camera's ready. I'll get it later on my way home."

"Thanks. How much?"

"A lot. About three hundred dollars. It was really smashed. And the new lens is at least a hundred and fifty dollars. I'll let you know."

"Now, tell me what I'm missing at the office." My real life is still the magazine, even when I'm not there.

Not much happening there. Val recounts the stale but recurring rumor that Calvin has bid on the *Los Angeles Herald*. The former New York bureau chief, who left last year to join a dot-com company, wants his job back before his new company folds, but Leslie's not inclined in that direction. The wife of the macho assistant managing editor appears to have left him for a woman. "That should destroy his last tiny shred of self-esteem," Val says. "Consider yourself lucky he's not getting his hands on your copy this week."

I'm not surprised by the lack of intrigue. The staff consensus is that the level of daily scheming and deception at *Nationweek* has dropped sharply since Leslie restored peace and tranquility to our corridors. Our workplace has become drab and boring. I remind Val about meeting Rob for dinner next time he's in town.

"As if I could forget," she says. "Thanks again. If I get any work in Hollywood, I'm going to take us, and Alex and Aaron, to a great dinner."

"The hell with dinner. Let's go to a spa. My grief-induced appetite loss only lasted a week."

"Okay, now, spill. I want to hear everything you've found out so far about Lydia."

Val listens attentively. One of the things I love about her is that she's virtually unshakable. I can confess my deepest, darkest secrets to her, and she nods in agreement, as if I am giving voice to her own hidden depravities. Which has the effect of making whatever I'm owning up to seem downright normal. With Val, I never have to edit my version of events, the way I do with other people. She doesn't register emotion at anything I tell her, until I get to the uncertainty over Colin's paternity.

"Wow. No wonder Lydia was depressed. That's a huge secret to live with all those years."

"So what do you think? Murder or suicide?" I ask, dipping a piece of California roll into soy sauce.

"I'm not sure. It doesn't sound to me like you really got the coach on anything. Don't you think you'd pick up a strong vibe if he were a sleazy child molester? You make him sound too nice to be guilty."

"I know. He has a motive, a good one, but I'm not convinced. And he's the only candidate at the moment."

"Well, what if Jill and Mathew really are having an affair? Maybe Lydia found out. If Jill loves Matthew, and wants to marry him, that gives her a strong motive."

"True. Problem is I have trouble seeing her as a homewrecker. She's such a straight arrow. She doesn't strike me as a person who thinks her needs should take precedence over anyone else's. And she cared about Lydia an awful lot."

"Sounds dreadful, like a grown-up Girl Scout."

"Then I'm not describing her well. Jill's a kind, solid person. Although she gets distracted sometimes by her work. It's as if she leaves the planet for awhile."

"You know, you always think the best of people," Val says, sipping her beer. "You should be more cynical, like me. It leads to less disappointment."

We bat it around for awhile, not having much to go on except that Jill and Lydia were together the Sunday before Lydia died.

"Maybe Jill told Lydia that day that she and Matthew were in love. And that drove Lydia to suicide. Maybe Lydia would have rather killed herself than kill Matthew for cheating or go through a divorce. Especially if Lydia thought Matthew was going to discard her and try to win custody of Colin," I suggest.

"Lydia had a history of mental illness. She might have been scared that a judge would give Matthew custody of Colin. He's a doctor, after all, a pillar of respectability," says Val, but she looks skeptical.

"Maybe not such a pillar, if he's sleeping with Jill. Do you think it's possible that the reason Lydia called me, and sent me the financial statement, was because she wanted me to help get dirt on Matthew to use against him in a divorce?"

"Could be," Val says, "but what if it wasn't suicide?"

"For the life of me I can't figure out how or why Jill would kill her and make it look like a suicide. Although she is a doctor and a scientist."

Our inevitable conclusion is that I'm going to have to do a lot more digging.

"Go see Jill again. Confront her about her affair with Matthew. That should unnerve her enough to tell you more," Val says.

"I can't. I'm starting to feel like a sleazeball myself. So far, I've accused Roger of being a child molester without having any proof, broken into Matthew's financial records, and been less than upfront with my husband about my investigation."

"You know, Claire, if it were only a story at stake here, I would agree. I know you better than that. We're talking life and death here. Maybe even murder. Anything you've done wrong so far is small potatoes." Val echoes Rob's warning: "Whatever you decide to do next, be careful. And call me if you think that you're in any danger."

It's not an idle offer. Before trading her flak jacket for a diaper bag, Val had dodged bullets in war zones in Central America, including Nicaragua and El Salvador. She says that she sometimes misses her youthful adventures, but war photojournalism is not compatible with the goals of motherhood.

"I'm not going to do anything yet," I say as we leave the restaurant. "I need a plan, some fresh ideas. I'll call you tomorrow."

"I'll think about it, too. I promise," Val says.

* * *

By evening, I'm struggling to figure out Allison's math homework, much less any new theories about Lydia's death. Math is a strain because I refuse to let on to my daughter that I was math-phobic as a child, afraid it will affect her self-confidence and stellar grades. This is one of those many nights I wish Aaron were home. I ignore the phone when it rings, afraid I'll lose my momentum.

"Mommy, it's Val," Max calls.

Good. Maybe she has had an inspiration. "Claire, about the camera. When I went to pick it up, Billy, the guy from the store, had managed to pry open the back. He found a roll of film inside."

"You're kidding," I say mildly. "Well, it's probably nothing. Pictures of Colin's soccer team, or the PTA picnic. Is Billy going to develop it?"

"I wouldn't let him. Luckily he put the camera in a black bag before he forced it open so the film wouldn't be exposed. He rewound the film. I have some darkroom stuff to do, so I'm going to develop it, tonight, after the kids are in bed. I thought you wouldn't want to wait."

"Thanks, that was smart. I really appreciate all the trouble you're going to. I'll come over later and watch you. Not that I'm expecting to find any clues, but you never know. I'll try to get the kids tucked in by nine. Is that okay?" I walk over to the refrigerator, eye the white wine, and remove the seltzer bottle instead. If I drink half a glass of wine, Allison will give me a hard time about driving five minutes to Val's house. The antidrug indoctrination they get starting in elementary school is a bit overboard.

"Perfect. See you in an hour."

"The film is drying. Come downstairs." I follow Val into her darkroom, a small room off of the playroom in the basement. The negatives are hanging in long strips from silver metal clips. With her left hand, Val picks up a small black cylinder and holds it to the negatives in her right hand.

159

"What a cute little thing. It looks like it belongs in a doll house."

"It's called a loupe, and it's a magnifying glass, you idiot."

Perching on a stool next to Val, I watch as she moves the loupe along the strip of negatives. Except for the hum of the developing machine the room is silent. "Oh, my God," she shrieks. "Claire, why didn't you tell me Lydia was into nude photography?"

"What are you talking about?" Val isn't smiling the way she does when she's teasing. "Here, take a look." Val offers me the loupe. "I have no idea who this guy in the picture is, but from your descriptions of Matthew, I'm guessing it's not him."

I hold the loupe to the negatives. "You're crazy, Val. All I can see are little X rays." A few seconds later, I make out a man's torso and a beard. "Holy shit. That's Randy. Naked. In six different frames." The next four frames are of a woman. The curly hair, the mouth, the shape of the eyes are unmistakable.

"Val, why is this last frame so out of focus?" All that's visible is the bottom part of Lydia's face. Her arm is reaching out of the frame as if she's touching the camera.

Val grabs the loupe from me and studies the negative. "It looks like those are self-portraits. In that shot, Lydia is reaching for the shutter. The self-timer probably went off."

"Why would she need to do that? Clearly, Randy was in the room with her."

Val shrugs. "Beats me. Do you want me to print these? There are only ten. The rest of the roll is blank. It's never been exposed."

I nod my head, still in shock from the images and what they suggest about the nature of Lydia and Randy's relationship. Was there any male in Lydia's life that she wasn't sleeping with? For the next hour and a half, I watch Val as disturbing images of Randy and Lydia float to the surface of the developing pan, which Val has placed under a red light. Each black-and-white print adds a few more details to a scene I could never have imagined. Randy's stiff, uncomfortable expression. The glint, probably from his belt buckle. "I don't think he's completely naked. He has to be wearing pants in this shot. That has to be his belt," Val says, pointing.

Despite the surprises I've discovered about Lydia lately, the photos of her wearing a low-cut black lace bra, with her tousled hair draped over one eye, astound me. I can't decide if the expression in her eyes is an attempt at looking seductive or a vacant stare.

Val, focused on her work, doesn't try to make conversation. "I'll make three copies of each print. It's easier if I do it now."

"Thanks. I'll take one set. To show Randy. Will you keep the other prints and negatives here? Hide them in a drawer or something?"

"Of course I will," Val says. "Should I keep the camera for a few days, too?" She realizes how uncomfortable the camera makes me.

"Good idea." I'm not ready to return the camera to Colin yet. Val puts one set of prints in a manila envelope and hands it to me. "It's really getting late. Drive home carefully." She gives me a hug and keeps her arm around my shoulder as she walks me to the door. "Would you rather I drive you home? You look pretty shaken."

"No, I'm fine. I can make it home. Val, thanks a million. As much as they disgust me, these pictures could be the breakthrough I need."

Val raises her eyebrows. "Maybe. Maybe not. Say Lydia and Randy were having an affair. It certainly looks that way from these pictures, but that doesn't necessarily mean he murdered her."

Randy and Lydia. Lydia and Rob. Lydia had a busy secret life as the belle of Bethesda. My stomach is as queasy as if I stepped off a roller-coaster ride. I don't remember driving home from Val's, but suddenly I'm parked in my own driveway. Once inside I pour myself a generous shot of brandy and bring it upstairs.

SIXTEEN

The photos repulse me. Not their content exactly. I'm no prude, and Randy and Lydia were consenting adults. Many people expose more flesh on an ordinary day at the Bethesda Swim Club. These photos, however, make me feel dirty, sneaky, like a voyeur, because I know they weren't intended for anyone else's eyes.

I'm tempted to take a match and ignite them, turn them into a satisfying heap of gray ash. No one would be the wiser then, except Val, and I could swear her to secrecy. If I burn them, there's a chance that in five or ten or twenty years the black-and-white images will recede from my memory. In their place will be the familiar images: Lydia in her flowered minidress at her sweet-sixteen party; in her flowing cap and gown at our high-school graduation; in her delicately beaded, ivory silk-and-lace wedding gown. Those innocent images no longer match the pictures of Lydia the seductress that are now firmly planted in my head.

The journalist in me won't light that match. The photos may be all there is, the only tangible evidence linking Randy to Lydia's death. So, after a long night of watching the digital numbers change, I pick up the phone the next morning, and call the person whom, in all the world, I want to talk to least.

* * *

I leave a message on his office voicemail: "Randy, this is Claire Newman. Please call me back as soon as possible. It's important." As I wait, I think about what I'm going to say. An hour later, I call again. This time, Randy answers on the second ring.

"Claire, I just got in and heard your message. I was about to call you. What's going on?"

"Randy, I need to see you today. There's something I want to talk to you about. It's important." My annoyance is unmistakable.

"Sorry, Claire. Today's impossible. I have patients back to back all day. How about next week, maybe Thursday or Friday?" He sounds patient, reasonable.

How dare he? Although it will ruin the lovely element of surprise, I can't resist. "Randy, I found some photos."

His voice drops to a whisper. "Photos. I see. Claire, it's not what you think. I can explain. Come in at two. I'll switch a few things around."

"See you then." Remaining cordial requires every bit of self-control, but I don't want to tip my hand before I get there.

Randy is waiting in the reception area when I step off the elevator. "Claire, please come in," he says, extending his hand. I ignore it, and follow him into his office. He sits behind his desk and motions me to sit down.

I don't waste any time removing the manila folder from my bag. I watch his face as he opens the folder and carefully studies each photograph. He doesn't register surprise until he sees the photos of Lydia.

"I had no idea Bethesda was such a swinging place. How long were you and Lydia sleeping together?" Clearly I'm angry.

"Claire, I know what this looks like, but don't jump to conclusions. We weren't having an affair."

"I see. You just liked to undress and take kinky photos. But no sex."

"You're wrong. I was wearing my pants. And I didn't take these pictures of Lydia."

"You mean someone else was there, too?" I say. "That's kinkier than I thought. Let's see, who could it have been? Matthew? Karen? Colin? One of your daughters?" The sarcasm doesn't mask my fury.

"Just give me a chance to explain, okay? I knew these pictures were on the roll of film in Lydia's camera. I didn't know about the ones of her. She must have taken them herself, after I left."

"You expect me to believe that?" I recall, however, Val's explanation of the photo where Lydia's face is too close to the camera, the one where her arm is reaching out as if to touch the self-timer. I sit back in the chair and fold my arms over my chest. "I'm waiting."

"I know this looks bad," Randy says, "but just give me a chance. Let me put these photos in their proper context." He's squirming now.

"It was a Saturday morning, a few months ago. Must have been the end of February. I was home reading. Karen had taken the girls shopping. Lydia called looking for Karen. I asked how she was feeling. Sometimes she would talk to me about her medications, the side effects. She said she wasn't feeling great, kind of headachy, nauseous and weak. I went across the street to check on her."

"Was that unusual? To go there when Matthew and Colin were out?"

"Not at all. Our families are always in and out of each other's houses. We keep spare keys for each other. When Matthew goes out of town sometimes, he asks Karen or me to keep an eye on things.

"When I got to Lydia's, she was fooling around with her camera. It was just like one I used to have about fifteen years ago, a Nikomat. I traded mine in awhile ago. Lydia had bought hers during one of her former flings with photography."

His account has a ring of truth. Lydia adopted and dropped hobbies as frequently as other people changed socks.

"She'd gotten interested in photography again. Enrolled in a class at the Corcoran. Studying the human figure, or something. We talked about photography and she asked me to pose for some photos, for a class assignment. Sure, I said, thinking it would distract her. The first thing she asked me to do was take off my shirt. I got mad and told her to forget the whole thing, that I wasn't a model, but she wouldn't drop it." Randy rubs his temples as if the memory is causing a headache.

"Instead of dropping it, Lydia began to mock me, saying she had no idea I was so prim and proper. 'It's not like I've never seen your bare chest,' she said. 'We go swimming together all the time.'"

"That's different, I told her. The pool is a public place." He looks at me to see if I'm buying his tale. I keep my expression blank on purpose.

"She wouldn't let it go. She said it was for a class assignment at a museum, not a *Playgirl* centerfold.

"I asked her what would happen if someone in our families saw the photos, and she promised me no one would ever see them. 'It's not as if Matthew takes much interest in my hobbies,' she said.

"Finally, I relented because she seemed so intent. Although I was nervous the whole time, I let her take five or six shots. I was worried someone would walk in and get the wrong idea. And I was pretty steamed at how she manipulated me into posing. Next thing I know, Lydia is pulling her sweater up over her head." Randy grimaces as he recounts the unpleasant scene.

"I asked her what the hell she thought she was doing. She told me to relax. She wanted me to take a few photos of her now.

"I was getting more uncomfortable. Lydia had a funny expression in her eyes, like she was taunting me. Or, at least, that's what I thought at the time. I guess I lost my temper."

Randy sighs. "I told her to get dressed; she was acting like a petulant child and I'd had enough. I walked downstairs. My hand was on the knob of the front door when Lydia caught up with me. She was in such a rush to catch me she was wearing only her bra and jeans.

She put her hands on my hands to stop me from leaving." I'm riveted, keeping my eyes fixed on Randy's face, not breaking eye contact with him.

"Lydia seemed to come to her senses. She apologized, and said that she didn't know what had gotten into her. She asked me to stay for awhile.

"I agreed because I thought we both should calm down. I didn't want things between us to be strained; Karen or Matthew would have noticed. So, I told Lydia I'd wait in the kitchen while she got dressed. If you're not down in two minutes, I warned her, I'm gone."

I watch Randy studying the photos, staring at the one where Lydia's bra strap is suggestively pulled off her shoulder.

"Claire, she was back in the kitchen within two minutes. I can't believe that she had the time, but she must have snapped those self-portraits first. It's the only explanation I can think of."

"How did she act when she came downstairs?" I ask, trying to put the pieces of the story together.

"Completely normal. She came into the kitchen carrying the camera, looking contrite. I told her that on second thought I'd rather she didn't use those photos for her class. What if someone there was a patient or someone I knew?" He looks at me sheepishly. "I know, I should have thought of that before I let her take them."

"I asked Lydia to destroy the film," he continues. "She promised and I believed her. She gave me coffee and blueberry muffins, and we talked as if nothing unusual had happened. Then, somehow, we got on the topic of the photos and she started badgering me all over again."

"Her moods changed so quickly," he adds. "She was so mad her voice was shaking. I thought she might hit me. Instead, she threw the camera at me. I moved out of the way and it hit the wall, then landed with a thud, on its back on the tile. A little black knob rolled across the floor. I got out of there as fast as I could."

"Randy, it's hard for me to believe that Lydia went from calm to camera flinging within minutes," I interject.

"It wasn't pretty," he nods. "Ever since she died, I've been afraid that those pictures would surface. They were innocent but they can really hurt me. If a patient saw them, or my family, it would look bad." He puts his head on the desk, pausing for a few seconds. "The worst part of the whole mess is that Lydia and I never really patched things up. We were still mad at each other the night she killed herself. I can't help thinking that if we hadn't had that fight, if she could have talked to me, I could have helped her. That she might still be alive. I failed her."

He gives me a penetrating look, appealing to my sympathy. I'm verging on believing him because his story explains, logically, how the camera got wrecked. "Claire, I'm begging you not to tell anyone about these pictures. For obvious reasons. But Lydia and I were not having an affair. Do you believe me?"

"I don't know. These photos are incriminating." If Randy and Lydia were having an affair, it opened up possibilities I hadn't considered. Randy had a motive to get rid of Lydia. If Karen knew, she had a motive, too.

"Claire, will you give me these photos and the negatives? So I can stop worrying about where they may turn up next?"

"I don't have the negatives with me. But, yes, I'll bring them to you. You can have these prints." No need to tell him that Val had printed two extra sets of the pictures and was keeping them in her basement for me, along with the camera.

"Look, Randy, I have to think about what you told me. I'll be in touch." I leave the photos on his desk.

Randy looks at them and manages a small smile. "Thanks, Claire. Call me whenever you feel like it."

"You can count on it." I walk to my car and think about Randy's explanation. Means, motive, opportunity. If they were having an affair, and Randy wanted out, he had all three.

As a psychiatrist Randy has plenty of expertise in antidepressants. If they were having an affair, and Lydia told Karen or Matthew about it, Randy's nice life with Karen would probably be over. And he could have gotten into Lydia's house easily that night if he wanted to slip her some lethal drug while she slept.

If Randy killed Lydia, how did he make it look like suicide?

Saturday is unseasonably cool for the last weekend in April, heavy-sweater weather. I turn the heat up in the car on my way to pick up Colin. He'd told me to come at one. Aaron had taken our crew to McDonald's, which is why he's known as the fun parent. My stomach rumbles. My lunch was a fat-free vanilla yogurt. Might as well just melt some chalk and swallow it. Matthew's car is not in sight, I notice, as I pull up to their house. Colin answers my knock, his mouth full of peanut butter and jelly.

"Hi, Aunt Claire. Dad just left for the hospital. He says hi."

He looks drawn. "Hi, honey. Are you getting enough to eat? I can make you an omelet or a grilled-cheese sandwich."

"I'm almost full. This is my second sandwich. Claudia left a pot of chili for the weekend, but I don't like her chili."

"How's Claudia's cooking?" I have asked him several times how he likes the new housekeeper but his answers have been politely noncommittal.

"Not too bad. A little spicy. And she makes rice with everything. I'm starting to miss potatoes."

"Welcome to the club. Allison jokes that Trini would put rice in the cornflakes, if we let her." He smiles. "Maybe you could mention to Claudia that you prefer potatoes or pasta once in awhile. I'm sure she wants to please you."

I make myself at home, opening the refrigerator door. "Colin, how about some cheese or fruit? Grapes? An apple?"

"Okay, grapes." Colin's a typical kid who will only eat fruit if someone else washes it and puts it in front of his face. As I dry the grapes with a paper towel, I pop a few into my mouth, then sit across from Colin at the table.

"How was school this week?"

"Okay." He tells me his ideas for an oral-history project and about a Spanish test that he thinks he aced. Lydia's death does not appear to be affecting his grades.

"Your camera's almost ready. I will return it to you in a few days."

"Thanks. It's funny, Mr. Kline was looking for it last week."

"Oh," I say. "Why? Did he want to borrow it for some reason?" I keep my tone neutral.

"He came over, said my mom had mentioned that it was broken. He wanted to get it fixed for me. I thanked him, but told him you were already taking care of it."

"That was considerate of him." Nice try, Randy. What a slime. So, he already knew I had the camera before I called to tell him about the photos, which means that my phone call wasn't the surprise he pretended it was. "How about some more grapes? Or something else?"

"I'll just have some milk and cookies." I watch him pour the milk and grab four Oreos. "Want any, Aunt Claire?"

"No thanks." He's wearing Topsiders. "Colin, Allison is expecting you to help her with those soccer kicks. Wouldn't it be easier with sneakers or cleats?"

"Uh-huh. I'll go change."

"Finish your lunch. I'll run up and get them for you. Are they in your closet, or do you keep them under the bed, like my kids?"

"The closet. In a white box. Thanks."

I walk down the hall to his bedroom, taking note of the house's pristine interior. It looks more like a house featured in a magazine than a real home. No one would ever consider our household—littered with toys, tennis balls, art projects, magazines, and soiled sweatshirts—for a photo spread.

Claudia's probably the first Finelli housekeeper who stands a chance of long-term employment. She probably doesn't vacuum and scrub the toilets twice a day, like Lydia did, but Colin and Matthew are unlikely to notice, or care. The condition of Colin's room is impressive, with hospital corners on the twin beds, and no clothes or sports equipment lying on the floor. In contrast to Allison, who makes her bed by lifting the quilt off the floor and hiding her dirty pajamas under the sheets.

I spot three white shoe boxes stacked in Colin's closet. I open the first one. Not at all what I'm expecting, but I know exactly what it is. The box contains a chunk of black soap—at eighteen dollars per bar, one of Lydia's few extravagances; two maroon bottles containing shampoo and cream rinse; and a tube of prescription toothpaste called Gingavent.

I pick up the tube, examining it closely. My periodontist recently recommended that I start using it; it's supposed to slow down the degeneration of gum tissue. Another one of the joys of turning forty. The prescription is still in my wallet, unfilled. I put the lid back on the shoe box, and find the sneakers. On my way back to the kitchen I debate mentioning Lydia's toiletries. Maybe Colin needs to talk.

"Colin, I opened the wrong shoe box by mistake. I found your mom's shampoo and stuff."

"Oh, yeah, I forgot that was in the closet, too." He looks embarrassed. "Dad threw out her stuff right away, her makeup and hair junk and everything. When I saw her soap and shampoo and toothpaste in the trash bag, they seemed so much a part of her," he says, his voice breaking. "When Dad wasn't looking, I took them out of the garbage. The shampoo smells like her hair used to." He looks worried. "I know it sounds weird. You won't tell anyone, will you?"

I pull him close. "Colin, I don't think it's weird at all. Not in the slightest. I would have done the same thing. In fact, your grandmother gave me a pair of your mom's earrings and sometimes I open my jewelry box and take them out and hold them. I promise I won't tell anyone about the shoe box. Do you promise not to tell anyone about the earrings?"

"Sure, but it's not the same thing. You didn't pick the earrings out of the trash."

A minor point. "Colin, I have some old pictures of your mom, which I also keep in old shoe boxes. I keep meaning to put them in albums. How about if I go through them this week and give you whatever photos I can find? And I may have some of her books on my shelf, too. We traded back and forth a lot. You can have those, too, okay?"

"Sure, that would be nice. But we better go. Allison said her game starts at four."

I follow him out, overcome by this brief glimpse of his private pain. Matthew has told me that Colin has plenty of friends, despite the many hours he spends alone, on-line. He's a decent athlete, is on teams, and gets invited to parties. Still, Matthew says, he has a zone of privacy that no one can penetrate. Like other only children. Like Lydia.

I can barely remember what it's like to be twelve, on the excruciating cusp between innocence and adulthood. How much worse it must be to arrive at this confusing juncture without a mother.

Finding Lydia's toothpaste spooks me. Dental woes were a bond we shared. We were each other's most sympathetic audience: Matthew has nearly perfect teeth, one cavity in his entire life, and Aaron's too stoic to empathize much with my pain and suffering.

We never went to the same dentists—I go to ones who practice downtown, within walking distance of my office. Lydia preferred dentists in the suburbs. We constantly compared notes about different procedures, how much they hurt, how long they took, how much they cost.

I glance at Colin, seat belt buckled, looking serenely out the window. "Colin, how are your teeth?"

"What do you mean? I didn't say anything was wrong with my teeth."

"I don't mean this minute. I mean, do you get cavities? I have terrible teeth and gums, like your mom. We used to say we hoped our kids would inherit their dads' teeth. My kids are lucky that way. Allison has had one cavity so far, the twins none."

"I lucked out, too. My dad says I look like the Marcos side, but at least I got the Finelli teeth."

I lean over and pat his hand. "Good. I'm glad to hear it." I don't say anything for the rest of the ride. I'm thinking about my family. My mother feels personally responsible for passing on her defective gums to me. Rob, like my father, has strong, healthy teeth.

Sharing my suspicion with Aaron that Randy Kline may have been sleeping with Lydia, and possibly killed her, is not a formula for a peaceful weekend. So, I keep this information to myself, until I have more substantial evidence to offer Perry Mason. Aaron is too preoccupied with the kids and his case to notice my uncharacteristic silence.

Monday morning, I run errands and mull over how to proceed, hoping my stealth method of problem solving will kick in. it. When I'm busy with an unrelated activity, answers often come to me. For instance, I can be stuck on a lead for a story all day, then it will occur to me when I'm taking a shower or chopping carrots for dinner. Thus, I decide that shopping for the kids' camp clothes is the best use of my day.

I head out at ten, armed with a long list. "Trini, tell the kids I'll be back by three-thirty. See you."

"'Bye, Claire. Have a nice day. Don't spend too much money," she jokes, imitating Aaron's constant rejoinder.

The day passes pleasantly enough. I browse around Borders, stock up at the pharmacy, and eat a bowl of *pho* for lunch at a Vietnamese hole in the wall near the mall. I buy stacks of brightly colored cotton shorts, T-shirts, and socks. Loaded with shopping bags, I return to the empty house around three. On mild days like this, Trini and the twins leave early to pick up Allison, so they can play on the schoolyard swings.

I bring the clothing bags into the kids' bedrooms and divide the new toiletries between their bathroom and ours. At the entrance to our bedroom, I stop. The contents of our bureau drawers have been upended onto the floor. In one corner lay hats, purses, and a pile of Aaron's dirty shirts for the dry cleaner. The dust ruffle on our bed is disheveled, as if someone had pulled it up to search underneath it.

My first thought is that the twins have played an unusually wild game of hide and seek. There's nothing playful, however, in the way the room was trashed.

My jewelry box, which I keep on top of the dresser, looks untouched. How strange that a burglar wasn't even mildly curious. I run to the study, where another big mess awaits. File cabinets are wide open, some dumped on the floor, with financial records and dozens of manila folders scattered around.

I retrace my steps downstairs, realizing that I missed any signs of forced entry on my way in because I came straight through the front door and upstairs. The contents of the hall closet have been dumped on the floor—a mountain of winter jackets, rain slickers, scarves, and boots.

The silver, stored in a velvet-lined box in the bottom of the dining-room breakfront is in its usual place, all accounted for. In the family room, the stereo, CD player, and television are unharmed, but shards of broken glass from the sliding-glass doors to the back-yard line the blond wood floors. The shattered door reveals the forced entry. From the looks of it, the intruder used a sharp rock to break the glass. The broken glass didn't trigger an alarm system because we don't have one. Aaron has long resisted a security sys-tem, as he considers it too expensive.

Choking back tears, I sit on the floor and survey the damage. I tell myself to stay calm, don't cry, the kids will be back any minute. Nobody got hurt. It's just a bunch of things, a big mess that we can clean up. Reaching for the phone, I call the police. Then I go outside to wait and to intercept my family. I don't want the kids to see our home in disarray, to feel like I do, violated and alone.

SEVENTEEN

A break-in? In *our* neighborhood?" Aaron's voice practically cracks. "I can catch the next plane home."

"Aaron, it's midnight and you're in the middle of a trial. Relax. The situation's under control. The police said it was probably teenagers pulling a prank. That there have been a few incidents around here lately." I don't feel nearly as calm as I sound. "They didn't take anything, they just made a mess. And violated our home."

"Any fingerprints?"

"It's odd, but there weren't. The cops said that these days even amateurs, including teenage pranksters, wear gloves. They learned from watching the O.J. trial."

"Why'd they pick our house?"

"Probably because we are one of the few houses on the block without an alarm system. At least that's what the cops said." I keep the "I told you so" to myself.

"Okay, you're right, I've been a jerk. We need an alarm. Get one installed tomorrow. Buy the most expensive one you can find, with all the bells and whistles. Whatever makes you feel safe. You sure the kids are okay?" He sounds humbled.

"They're fine now. Trini took them back to the park, so they weren't here when the police came. I called Val and she came straight from work and helped me. I took the kids out to dinner while Trini finished cleaning up. Allison seems a little anxious, but the boys thought it was pretty cool that bad guys got into our house. They're sleeping with their plastic swords. They're asleep now, but I won't be surprised if all three of them wake up in the middle of the night and wind up in our bed."

"I'm sorry you have to deal with this, especially so soon after Lydia." For the first time in weeks, Aaron doesn't seem impatient with me.

"I'm okay, really. I'm going to try to get some sleep. I'm wiped. You should too."

"I'll call you first thing in the morning, before the kids leave. I love you."

"I love you, too." I hang up, wondering if he'd love me as much if I told him the real reason I'm spooked. I don't think it was teenage vandals; I think Randy ransacked our house, in pursuit of the camera and negatives. Val agrees with me. Randy wants those photos pretty badly. And perhaps he's also sending me a sinister warning to stop asking questions about Lydia's death.

I gulp from the snifter of brandy I keep refilling. I won't admit this to Aaron but I'm scared. Seeing our house ransacked drove home an obvious point, one that I've been denying to myself pretty hard: Investigating murder is dangerous. I'd like to climb into bed with Trini, or sleep with my own sword. I have to nail Randy and soon. It's the only way I'll ever get a decent night's sleep again.

By morning, the kids are acting as if the break-in was in the distant past. I'm not nearly as resilient. I don't think it will hurt if I take a few hours off to regroup. May as well try a little self-improvement. I call my periodontist's office and speak to the hygienist. "Cathy, Dr. Nadicki gave me a prescription for Gingavent toothpaste several weeks ago, and I haven't gotten around to filling it. He said not too many drugstores stock it. Where should I go?"

"The best place is Oliver's in Chevy Chase. Know where it is?"

"Sure. In that medical building off Wisconsin Avenue near Mazza Galleria, right? Across the street from the Gap. What does it cost, fifty dollars a tube?"

She laughs. "Not quite that much. And it's probably covered by your insurance."

Grateful for an excuse to leave the house, I drive over. Oliver's is a throwback, a tiny, old-fashioned apothecary, owned by the same family for generations. It competes against the large discount chains by carrying exotic items, providing delivery service, and charging higher prices, which is why I don't shop there much.

The pharmacist isn't there, but I recognize the clerk behind the counter. Susan Glazier grew up in our neighborhood, and two summers ago baby-sat my kids a few times. "Hi, Susan. Aren't you in college now?"

"Claire, hi. Nice to see you. No, I took a semester off to earn extra money. College is pretty expensive and I want to go to Europe this summer." She looks around to make sure we are alone. "This isn't what I had in mind, but I don't have any marketable skills. What can I do for you? Tell me about your kids and what they're up to these days. How old are the boys now, three?"

I hand her the prescription. "No, they're four. Practically shaving. Stop by and say hello to them when you have time. They remember you."

"I'd love to. Let me bring this to Doc Oliver. He's in the back. It shouldn't take more than ten minutes. Are you going to wait?"

"Sure. I'll go look at the magazines." The selection is so narrow that I'm back at the counter within five minutes. To pass the time, I make a small pile of items to buy. A tin of imported lemon drops, a tube of navy-blue mascara, three bars of glycerin soap. I envision Lydia at this counter, waiting for her toothpaste. How it would irk her to be overcharged. She wouldn't have filled the wait by picking out other overpriced items she didn't need. That was Lydia: Why buy an unnecessary stick of gum just for the transitory pleasure of the purchase?

Suddenly, I'm curious to see if my mental image is right, if in fact, Lydia did buy her Gingavent at Oliver's. Usually, I laugh at superstitions, the way I do at the e-mail chain letters I always break. If Lydia did buy the toothpaste here, I'll take it as a sign from above that I'm on the right track about Randy.

My days covering the police beat at the *Montgomery County Bulletin* taught me that, after a suicide, normal police procedure is to pull the victim's prescription records and check them against the pills and medications found at the dead person's home, in medicine cabinets, clothing pockets, briefcases, and purses.

Yet, the odds of the police tracking down Lydia's prescription records to this little store to check on a harmless tube of toothpaste seem virtually nil. I wouldn't risk the embarrassment of checking with Doc Oliver, who might have heard of her death, or recognize her name from prescriptions he filled for Matthew's patients. Asking Susan, however, is a safe bet. Her parents, Christian Scientists, aren't in the Finellis' social loop.

"Susan, can you do me a favor while I'm here? A friend of mine has the same prescription. I bet she fills it here. I'm going to see her later, so maybe I can bring her a tube and save her a trip. The prescription is refillable three times, right?"

"Right. Let me check on the computer. What's her name?"

"Lydia Finelli. With two *l*s. She lives on Highland Manor Road." I give no outward sign that this is an unusual request.

Susan clicks a few keys. "Claire, I don't think she'll be needing a refill."

"Why not?" I'm stalling. If Susan knows Lydia's dead, it's going to be embarrassing.

"She got two tubes a few weeks ago and each one lasts for about six weeks."

"Really. Two tubes. I wonder why. Can I see?"

"Sure. She bought one on April sixth. And another one on April thirteenth."

April 13th? Lydia died early in the morning on Monday, April 15. Why would anyone contemplating suicide worry about her gums? Under the circumstances, it would be understandable if she stopped flossing altogether, but not Lydia the perfect. Her personal hygiene habits must have been too entrenched.

"You sure that's the right date?"

"Absolutely. It says so right here. It looks like her husband signed the receipt."

I look over Susan's shoulder and recognize Matthew's indecipherable scrawl. "If my handwriting was better, I would be a lawyer," he liked to joke. Matthew must have been here on an errand and thoughtfully picked up another tube, not knowing Lydia didn't need it. Although he could have asked, like I did, and found out she had just bought one. Probably a guy thing, thinking it's a sign of weakness to ask a simple question of a pharmacist, like asking for directions at a gas station.

A few minutes later I walk out with my tube—eighteen dollars for toothpaste that probably contains two dollars worth of ingredients. One more errand to cross off the list.

Next stop is the library at the National Institutes of Health to research blood types for Rob. I'd also like to find more information about monoamine oxidase inhibitors, the class of drugs that includes Nardil, Lydia's antidepressant. I haven't had much luck online.

The NIH librarians are extremely helpful steering me toward information about genetics and blood types. Within a few hours, I have an answer for Rob, but it's ambiguous. Colin could be Rob's son. It's equally possible that he's Matthew's son. Only genetic testing will yield a definitive answer. Poor Rob may never know.

Information is far sketchier on MAOs. All I find is one more citation in last year's November–December issue of the *American Journal of Neuropharmacology*. A psychiatrist in Ames, Iowa, described how an obese thirty-five-year-old patient, who was taking Nardil for depression, suffered a fatal stroke after gorging himself with Chianti, blue cheese, and sauerkraut. The description of the case echoes Lydia's death, but yields no new information. I wonder what role the obesity played in his death.

I stop for groceries on the way home, looking forward to the mindless task of cooking dinner. Fresh salmon fillets, corn on the cob, a strawberry tart. Maybe I can entice Colin into joining us.

At home, I unload the bags. It's late enough to call the West Coast. Rob's in a meeting but his assistant says he'll get back to me within the hour. I marinate, husk, and toss a salad. The phone rings as I'm changing into sweats.

"Hi, it's me. What did you find out?" my brother asks.

"You're not going to like it. Maybe he is your son, maybe not." I repeat what I've learned.

"I hear you." I cringe whenever Rob uses California expressions, like he's turned into an escaped alien from Planet Laidback. "I know you're right, Claire. It would be cruel to disrupt Colin's life. The more I think about it, though, the more convinced I am that I'm his father. It's the only explanation that makes sense, considering Lydia's behavior toward you."

"I know. That's what my gut tells me, too." It would explain why Lydia cut off her relationships with Rob and with me, why she kept me as Colin's guardian all these years, even why the Finellis never had more kids. Maybe Matthew was the infertile one, not Lydia, as I'd assumed from her reluctance to talk about it.

"Listen, Rob, this is a big one. Say, for the sake of argument, that Colin is your biological son. Matthew's still his father in every sense. You have no claim on him. Matthew raised him. He's a devoted father and they love each other. The best way to express your concern, your love for Colin, might be to keep quiet about this, maybe forever. Can you live with it, if it comes to that?"

"Claire, give me some credit. I've thought of those things, too. I'm not making any hasty decisions here. But, sooner or later, I'm going to have to know for sure. I think we've talked this through enough for one day. How are you? Anything else going on?"

Rob is sympathetic about the break-in, but dubious about my suspicions of Randy. "The police are probably right about youthful vandals. Claire, gotta go. My next meeting walked in early. Quick, tell me the plans for next Thursday night."

We agree to meet at the restaurant at 6:30. "I'll make reservations and remind Val. I hope Aaron can join us."

"Claire, one more thing. Be careful, okay?"

"I know. Life is a wicked intersection." It's a family joke, based on our mother's dramatic warnings to Rob when he was learning to drive.

Exercise is probably the best outlet for my pent-up uneasiness about the break-in, as well as my frustrations with my investigation, which seems to be going nowhere. Plenty of time to invite Colin over when I get back. The school bus doesn't drop him off until three-thirty.

Colin sounds surprised. "Gee, I was just at your house on Saturday."

"You mean you're sick of us already?"

"No, I mean aren't you getting sick of me?" I sense a seriousness underneath his teasing manner.

"Colin, we have five years to make up for. Consider us part of your family now, all of us. That means even if we're sick of each other, we eat dinner together and fight over who has to clear the table. Do you like salmon?"

"Sure. And Claudia didn't come today. I was going to eat leftovers. My friend Paul is here doing homework and stuff. His mom is picking him up at five-thirty. Let me call and check with Dad, but I think he's going to be late tonight."

"Okay, I'll pick you up at five-thirty unless I hear otherwise from you. I'll drive you home by seven-thirty since it's a school night. Okay?"

"Thanks, Aunt Claire. See you then."

As I pull into the Finellis' driveway, after a stop at the bakery for dinner rolls, Paul and his mother are driving away. "Come in. I'll be ready in a sec," Colin calls through the open door. I hear him signing off the computer.

"Aunt Claire, I'll be right down. I want to grab a water bottle from the refrigerator."

"I'll get it for you." There's a nearly empty bottle of Chianti in the refrigerator door. I'd seen it there last Saturday when I took out the grapes. It's the bottle from Lydia's last meal; I remember seeing the colorfully labeled bottle in the kitchen the day I found her body. I bet Matthew doesn't know it's here. Some well-meaning neighbor, trying to be helpful, must have put it away after the ambulance came. No way would Matthew drink an old, open bottle of wine. I dump the remains in the sink, rinse the bottle, and place it in the recycling bin.

The price sticker is glued on the bottom: $19.98. It's overpriced, but no wonder. The sticker says POTOMAC PLACE, a gourmet store on River Road, which sells wine, cheese, caviar, prepared food, and selected kitchen gadgets at a huge markup. Lydia must have loosened her purse strings to be shopping there.

Potomac, the town adjoining Bethesda, is filled with large, expensive old homes and newly built McMansions. The store is a twenty-minute drive from my house and I rarely go there, unless I'm passing by on another errand, or need a hard-to-find ingredient for a recipe. Price-conscious Lydia certainly wasn't the typical customer. The store, which does a thriving takeout business of readymade delicacies, caters to customers who don't cook much in their huge designer kitchens, but might invite friends over for drinks and hors d'oeuvres before going to dinner.

Colin comes downstairs. He's run a wet comb through his hair.

In the car, he's silent, but I sense something's on his mind. "Colin, I didn't get a chance to go through my boxes of pictures yet, but I promise to get to it later in the week."

"That's okay. No rush. Aunt Claire, can I ask you something?"

"Sure, honey, anything at all."

"Was it horrible to, you know, to find Mom?"

"It was a shock, sure. But not horrible. I think it's better that a grown-up found her. Not you."

"I keep thinking, if only I had gone in to say good-bye that morning. If only I wasn't worried about waking her."

I reach for his hand. "Honey, it would have been too late, anyway. She was already gone. I'm sure your mom would have preferred things to unfold the way they did. I know I wouldn't have wanted my kids to find me like that."

Immediately I'm sorry. My comment implies that Lydia was at fault, not thinking of her son, that I'm a more thoughtful mom. "Is there anything else you want to ask me? About her death?"

"No. I just can't believe she committed suicide. She didn't go to church anymore, but I thought she considered herself Catholic."

"I know. I'm having a hard time with it myself. So is your grandma," I say, pausing for a few seconds. "Colin, I don't want to dwell on unpleasant memories, but do you remember anything unusual about that night? Did anyone come over? Like Karen Kline? Or Jill?"

"Nope. It was just me and Mom. I went into her room around ten to say good night, like I usually do. She was already in her nightgown, brushing her teeth. A little while later Dad called to say good night. We both talked to him. Then I stayed up too late playing Sims on my computer. That's all I remember."

What if Randy came over after Colin fell asleep? All he had to do was cross the street. He has a key. I ponder that scenario, one hand on the steering wheel, my other hand squeezing Colin's hand. He doesn't pull away from me until I turn into our street.

Later that evening, after driving Colin home, I'm tempted to drop in on Karen. I haven't had a chance yet to fill her in on my latest encounter with McCaffrey. It's only seven-forty. What if Randy's home? I don't want to risk losing my cool. Accusing him of breaking and entering wouldn't be a smart move. I need to lay a clever trap. I check the Klines' driveway. Only one car is parked there, a Jeep. Karen's car.

I pull in. If Randy comes to the door, I'll simply leave a message for Karen. It's a relief when Karen answers.

"Claire, what a nice surprise. Come in." She looks perfect, as usual, in a simple white-linen top and a long, straight periwinkle skirt.

"I hope I'm not interrupting your dinner. I dropped Colin off and thought I'd catch up with you. I spoke to McCaffrey," I say in a low voice so that her girls won't overhear.

"Come in. The kids and I ate an early dinner. Randy has a group tonight. He won't be home for awhile. Coffee? It's decaf."

"No, thanks." I drop my purse on the front hall table next to hers and a stack of mail.

"I meant to sort that mail," she apologizes, as if I'd be offended by a mail pile. Karen rifles through the mail, placing a *New England Journal of Medicine* and the *American Journal of Neuropharmacology* back on the tabletop. Of course, Randy reads that journal. The same journal that had the article about the obese man who died of an interaction between Nardil and the foods with the high tryamine content. *That's how Randy figured out how to kill Lydia.* I steady myself on the banister.

"Claire, are you okay?"

"Just a little dizzy. I'm fine now, really. I haven't been sleeping too well. I guess I shouldn't have had that glass of wine with dinner."

"Let me get you a cold drink." I follow her into the kitchen, where the girls are doing their homework around the table. I wonder how such a vile man could have such a picture-perfect family.

"Sit down, and drink this slowly."

"Thanks." I plaster a fake smile on my face. "I'm fine now."

We walk into the study and Karen closes the door. I fill her in on what I found on-line about the coach, and his reaction when I confronted him.

"The poor man. He's been through so much and he seems so nice. I'm inclined to give him the benefit of the doubt," Karen says.

I am, too, now that I suspect that Randy, not McCaffrey, played a part in Lydia's death. "You know, I've been thinking about the night Lydia died."

"I often think about it, too," says Karen.

"Did you happen to notice any cars, or visitors at Lydia's that night? I mean, if you were home."

"Oh, we were home. Lizzie had an awful stomach virus. Randy was on his way to the gym, but he stayed home to hold Lizzie's head over the toilet. He's such a worrier."

"So, you guys were home all evening?" I ask, as if the question is merely casual conversation.

"Uh-huh. Lizzie stopped throwing up around midnight and we got some sleep. You know, around nine, I ran to the store to get some ginger ale for Lizzie. If there were any cars parked outside of Lydia's house, it would have registered with me."

"You must have been so tired. My kids' illnesses always wear me out." I'm doing my best to draw out the conversation.

"Actually, I didn't sleep very well that night. I'm a light sleeper to start with, and I got up to check on Lizzie at least three times."

So, Randy was in clear sight until midnight, and then Karen slept fitfully. Surely she would have noticed if she woke up and her husband wasn't home. "Karen, thanks for the drink. I better run. My kids are probably wondering where I am."

She walks with me to the door.

"Please give Randy my regards. How's he doing?"

"He's been taking Lydia's death pretty hard, too. He seems distracted. He and Lydia were very good friends. He thinks he failed her somehow. I keep telling him that if Lydia's own psychiatrist couldn't save her, how could he? I guess it's going to take time for all of us."

"It's a tough one, all right. Thanks for everything, Karen."

"Sure. Good to see you, Claire. Drop by anytime you're in the neighborhood. And don't fret about your dinner party. I have it covered." She smiles pleasantly, glad to reassure me.

If Karen only knew how little I'm fretting about the party. I'm far more concerned that her husband is a killer.

EIGHTEEN

Randy takes my call but tries, unsuccessfully, to fend off my visit. I'm not buying it. "I want to show you something. It's important. We can do this a few ways. I can barge in on a therapy session, or bother you at home in front of Karen and your kids. Or you can tell me a good time to come to your office. Your choice."

"Okay, how about four today?" He sounds resigned, as if I'm a pesky telemarketer he's trying to hang up on.

"Sorry, that's too late. How about ten-thirty?" That gives me time to drive back to the National Institutes of Health and photocopy the journal article. I could kick myself for not doing it yesterday.

"Eleven. I have a fifteen-minute break between patients."

"That sounds fine. See you then." I'll be damned if I say thanks to Lydia's murderer. I reconsider, yet again, going to the police with my suspicions. You're almost there, Claire. Don't blow it now, I chide myself.

Sitting in a chair in his waiting room, looking annoyed, Randy doesn't rise to greet me. I practically fling the journal article at him. "I know you subscribe to this, so don't waste my time trying to deny it. I saw a copy at your house. This particular issue must have been especially fascinating."

He looks at the article, skimming it. "I don't know what you're talking about. For a change. Claire, where did you find this?" He's talking to me as if I'm an errant child.

"At the NIH library, where I was catching up on my scientific reading. This article gave you the idea how to kill her, didn't it?" I speak softly, but look him straight in the eyes.

A look of pain crosses his face. Guilt? "I haven't read this article yet. Someone borrowed this issue from me."

"Sure. And your dog ate your homework. My four-year-olds can come up with better excuses." I examine my fingernails, as if I'm contemplating a manicure. I want him to get the message that I'm in no hurry to leave.

"Look, Claire, I don't have to justify myself to you. Now, if you're done playing Nancy Drew, I have work to do." He stands up.

"Sure, Randy. And you didn't break into my house looking for Lydia's camera, either."

"Claire, I know you loved Lydia. I did too. It's your right not to like me, but let me give you a bit of professional advice. You're delusional. Lydia committed suicide. Making wild accusations against me won't bring her back. You can torture me with those photos if you want. But, for your own good, as well as mine, move on. You will never, ever, be able to prove that I had an affair with Lydia. Or that I had anything to do with her death. Because I didn't. And that's the truth. And I'm certainly not a cat burglar. The idea that I broke into your house is ludicrous."

"You're an arrogant liar. But I will nail you. I promise you that. If you don't believe me, you're the delusional one. Save the psychobabble for your paying customers."

On my way out, I slam the door for punctuation. In the elevator, reflecting upon Randy's words, I have to admit they sound plausible. Oh, of course he sounds reasonable. Psychiatrists are expert dissemblers.

* * *

When I get home I retrieve Matthew's financial records from the drawer where I'd stuffed them. A little voice in my head, that I try to shut up, whispers that I may be on the wrong track with Randy. So, once again, I'm on the lookout for any clues from Lydia embedded in those financial records. I can decipher records better than most, but I'm stumped. There are pages upon pages, transactions upon transactions. I don't know if I'm reading the statement correctly. I need help.

Scooping up the records, I head downtown. I call Gary Swensen from my car. He doesn't pick up. "Gary, it's Claire. I'm on my way into the office. Do you have some time to help me with something today? I'll be there soon."

I hope he'll be around. Gary, who's older than most of the staff, is sharper than anyone. He's not overly fond of the rest of his colleagues, expressing disdain for the Ivy League crowd Calvin's brought in at inflated salaries. Most of the time he conveniently forgets I'm one of them. He jokes about the "little lad" reporters who dress like investment bankers, summer on Nantucket, and swill sparkling water instead of scotch.

Gary's door is half closed; he's typing at the word processor, an unlit cigarette dangling from his mouth. He looks up and smiles.

"Got your message, Carrot. Where've you been? Been missing you. The hall isn't any fun when you're gone. Just a bunch of boring guys telling dirty jokes. Sit down, take a load off. Is that yupster husband out of town again?" He motions me to his extra chair.

I shut his door. At *Nationweek,* that's usually the prelude to juicy gossip. Gary looks up expectantly.

"Gary, are you on deadline? I could really use your help, if you're not too swamped," I ask. I'm ashamed of myself for using the helpless female ploy. Except it's foolproof with Gary.

"Sure, I'm on deadline. Otherwise, I'd already be at lunch. But it's early in the week." Gary makes it a practice to file his stories as late in the week as possible, to protect his prose from an assistant managing editor who doesn't practice the editorial Hippocratic oath. Tim only does harm to our copy. We all push the deadlines but Gary can get away with delivering his stories a day or two later than the rest of us.

"Gary, would you mind coming to my office?" I feel better as he follows me down the hall. I pull out the records and explain what I've deciphered, leaving out several crucial details, such as how I acquired the trading records. I don't fool Gary, but he doesn't ask. "My, how far you've come, my dear, under my guidance," is his amused comment.

He studies the transactions for a few minutes, whistling. "I haven't seen anything this good in ages. Hand me a yellow pad. Okay, now let's see if anything I've taught you has sunk into that pretty head. What have you got so far?"

I let the reference to my pretty head slide. Some women staffers find Gary's comments hopelessly chauvinistic. A few unenlightened remarks, however, are a small price to pay for Gary's help in moments like these. I hate when he tells me that I've got to get over my childhood math phobia and learn to wield a calculator like the big boys, but I have to concede that he may have a point.

"Okay, here's my theory, but check me on it. Over four days, the guy who holds this account sold short about fifty thousand shares of HCC. Maybe he used the other securities in his account as collateral."

"Get out your calculator," Gary says. "When he sold short fifty thousand shares of HCC, it was selling at forty dollars a share. How much was that position worth?" I quickly multiply fifty thousand times forty. "Two million."

"Stay with me here. Lots of zeros. When he bought the shares back at the end of the month to close out his position, the stock was selling at twenty dollars a share. So how much did the stock cost?"

I multiply fifty thousand shares times the purchase price of twenty dollars per share. "One million dollars. Wow. We're talking real money here."

"Good girl. He buys for one million dollars and sells for two million dollars, making a million in profit in one month. And you think he's not sharp?"

The beauty of selling short is that the investor—in this case, Matthew—gets to sell the stock before he buys it. "What about collateral?" I ask. Since the investor doesn't own the stock, he has to put up collateral. "Is that the Theragenics?"

"Now you've got it," Gary says. "My work with you has not been in vain. I can go to my grave happy." It looks like Matthew used Theragenics as collateral. That is, until it dropped in value. "See how Theragenics was worth one million dollars at the beginning of the month, and how it fell to five hundred thousand dollars?" Gary points out.

Okay, now I get the significance of the midmonth flurry of transactions. When an investor sells a stock short, he's betting that its price will fall and he can buy it back at a lower price. The price of HCC Inc. was falling, so Matthew's bet was paying off. The problem was that his collateral was eroding as Theragenics' price fell.

Still, I don't understand why Matthew didn't dump the Theragenics stock. Especially since he was privy to inside information about the failed merger and the fudged results on the drugtesting program. And how had he managed to be so savvy about HCC?

"Gary, what do you know about HCC?"

"I think it's an upstart telecommunications company in Colorado. Now, this guy whose records you are delving into—whoever he is, I don't want to know—is he in any position to have inside information about HCC?"

"About telecommunications? Absolutely not. He's in the medical field. I bet he can't program his own VCR."

"A doctor? Claire, get the newspaper from my office. Why would he be so interested in HCC?" Gary looks like I've gotten his curiosity juices going.

"Maybe HCC is expanding into medical technology?" That's my best guess. I grab the stock listings from Gary's office and return in a hurry.

"Should we do an on-line search on HCC?" Gary suggests.

"Takes too long. I have a better idea." I go to my Rolodex and look up the number of Barbara Greenberger, a source of mine who's a financial analyst on Wall Street.

"Barb, it's Claire, with a quick question. Off the record." I ask her about HCC Inc. and whether they are expanding into medical technology.

Her answer surprises me. I grab the stock listings from Gary's hand. "You're right. There are *two* HCCs." Barbara tells me the telecommunications company trades under plain HCC; the drug company under HCC Inc., which stands for Healthy Care Corporation Inc.

"Barbara, this is important. You know where Healthy Care Corp. is located?"

"It's in Rahway, New Jersey. I pass it sometimes on the turnpike. There was an interesting development with HCC Inc. in the last few months. The stock price took a dive. Rumor was that it was going to acquire a small biotech company, I think in Washington. I don't know the small company's name. Anyhow, the deal went sour."

I connect the dots in my head. So, HCC Inc. was going to acquire Theragenics. Then, HCC found out about the flawed research. Matthew and Jill both knew that HCC's stock would fall when news of the failed acquisition became public.

"Barbara, I'll call you back when I get off deadline. Thanks a million." Literally. Barbara's information means that Matthew, probably acting on advice from Jill, had made a million dollars trading on insider information.

I fill Gary in on the failed acquisition. I'm so nervous that he will abandon me for his own work that I let him light up four cigarettes over two hours, in clear violation of his doctor's orders and *Nationweek* policy.

Eventually, we come up with a hypothesis: Matthew, alone or with partners (i.e., Jill), had sold short fifty thousand shares of HCC Inc. stock over four days. He sold short the stock at forty dollars per share, betting that it would fall to twenty dollars. The accounts show a profit in excess of $1 million, more money than Matthew might have made had the acquisition gone through.

Not a bad scheme. Especially if Matthew, for instance, and not Chris Klarman, blew the whistle on the fudged research. He had to know that that information would likely postpone or quash HCC's acquisition of Theragenics. And, if it didn't, and the deal went through later, as a major stockholder of Theragenics, Matthew would profit again. What's more, no one was likely to suspect Matthew of going to HCC with the damaging information about the research. He and Jill stood to gain the most if the deal went through. It was clever. Illegal, but definitely clever.

"Claire, this has been loads of fun. And I can't wait to hear where you're going with this story. But I better get back to my rabbit hole and do some of my own work."

"Gary, I can't thank you enough. Dinner and martinis next week. On me."

I shut the door and wish I knew what to make of this new information, or how it fit into the puzzle of Lydia's death.

NINETEEN

The day's practically gone but, despite my confusion over Matthew's financial dealings, I'm not ready to give up. From my cell phone, I call Trini: "I'm going to be a few more hours. Please give the kids dinner. Tell them I'll be late, but I should be home to tuck them in."

"Take your time. Don't worry about anything. They'll be fine," she assures me.

Aaron's not due back from Cleveland for a few more days and, rather than missing him, I'm relieved I won't have to explain my whereabouts.

Normally, I enjoy the peace of being alone in the car, but after an hour of barely moving traffic, I'm ready to jump out and walk. I haven't even gotten as far as the Old Georgetown Road entrance to Route 270 in Bethesda. At this rate, I won't reach Gaithersburg until after seven. Relax, I remind myself, Jill will be there, probably until midnight. Listening to *All Things Considered* on National Public Radio isn't having its usual soothing effect.

By the time I pull into the Theragenics parking lot, it's nearly empty, but I recognize Jill's beat-up Ford Escort. If my hunch is right, and she and Matthew split his insider trading profits, she's doing a great job hiding her newfound wealth.

There's no receptionist to block my quick stride into Jill's office. Bent over a computer printout, she looks up, startled, at my knock. "Claire. What a surprise. I don't get too many drop-ins in this neighborhood. What brings you here?" She looks as ragged as last time, with her stringy hair clasped in a plastic barrette, the shirttails of her wrinkled denim workshirt hanging over mush-colored corduroys.

"This isn't exactly a social call." Without waiting for an invitation, I plop myself into the folding chair facing her desk. Not exactly a lavish executive suite; the lowly researchers at *Nationweek* have plusher office furniture in their windowless cells. "I want to talk about your partnerships with Matthew. Business and personal."

"I don't know what you're talking about," she says, but stripes of red flush her cheeks.

"Jill, I know you two are having an affair. So let's lose the Little Ms. Innocent act." I'm bluffing but, so far, she hasn't called me on it.

"Okay, Claire. I'm not going to play dumb with you. I knew you'd find out. You're so dogged." She's not paying me a compliment. Dogged is her way of saying I'm becoming a big pain. "How'd you find out?"

"It doesn't matter how. How long, anyway?" I don't know why she's answering my questions, which are none of my business, but I continue to pretend I'm entitled to the information.

"For almost a year now. Is this where you give me the moralistic lecture about Matthew being married?"

No need for me to interject when she's doing such a good job interrogating herself. I use the reporter's trick of keeping quiet for a few beats, letting her fill in the gaps.

"You must know, then, that he says he loves me. Although I've told him over and over and over again that I won't marry him. Before, it was because I'd never do anything to hurt Lydia or Colin. Her death doesn't change how I feel."

"What high moral standards. For someone sleeping with a friend's husband, that is." It's hard to muster much indignation when I've been transgressing some ethical boundaries myself.

"I wasn't taking anything away from Lydia. She was the one who rejected Matthew, emotionally and sexually. They hadn't slept together for years."

"Come on, Jill. Don't tell me you fell for the old my-wife-doesn't-understand-me routine. You're just trying to justify your behavior."

"No, Claire. I'm not. Look, I knew he was married. Lydia was my friend, too. By conventional standards, what I did was wrong, but I didn't seduce Matthew."

"Conventional standards don't apply to scientific geniuses like you? They're only meant for us ordinary dummies?" She ignores the sarcasm.

"That's not what I mean," she says evenly. "At first, when Matthew suggested we change our relationship, take it to a more intimate level, I was shocked. And insulted. I thought it was a terrible idea." She sighs. "But he's so damn persistent. And he knows my weak spots. Look, I'm not blaming Matthew. I'm a responsible adult. I'm attracted to him, always have been. Sometimes, I think that's why I never married. Nobody ever measured up to him. Yeah, I was lonely. You try going home to an empty apartment every night, year after year. Watch as your friends, your sister, your cousins all get married, have babies, make pointed remarks to you about ticking biological clocks. Then judge me."

"I don't get it. How could you betray Lydia like that?"

"I wanted to protect her. And Colin. Don't you see? If not me, Matthew would have found someone else to fall in love with. Someone who didn't care about Lydia and Colin. Someone who very well might want to break up his marriage."

"So, you had an affair with Matthew out of selflessness?" I wonder if Jill actually believes what she's saying.

"I'm not going to pretend my motives were noble. Matthew and I have been close for twenty years. Lydia's troubles brought us closer. We have a bond based on shared interests and experiences. In many ways, we've been like a married couple for the past twenty years. Except for the sex, I mean."

Why bother to disabuse her of the notion that longtime marriages are hotbeds of sexual activity? Let single people keep their illusions. "It's amazing the lengths that people go to rationalize their behavior," I say, but I'm thinking of myself—and some of the shady stunts I've pulled lately—as much as Jill and Matthew.

"Obviously, since Lydia killed herself, I've rethought the situation," Jill says in a whisper. "I never meant to cause this tragedy."

"I don't understand how you could do this to her," I repeat, though why should Jill take the blame? Matthew was the married one. I'm impatient to steer the conversation toward the insider trading.

Jill lapses into clinical language, as if she's discussing an anonymous patient, not her lover's wife, or our late mutual friend. "You know that Prozac, which Lydia was on for years, can cause anorgasmia in women?"

"You mean the inability to reach orgasm? Don't MAO inhibitors have the same effect?" I can't compete with Jill's medical knowledge but, like any halfway decent reporter, I'm not bad at leveraging a few hastily read articles into sounding like I know what I'm talking about.

"Lydia suffered from atypical depression. Her doctors thought she'd do better with a MAO inhibitor, so they switched her from Prozac. The MAOs helped, or so everyone thought. Except for her libido."

So, Matthew and Lydia weren't having great sex, or even any sex. Is that enough to destroy a marriage? Possibly. "What really happened that Sunday afternoon at Lydia's house? Did you tell her about you and Matthew? Is that why she killed herself that night?"

As I voice this theory, I reject it. It doesn't sound right. Lydia wouldn't give up that easily.

Jill winces. Obviously the thought has occurred to her. "Of course not. I don't think she knew about Matthew and me."

"I wouldn't be so sure of that," I say, without mentioning the financial statements and Lydia's cryptic note. "I don't understand why, if they weren't happy, they didn't divorce. People do it all the time. Or were they planning to?" Like Val said, that could have been the reason Lydia called me—to recommend a sharp lawyer or help her track down what she obviously suspected were Matthew's hidden assets.

"No, divorce was out of the question for them. For lots of reasons. As depressed as she was, Lydia didn't want to leave Matthew. Her identity was based on being his wife and Colin's mother. She would never have done anything to hurt Colin or risk losing him. Don't forget, with Lydia's history of depression and attempted suicide, Matthew probably could have won a custody fight. Anyway, I didn't want Matthew to leave Lydia for me. Colin would have hated us both. We didn't want that."

Jill's logic sounds pretty muddled to me, especially considering how things turned out. I pull a sheaf of papers from my bag. "Jill, on that last Sunday, did you and Lydia discuss investments?"

"Investments? Don't be silly. That would be like Lydia asking me what she should wear to a party or cook for dinner." She looks bewildered.

"Well, you may be interested in these." I hand her the trading records. "By the way, I figured out your scheme. Only I'm not quite clear on who did what."

"What scheme?" She scans the papers.

"You know, Jill, I used to buy your act. The holier-than-thou, money's-not-important-to-me, I'm-a-pure-scientist routine. But what were you and Matthew planning to do with your newfound fortune?"

"Claire, you've barged in here with a lot of crazy accusations. What the hell are you talking about?" Her confusion seems genuine, but she could be acting.

"Jill, look at these trading records. They're copies of stock transactions in Matthew's account. Look at the dates, and the trades involving HCC. Surely you remember HCC in Rahway, New Jersey?"

Mentioning HCC catches her attention. She bites her lip as she studies the documents. "Claire, these might as well be in Chinese."

I grab the papers impatiently. "Jill, look at these dates in March. Do they ring any bells? Like matching up to the same day that your deal fell through?" Slowly, I explain to her about the insider trading. Jill grips the arms of her chair, as if it's a lifeboat keeping her afloat.

"I don't get it. Explain it again, please."

"Oh, please. Cut the act." But Jill looks so pale and sad that I pity her. I go out to the hall and bring back two paper cups of water from the cooler. Then, I repeat my explanation of the trading records.

We drain the cups, not speaking. Jill crumples the cup and buries her head on folded arms, the way children do when they take a rest at school. I wait until she stops crying. A few minutes later, when she lifts her head, and looks at me, her mouth is set in anger.

"Claire, I'm trying to absorb all this. If what you're saying is true, then Matthew betrayed me. Matthew. For weeks, I have been blaming Chris Klarman for my problems, but it must have been Matthew all along." She meets my gaze. "How could you think I'd be involved in this scheme? Why would I sabotage my own company, my future, my dreams? You've misjudged me, but not nearly as much as I misjudged Matthew."

If Matthew acted alone, without her, I really don't understand what he'd been up to. Still, his financial finagling isn't why I'm sitting here. I'm not sure whether Jill's innocence is for real, but I decide, at that moment, to take her into my confidence. Even if it is a risk. Otherwise, I can't get to the next step. I need her to help me trap Randy. "Jill, if I'm right, then Matthew is responsible for some misguided, greedy, illegal financial maneuvers. But whatever wrongs he committed, for whatever reasons, they pale in comparison to Randy's actions."

"Randy Kline? What's he got to do with anything?"

"I think Randy killed Lydia."

"Come on, Claire. That's not funny. Things are bad enough without your sick jokes."

"Jill, why do think I am here? Over money that Matthew may have obtained illegally, with knowledge about your company? I don't care about any of that—unless the insider-trading scheme with Theragenics is somehow connected to Lydia's death, although I don't see how. Lydia sent me some financial records before she died. I didn't know why, though. I thought maybe they would offer some clue about her death."

"Wait a minute," Jill interrupts. "You mean it. You've snapped. You actually think Randy murdered Lydia? That's crazy."

"I know it's hard to believe. I thought Randy was one of those touchy-feely sensitive guys myself. There's stuff you don't know about." I recount the evidence: the lewd photos, the break-in. "Sure, there are holes in my theory. Big ones, like how Randy got into Lydia's house that night without his wife finding out. And how he killed Lydia without raising red flags to the police."

"Claire, this is ridiculous. You're a reporter, not a detective."

"Jill, this is not a game. I think Lydia was murdered. Are you going to help me figure out what happened to her?" It's the least Jill can do after sleeping with her husband, I think, but I hold my tongue.

"Claire, if Lydia's death seems suspicious, go to the police and tell them what you've told me. Let them sort it out."

"I'm planning on going to the police. But not yet. Not until I have enough evidence for them to take me seriously. I haven't come this far to be labeled hysterical by the police. Let's get the proof ourselves. We're almost there. Come on, we make a great team." I'm counting on Jill's medical expertise to figure out how Randy could have murdered Lydia and made it look like she committed suicide.

"Sorry, I'm having trouble getting past what you've told me about Matthew. I'm not thinking straight."

I appeal to her guilt. "Jill, if I'm right—and I know it's a big *if*—then you'll know for sure that Lydia didn't kill herself because you were fooling around with Matthew. Wouldn't that be reassuring?"

Jill thinks it over. "Okay, I'll help you with Randy. Only don't expect me to do anything illegal." She hesitates.

"What is it? What aren't you telling me? We're partners now. Don't hold back."

"Claire, there's something else, something that's been bothering me for weeks. You know the police questioned me, and Matthew, after you found Lydia. The police asked me something and I glossed over it, but maybe it's significant." She looks like she's going to burst into tears so I wait, saying nothing. Finally, she takes a deep breath. "Randy may not be your villain."

"What do you mean?"

Jill pauses before speaking. "Remember why Matthew went to the Eastern Shore the night Lydia died? He was presenting neurological research at a conference the next morning. Well, before he left, he asked me a technical question, related to some data on clinical trials for Alzheimer's patients. I didn't know the answer. Sunday night, I was mulling it over. I had an idea, so I called Matthew at the inn. The first time I called, around eleven, there was no answer. I thought he'd gone downstairs for a drink or to meet some other people from the conference. I tried again at eleven-thirty, and then at twelve-fifteen. Still no answer. I left a message the last time. Then my cousin Betsy, who lives in California, called. She knows I'm a night owl. By the time we hung up, it was after one."

"By now, I was worried. My call waiting hadn't clicked so I knew Matthew wasn't trying to call me back. I called him again. He picked up on the sixth or seventh ring, sounding groggy. He said he had taken a shower and must have fallen asleep. He said he hadn't noticed the message light on the phone or that it wasn't on or something. I told him about the data and we got off the phone pretty quickly." She pauses, catching her breath. "A few days later, the police asked me what time I'd spoken to Matthew. I wasn't sure, I told them, but late, around midnight."

"You mean you deliberately misled them? Why did you lie?"

"It's silly. I was afraid if they knew I had called him several times that night, especially so late, they would guess we were having an affair. I was embarrassed, so I fudged the time, thinking I could always correct it if it came up again. But there was no next round of questioning. And being off by an hour or so seemed like such a tiny detail."

"Hmm." I take out a note pad to jot down numbers. "Say Matthew was gone from eleven to one-fifteen. Of course, we don't know when he left, only that you first tried him around eleven. Even if he left at eleven, he could have driven to Bethesda and back from the Eastern Shore. Port Chatham, where he was staying, is about an hour and a half away. Aaron and I have been there."

"It's about a hundred miles away from Bethesda. I've driven there myself in an hour and a half," Jill says.

That sounds right. Matthew could have made it home and back to the hotel, but it would have been tight. "He couldn't have been home long, but it's possible. Especially on a Sunday night with no traffic. That Porsche really flies." Wouldn't the police have questioned Matthew more carefully about the distance? Probably, if they were suspicious of him. Which they obviously weren't. The police didn't seem to question that Lydia's death was a suicide.

Jill's upset with Matthew, so I'm humoring her. There's no way Matthew drove home, murdered his wife, then drove back for his meeting. It's preposterous. I know him too well. Anyway, I saw how upset Matthew was the day I found Lydia's body. That wasn't play-acting. Randy's the bad guy. "It's getting late. I have to get home to my kids," I say, leaving aside my anger, for the moment, my outrage over Matthew's infidelity and Jill's betrayal of Lydia. I don't know where to put those feelings, so I block them out. All I know is that I need Jill's help.

We make a plan, with Jill volunteering to research fatal food reactions from MAO inhibitors. I tell her what I remember from the journal article so she can look it up on-line. As far as I'm concerned, Jill's doing the busy work. I'm still intent on trapping Randy.

"Claire, I gave you my home number, didn't I? I had it unlisted when those reporters were hounding me."

I pat my bag. "It's in here." We walk out to the parking lot together. "Jill, I know this insider trading stuff has been shattering. I'm truly sorry about it. I can't believe Matthew has changed this much, that money has become so important to him. Together, we'll figure this whole mess out."

"Female solidarity. It's the only thing we can trust," she says. I don't blame her for feeling bitter. Exhausted and hungry, I drive home as fast as I can. Without traffic, the drive is easy. Twenty minutes door to door.

TWENTY

Allison is curled in her favorite position, on the blue-chenille couch, under her ratty patchwork quilt, reading the latest Lemony Snicket book. I can see the top of her cotton pajama tank top, with the moon-and-stars print, from an exposed patch in the quilt where the fabric has worn through. She has slept with this quilt every single night of her life. It has accompanied her on every sleepover date, and in every hotel room on family trips. I've told her that her future husband may not want it on his honeymoon, but she's assured me that she wouldn't marry anyone who would come between her and her blankie. For once, she's remembered to remove her rollerblades before putting her feet on the upholstery. The twins are standing on their heads, their preferred position for television viewing. All three heads are wet, a good sign.

"Hi, guys," I say, hugging each one, inhaling the fresh scent of clean child mixed with shampoo. "You smell delicious, all of you. Thanks for getting them bathed, Trini. I know it's not easy." She shoots me a knowing glance. Trini maintains that the kids never misbehave with her, which used to make me feel incompetent until Max confided that Trini lures them into the bathtub with a secret stash of Hershey's Kisses.

"Mommy, where were you? You didn't tell us this morning you were going to be late. We've been waiting for *hours,*" Zach says.

"Sorry, sweetie." I kiss his forehead. "I didn't realize I'd have to work so late. I'll let you guys stay up until nine-thirty. Who wants to keep me company while I eat dinner?"

"There's chicken curry and rice on top of the stove," Trini offers, understandably beating a quick exit to her basement sanctuary.

Opening the refrigerator I take inventory, removing salad and watermelon.

"Mommy, you need to go shopping. We're out of juice boxes and cookies," Allison reminds me.

"And granola bars," Max chimes in.

"Who wants watermelon? But you'll have to brush your teeth again."

I cut the melon in chunks, put small portions of rice and curry from the pots onto my plate, and zap it in the microwave for two minutes.

"Too noisy down here. I'm going upstairs. I have twenty pages left. Come tuck me in after the twins." Allison allows me a hug on her way out.

"I miss you, too, sweetie," I call after her.

The boys carry on their version of conversation, constant interruptions escalating into screaming. "Boys, let's chill a little. One at a time. Tell me about your day. Zach first, then Max."

"At recess, James called Teddy an idiot. So Teddy threw a bucket at James and hit him in the eye. Mrs. Edson gave both of them a timeout until they apologized," Zach reports. Nothing thrills him more than other kids getting into trouble.

"What happened? Let Max tell."

"James said he was sorry Teddy's an idiot but it's not his fault. It's Teddy's parents' fault. So, Teddy threw a shovel at James. Mrs. Edson took both of them into the hall for a serious discussion."

I smile, despite my discouraging day, glad to be home with my boys in our kitchen. I pick absently at the rice. "Did I ever tell you guys how I threw my bedroom slipper at Uncle Rob and he got a big lump on his forehead? I cried a lot more than he did."

"You've told us that a million times already," Max says, rolling his eyes at his brother.

"Sorry for boring you. That's what happens when people get old, like twenty-five or thirty. We lose our memories. Okay, go brush your teeth. I'll be right up. Pick one story. Only one. It's way past bedtime."

"Two. We always get two," Zach wheedles. "It's not our fault you came home so late." I'm too tired to argue, something the twins count on daily. "Okay, two, but they have to be short."

I put the dishes away and climb the stairs, making a short detour to Allison's room. She doesn't look up from her book. "How was your day, honey? I'll be back in ten minutes. I'll turn out the light and we can talk in the dark, okay?"

"Ten more pages, Mom." She continues to read as if I'm not standing there.

In the bathroom, the boys are in the midst of a heated discussion. Nothing's too mundane for them to turn into a competition. Last week they had a contest to see who could pee from farthest away without missing the toilet bowl. I lost; I had to mop the floor.

"Zach says the toothpaste tastes yucky, so he didn't use any," tattles Max.

"Come on, Zachary, do it again. It only counts if you use toothpaste."

"It tastes like medicine."

"That's just the taste from the watermelon in your mouth. Don't be ridiculous. There's nothing yucky in the toothpaste."

I sit on the edge of the bathtub and close my eyes. As the boys brush their teeth, an act I have witnessed hundreds of times, a series of images flashes through my mind, unreeling like a private home movie. The images are so clear I wonder if stress and fatigue cause hallucinations. In the first scene, Matthew is at Oliver's, buying the second tube of toothpaste, not as a husbandly act of love, but for devious purposes. In the second scene, Lydia is in her worn nightgown, bending over the bathroom sink, brushing her teeth. Scene three is Colin kissing Lydia good night. The phone rings. It's Matthew, the attentive father and husband, checking on the domestic routine he knows so well. Scene four: Matthew secretly returns home, parks his Porsche in the garage, out of the sight of neighbors, and tiptoes into the house through the basement entrance, careful not to wake Colin.

These distinct images are followed by a few reels of blank tape as I try to fill in the missing scenes: How did he murder her? Then, back to the movie playing in my head: Matthew gets rid of the toothpaste, which he has doctored with some potent drug that makes Lydia sleep, or possibly even kills her. Then, he replaces the toothpaste with a fresh tube, in the unlikely event that the police take the toothpaste and test it for evidence. Matthew speeds back to the inn in Port Chatham, pretending Jill woke him with her phone call. The next morning, Matthew participates in his meeting, thoughtful and well-spoken, as usual, then acts dazed and shocked over Lydia's "suicide." The bereft widower.

Or could it have been Jill all along? I push away the thought.

These new images won't leave my mind. It has to be Randy. I repeat this like a mantra. Or is it? How blinded am I by my friendship with Matthew? I think of Lydia's old letters. The proof I need may be lying in the sneaker box in Colin's closet.

"Mommy, why are you still sitting in the bathroom? Come tuck us in," Max yells. I get them into bed as if I'm on automatic pilot, replaying in my head everything I know about the night of Lydia's death. I close Allison's door, longing for a hot bath, a glass of wine, an hour of mindless television. Just one more telephone call.

Jill answers immediately. "It's me again. I had an epiphany while the boys were brushing their teeth." I narrate the scenes I had imagined, expecting her to laugh, and tell me how badly I need that glass of wine.

Beth Brophy

"It's one hell of a long shot," she agrees. "If you bring me the tube of toothpaste in the morning, I'll take it to a commercial lab and have it analyzed."

"Any ideas how I'm supposed to get that tube? Should I break in?'"

"Claire, you'll figure out something. This lab does comprehensive drug screening for the Montgomery County police."

"How long will it take?"

"Usually it takes a few days, but I can ask them to put a rush on it, maybe twenty-four hours."

"I'll get the tube to your office by ten. I don't know how yet, but I will."

One obstacle down, one to go. Matthew picks up on the second ring. "Hi, Matthew. Sorry to disturb you this late. Listen, I promised Colin I would drop off some old photos of Lydia and me as teenagers. Do you mind if I leave them in the morning, around nine? I'll be in the neighborhood."

Matthew's voice oozes friendliness, or am I imagining it? "Of course, Claire. You're always welcome. Colin and I will be gone, of course, but Claudia, our housekeeper, will be here. I'll tell her you're coming." His voice drops to a more intimate level. "Claire, I can't tell you how much I enjoyed dinner. I've been thinking about it all week. And I know Colin appreciates the attention from your family. It seems to be cheering him up a bit. You're a true friend."

"We love spending time with Colin. And as soon as Aaron's trial is over, we'll set up another dinner for the three of us. He was sorry he missed the last one. I'll call you in the next day or two, okay? Gotta go. I hear one of the boys."

Sleep is out of the question. I'm practically hyperventilating. I drink a few slugs of Pepto-Bismol straight from the bottle and go to my study to sort out the photographs.

Wednesday morning I wake up with a heavy feeling in my stomach, like the one I used to get in high school the day of a math test. If only my worries were so simple. I spring into morning routine: pulling clothes on the twins' wriggling bodies, pouring milk into cereal bowls, handing Allison lunch money, herding the three of them out the door.

I bring my coffee upstairs, alternating sips with showering, applying makeup, and dressing. Driving to the Finellis, my heart pounds and I can feel the sweat collecting in my armpits. What if Claudia isn't there? What if Matthew forgot to tell her that I'm coming? Worse yet, what if Matthew is home? I can't face him.

Claudia answers the door immediately, as if she were waiting for me. "You must be Mrs. Claire. Dr. Finelli said you were coming over."

She's dark-haired and trim, neatly turned out in a gray sweatshirt, black leggings, and white Keds, about thirty-five, maybe forty. I extend my hand. "Hi, I'm Claire Newman, an old friend of the family. Nice to meet you."

Claudia offers me coffee. Brewing coffee guarantees her presence in the kitchen for a few minutes, which would help, but my schedule is tight.

"No, thanks. I'm in a hurry. I'm just going to leave some photos for Colin on his desk." I walk toward his room. "Don't let me keep you. I know my way around. I can see myself out."

"I'll be in the laundry room if you need me. Mr. Colin has many dirty clothes." Claudia says cheerfully. I watch her disappear into the laundry room, which is separated from the kitchen by five steps.

I don't close Colin's bedroom door. It will look too suspicious if Claudia comes back upstairs. I leave the photos on Colin's desk and open his closet. The three sneaker boxes are stacked on the floor. Removing the lid from the first box, I find sneakers. The second box contains Lydia's toiletries. I grab the toothpaste and bring it, along with my purse, into Colin's bathroom. I had squeezed some Gingavent out of my tube this morning, but I want the tube to look exactly like the one I'm replacing. Closing the bathroom door, I run the faucet, pushing a bit more out. I run the water for another minute, cleaning the toothpaste off the sink with a wad of toilet paper. I flush the paper down the toilet, and listen for Claudia. No footsteps, but Keds padding across a carpeted floor wouldn't produce much noise. I switch the toothpaste tubes, place the lid back on the shoe box, and close the closet door, careful not to let it slam.

"Thanks, Claudia. I'm on my way," I say as I leave. I don't exhale until I'm sitting in my car.

By the time I reach Jill's office, I'm steadier. I hand Jill the tube, eager to get rid of it.

"How'd you get it?" she asks. "You must have nerves of steel."

"I'm still shaking."

"Okay, it's my turn. I'll bring it to the lab. Call you later."

"Try me at home this afternoon. I have a few errands." She nods. In the back of my mind, I'm still wondering about Jill and whether she's really on my side or not.

Had any of Jill's employees happened to walk past her door, they would've observed an ordinary scene: two women, planning to talk later, probably to confirm plans for lunch, a movie, or tennis. Nothing in our words or demeanor betrays the deadly seriousness of our business.

Generally, I go to great lengths to avoid backtracking. Inventing a shortcut brings me inordinate pleasure, as if the five seconds I shave off an errand to the dry cleaners will permanently enhance my life. There have to be two or three shorter routes to Potomac than the one I'm taking. For once, though, I ignore my handy road atlas of Montgomery County and drive the long way. I need the extra time to compose myself.

In the Potomac Place parking lot, my not-washed-in-weeks Camry looks shabby among the gleaming rows of BMWs, Acuras, and Lexus SUVs. I check my wallet for the slip of paper that has Matthew's credit-card number written on it, from when Colin gave it to me for the camera repair. I comb my hair and reapply lipstick. I'm wearing what Allison calls my "serious" clothes: black linen suit, white blouse, pearls with matching button earrings, heels. Not a thread of funkiness.

Wheeling a cart up and down a few aisles, I throw in a pint of raspberries (seven dollars), fresh tarragon (four dollars), and a jug of extra-extra-virgin olive oil (twenty-eight dollars). At the customer-service desk, I ring the bell. A young woman appears. "I'm looking for the manager," I say.

"He's not in. Can I help you? I'm the assistant manager," she says. The nametag pinned to her yellow shirt identifies her as DIANA.

"I hope so, Diana. You see, I bought a few things here in mid-April for an office party. I paid with my boss's credit card. I also bought a few things for myself. Now I'd like to reimburse him, but I can't find the itemized bill. Could you give me a copy of the original bill?"

"Let's see." She taps her silver-lacquered nails—the shade Allison and her friends favor—on the desk, a sign she's deep in thought. "As long as your boss has a charge account here, I can help. Does he?"

I can't imagine Lydia as a regular customer in this overpriced market, but a Finelli charge account is my only hope. "I'm pretty sure he does. But, like I said, I paid with my boss's credit card."

"That's okay. Come with me to the back. We'll check the computer."

I follow her to the office in the back and sit down, willing my legs to stop shaking. "The name is Finelli. Here's the credit-card number."

She clicks a few keys. "Highgate Manor Road in Bethesda?"

"That's it," I say. Lydia's spending habits must have loosened considerably. She used to comparison shop for ketchup between Giant and Safeway. "The party was the weekend of April thirteenth. I remember because we were joking about the guests finishing their tax returns."

"There are two bills here. Do you need the one from April twelfth or the one from April fourteenth?" Diana glances at her desk calendar. "Were you here that Friday or that Sunday?"

Good question. "Now that you mention it, I think I came back on Sunday, too, to pick up a few last-minute items. Could you possibly print them both out? I'd really appreciate it."

Diana gives me a skeptical look, but placating well-dressed, if slightly scatterbrained, customers is part of her job. "Sure," she says, pushing the PRINT key.

"Thanks so much, Diana." I continue the ditzy-customer routine. I doubt she could be any ruder. "That's why I like to shop here. Such good service. By the way, would you mind if I look at the printout while you're here, in case there's something I don't understand?"

"Of course," she says, pointedly glancing at her watch.

The first printout, dated April 12, is brief: a Grande Minceuer blender for $160, a bottle of Italian mineral water, $2.50, and a "subrbrn" for $7.95. "What's this, a subrbrn?" I ask, spelling out the letters.

"The suburban is one of our specialty sandwiches," Diana answers. "Corned beef, cole slaw, and Russian dressing on rye."

"Of course, now I remember. Delicious but messy." Diana hands me the second printout.

I scan it quickly. The bastard. Chianti, New York State cheddar, English Stilton, pickled herring, soy sauce, sauerkraut. A shopping list of aged, fermented foods that contain loads of tyramine, the protein that interacts dangerously, sometimes fatally, with MAO inhibitors, by causing sudden high blood pressure, or, as in Lydia's case, a deadly stroke. At the bottom of the second list is another "subrbn" sandwich.

"Thanks again, Diana. I have what I need."

Clutching the printouts, I walk to my car, dimly aware of abandoning my grocery cart inside the store. I don't understand the details, such as why Matthew spent $160 for a fancy imported blender when the KitchenAid on his pantry shelf was perfectly serviceable. All he had to do was scour it with hot soapy water when he was finished, dry it well, and put it back on the shelf. No one would be the wiser. I guess it's worth $160 to save yourself the chore of cleaning up the crime scene. And what if Colin, usually a deep sleeper, had woken up and seen his father washing the blender? No, it was $160 well spent. Except that it allowed me to trace his purchase. I guess even smart people like Matthew sometimes do dumb things. Far more troubling to me, however, is how anyone could think about his own lunch while shopping for ingredients he plans to use to kill his wife.

What were the odds of finding the smoking gun in a gourmet grocery? The idea almost strikes me as funny, but I'm trying too hard not to lose my composure before I reach my car. In fact, the only thing preventing me from throwing up my breakfast on the shiny black Range Rover parked in the next space is imagining the embarrassment it would cause.

TWENTY-ONE

W hat in the world is taking Jill so long? She'd promised to call this morning with the lab report on the toothpaste. I'm more jittery than an expectant mother waiting for amniocentesis results. The only call I get is from Rob, finalizing dinner plans for tonight. Never mind that we have call waiting; I rush him off the phone.

Rob's arriving from New York on the noon shuttle and checking into the Four Seasons. For reasons I understand completely—premotherhood, I, too, regarded an undisturbed night's sleep as a birthright—he prefers a hotel to our guest room, which he calls the Laura Ashley theme park. I admit I got carried away with the coordinating patterns. Rob says he expects his meeting to be short. An actress who hasn't starred in a decent movie since the 1980s and her current squeeze, a zillionaire senator from Idaho, are pitching a film project.

"Their idea is awful. I'm just being polite," Rob says. "A thriller about environmental waste."

"Hasn't that been done? *The China Syndrome, Silkwood?*"

"Thanks for pointing that out. It hadn't occurred to me."

I pace around the house, holding the portable in my hand,

watching it not ring for another hour. When it finally does, Jill's voice is thick, as if she's been crying. "Claire, you were right. Come to my office right away. Don't forget the autopsy report. I need to check it again."

"I'm on my way. What did you find?"

"Carfentanyl. I'll explain when you get here. Hurry."

I concentrate on driving within the speed limit to Jill's office. Carfentanyl. Never heard of it. Jill practically pulls me through her office door. "What took you so long? Come in."

I hand her the autopsy report, which she studies intently. "Yup, just what I thought. Food in the lungs. I thought so."

"Do you mind letting me in on this?"

"Okay, let's start with the toothpaste. The doctored toothpaste. You were right. The lab found traces of carfentanyl, a powerful anesthetic. There's no way it would have shown up in a routine autopsy. The medical examiner has to look for it specifically, has to order a gas chromatography and a mass spectrometry. Those are the tests I ordered."

"Jill, you're losing me. Try English."

"Sorry. Let me back up. The important thing is that Matthew probably injected a tiny bit of carfentanyl into Lydia's toothpaste before he went to the Eastern Shore, knowing she wouldn't brush her teeth until bedtime."

"If carfentanyl is so powerful, wouldn't Lydia be able to see it? Or taste it?"

"Nope, it's a white powder and would have blended right in to the toothpaste. It takes just a tiny pinch to do the job, so there wouldn't be any change in the Gingavent's taste."

"Because Lydia used prescription toothpaste," I think out loud, "Matthew knew there was no danger of Colin brushing his teeth with the doctored tube. But how did the carfentanyl knock her out?"

"Simple. When Lydia brushed her teeth, she absorbed it through her mucus membranes. Within twenty minutes she would have been sleeping deeply. Maybe even in a coma."

"Jill, when Matthew called at ten to say good night, Colin told him Lydia was getting ready for bed. Matthew knew her routine. He lived with her for twenty years."

"That's right. So let's say he left right away and returned to the house around eleven. Colin and Lydia are sound asleep. Especially Lydia. There was no chance she'd wake up," Jill continues.

"What if Colin woke up?" I answer my own question. "Matthew could say he came back because he forgot something and scratch his plan to kill her. But why not just give her enough carfentanyl to kill her?" The answer is obvious. "Because he wants it to look like suicide. Okay, so how did he actually do it?"

Jill puts her arm around my shoulder. "I'm warning you, it's horrible. But this theory takes into account the evidence, like the new blender from Potomac Place and the cheese wrappers that the police found. And the Chianti bottle you saw in the fridge. Matthew wanted Lydia's death to look consistent with a drug interaction caused by her eating those forbidden foods. So her death had to look like a CVA."

"A CVA?" I ask.

"Sorry; that's a cerebral vascular accident. It's the brain's equivalent of a heart attack, a sudden blockage of the blood supply to a portion of the brain that results in death to the nerve cells."

I translate: "A CVA is a stroke, right?"

Jill nods.

"Go ahead. Give me the gory details. I'm a big girl." With a stomach churning faster than a Mixmaster turned on high, I hang on every syllable out of Jill's mouth.

"Here's what I think. Matthew came home with the equipment he needed, an oral-gastric tube, a blender, the wine, the cheese and other food. He concocted a fatal last supper by pureeing the food and wine in the blender. The new blender must be a lot quieter than the KitchenAid. And he could dispose of the new one without Sallie or Colin noticing.

"He fed the nasty concoction to Lydia through the tube while she was knocked out by the carfentanyl. Next, he scattered the food wrappers around, took the tube and blender with him, and drove back the to Eastern Shore. Colin sleeps through it all. Lydia's death looks like suicide. Plus, she'd tried to kill herself before, so nobody questions the cause of death. In the unlikely event that the police got suspicious, Matthew has a good alibi, and a hotel room on the Eastern Shore, a hundred miles away. And I, unwittingly, confirmed he'd been there at midnight, which meant the police knew, if they were interested, that he didn't have enough time to drive back and forth and kill her."

"I don't know, Jill. It sounds so far-fetched. Wouldn't using the tube take too long?"

"It's actually quite simple, and inserting a gastric tube only takes fifteen seconds. Any first-year med student can do it. The procedure I just described, from start to finish, takes less than five minutes. Don't forget Lydia was unconscious, which makes everything easier for him."

"Wouldn't the tube have left abrasions inside Lydia's throat or mouth?"

"I thought of that. Not necessarily. Let me walk you through this while you look at this picture." Jill pulls a medical textbook off her desk and opens it to a diagram of the digestive system. "Say Matthew passes the tube orally, past the pharynx, down the esophagus, through the proximal gastric sphincter, and into the stomach. Lydia's unconscious, so maybe he strokes her neck to cause reflexive swallowing. Then he connects a fifty-cc syringe to the mouth end of an Ewald tube. Here, I brought one to show you." It looks like a wide tube with several openings on the end.

"With the Ewald tube, Matthew can quickly aspirate large amounts of Lydia's gastric contents," Jill explains. "It's what hospitals use to pump stomachs. Matthew's next step would be to inject air through the tube while he positions his stethoscope over Lydia's stomach. He listens for air whooshing into the stomach. That helps him place the tube in the right spot.

"Next he aspirates the stomach contents into his syringe, while emptying the contents into the blender. He blends the wine and foods containing tyramine with the contents of Lydia's stomach. Then, he reintroduces those ingredients into her stomach by drawing them into the syringe and plunging them back down the Ewald tube. You following?"

"I think so. But why do it that way?" I ask, keeping my eyes pasted on the textbook.

"Simple. Digestion begins in the mouth, and it involves all kinds of enzymes," Jill explains. "If he just mashed the food and injected it, it would be at a different stage of digestion than the other stuff in her stomach. It would lack the preliminary digestive enzymes, which the medical examiner might have discovered during the autopsy. Also, mashing the food with the digestive juices before injecting it would speed absorption from the stomach." Jill's voice breaks. "It probably killed her faster."

"How long?" I ask.

"There's no way to know for sure, but probably within three to five hours. Which is consistent with the time of death, which was between two and five A.M., right?"

"And you think Matthew was calm enough to perform this entire disgusting procedure without screwing up once? Not one single mistake? I can't believe that."

"He did make one minor slip, which is why was there was food in her lungs. It looks like he accidentally pulled the tube out in the middle of the procedure, and reinserted it without checking, injecting a small amount of food in Lydia's lungs before he realized his mistake." She pauses, as if debating whether to add the crowning detail. "You know, in med school, when we were lab partners, he never doublechecked his procedures. It used to drive me bonkers. He always just assumes he did it right the first time. None of my other lab partners were ever that arrogant."

"So, why didn't the medical examiner get suspicious about the food in her lungs?"

"Probably because people who are unconscious often vomit and breathe it in. My guess is that in the absence of other suspicious evidence, the medical examiner just figured that's what happened."

The cruelty is staggering. "It sounds disgustingly clever. Are there flaws in this theory?"

Jill thinks for a minute. "Let's see. First, there was the risk that Colin might wake up and see Matthew."

"Not if Matthew locked the bedroom door while he was in there with Lydia," I interject. "And Colin is a sound sleeper. But, Jill, what about the next morning or afternoon? Matthew had no idea I was coming over. It was pure chance that I found her. He said he planned to get back by two that afternoon, before Colin got home from school. What if he got stuck in traffic or something? Matthew was taking a risk, even if it wasn't a big one."

"I know. That's the second flaw," Jill says. We consider it for a moment: If we are right, Matthew murdered Lydia and left her to die, with no guarantee that Colin wouldn't be the person who found her. Lydia, at least, was sleeping or unconscious when he worked her over. But Colin would have had to live with the trauma of finding his mother's body for the rest of his life.

"You know, Jill, I'm a pretty good judge of character. But we are talking about a man, an old friend, who plotted his wife's murder in a bizarre and disgusting manner, bought the equipment he needed to do the job, executed a carefully thought-out plan, then dug into a corned beef sandwich."

Jill looks pained.

"Don't beat yourself up too much, Jill. I was his good friend, too. For a long time. How were we to know he was the devil incarnate?

He's a doctor, after all. A healer. A life saver. And he dresses well and drives a nice car." Under stress, black humor helps prevent me from losing it.

"You can make jokes, but at least you never shared your bed with a murderer," Jill says.

"You're right. You win. You're so damn competitive. Anyway, back to the flaws. What else?"

"I saved the biggest for last. There was no guarantee that Matthew's plan would work. Some people on MAO inhibitors are susceptible to fatal tyramine reactions. Like Lydia turned out to be. But other people could simply wake up the next morning with a bad headache. Matthew had no way of knowing what would happen in advance."

"Pure arrogance," I conjecture. "If she woke with a bad headache, he'd tell her it was just a side effect of her meds. Anyway, what did he have to lose? He could always try again, next month or next year." My instinct, honed by years of tight deadlines, is to focus on the immediate crisis, to defer thinking about the larger implications until later. My only goal now is to nab Matthew. "Okay, the other big flaw. What is it?"

"Motive," Jill whispers. "I had no idea he hated her so much. Why in the world would he do it? And in such a degrading way."

It's the same question I'd wrestled with last night, after my usual remedies for inducing sleep—a hot bath, a shot of brandy, an hour of mindless television had failed. Hesitantly, I say to Jill, "Only one person can tell us that."

We debate for hours whether now is the time to go to the police. Jill votes yes. I say hold out for a few more hours. Finally, Jill goes along with my basic plan, although she's not happy about it. She thinks I'm taking unnecessary risks, but I want to be sure I have the goods on Matthew. We spend more time revising and perfecting the plan. Jill keeps insisting that it's too dangerous and that she has to come, too, but I've come this close to solving the case, and I want to follow through on my own.

"Don't forget I have longstanding dinner plans at six-thirty," I remind Jill. "It's already past four." I would love to cancel, but won't do that to Val or Rob.

Jill sighs. "Okay, you win. You wore me down. You'd better head over there. His office hours end at five-thirty. Are you sure you called everyone you need to?"

Everything was in place. Aaron's secretary would remind him about dinner when he checked in with her from the airport. Trini wasn't expecting us home until at least eleven. I'd left a message for Val confirming our dinner plans, then called her back with Matthew's office address. "If I'm not at the restaurant by six-forty-five, come get me. Or send Rob. It's important. I'll explain later." I left Rob a similar message on his cell phone, along with Matthew's office address and telephone number.

"Okay. I'm off."

Jill hugs me. "Good luck. Be careful."

"You have the keys to his office, right?"

She shows them to me for the fourth time. "I'll be there at six, I promise. And remember, don't eat or drink anything. He may still have carfentanyl and, if he feels threatened, he might use it."

"Thanks, Mom." I don't want Jill to see how scared I am, or she'd insist on coming. I'm adamant about going myself because I'm sure I can get Matthew to confess. I do know, though, that generally speaking, going alone to confront a murderer is risky. But I have the upper hand with Matthew, I reassure myself. He has no idea I'm onto him. By the time he learns otherwise, Jill will be there as backup. Two against one, no contest. I try to hush the little voice that's reminding me I'm breaking Aaron's cardinal rule. Whenever associates ask him how he maintains his nearly unbroken string of courtroom victories, he replies: "Simple. I never underestimate my opponents."

TWENTY-TWO

Matthew's receptionist —ANDREA, according to the nameplate pinned to her white coat—eyes me suspiciously. "Office hours are over. Dr. Finelli is seeing his last patient now." She emphasizes the word *last*.

It's after five, and she's probably late to meet her friends for happy hour. The waiting room is deserted, no trace of the other doctor with whom Matthew shares the suite. "I'm a friend of Dr. Finelli's, not a patient. Why don't you tell him Claire Newman is waiting for him?" Grudgingly, Andrea gets up to deliver the message.

When she returns, her attitude's noticeably adjusted. "Ms. Newman, Dr. Finelli says to please wait. He'll be with you in a few minutes." She gathers her purse and keys and walks out. "Good night. Don't worry if you hear the phone. I already switched it over to out-of-office mode."

"Good night," I say. As she disappears down the hall, I check the locks on the office door. Three, which corresponds to the number of keys in Jill's purse.

Too fidgety to read, I notice a pile of *Nationweeks* on the magazine tables. I'll have to remember to pass on the word to the guys in ad sales: They love having doctors in the subscription base; it drives up the demographics. Wouldn't bother them to have murderers, either, as long as they earn six figures and buy luxury goods. To distract myself, I flip through a cooking magazine, but a photo spread of wine and cheese only adds to my agitation. I shut the magazine and check my watch again.

Hearing voices, I glance up. An elderly man shuffles slowly down the hall, supported by his wife on one side and Matthew on the other. Matthew winks at me and continues speaking loudly to his patient. "Everything checks out fine, Mr. Miller. We'll see you back here in three weeks."

"Thank you, Dr. Finelli," says the wife. Matthew courteously walks them to the elevator. He's grandstanding, no doubt, for my benefit. I bet he doesn't usually waste much precious time on amenities like walking his patients to the elevator. Fumbling in my purse, I press the RECORD button on my compact tape recorder. Sixty minutes and counting.

Matthew flops into the chair next to me. "Whew, what a day. One emergency after another. I'm so glad you dropped in. To what do I owe the pleasure?"

"Oh, I was in the neighborhood. I thought I would take a chance and see if you were around. I thought we could talk."

"Sounds good to me. How about a drink? I have a bottle of vermouth, a new Italian brand. You'll like it."

"Sure, I like to try new things," I say, following him into his consultation room. I'm relieved to get him out of the waiting area into a room where Jill can overhear our conversation without being seen.

I examine the photos on Matthew's desk—Colin and Lydia, alone and together in various poses—while he hangs his white coat on the hanger on the back of his door, rolls up his sleeves, and washes his hands. He removes two glasses from a shelf above the sink. "I'll be right back with the ice." My stomach sinks below my ankles as he clicks the locks on the outside door.

Matthew hands me a tumbler filled with ice and a maroon-colored liquid. I pretend to take a sip, then set my glass on the low table in front of the leather loveseat and matching chairs. "Sorry about the tumblers; they're the only ones in the cabinet." How typical of Matthew to apologize for serving drinks in the wrong glasses. He walks to the window. "I think I'll lower the blinds. There's a glare this time of day."

I watch him adjust the blinds. Matthew appears to be a man who's reached his prime with everything intact—looks, career, self-confidence. He actually appears more handsome than he did twenty years ago. Lanky as a youth, he's filled out, but there's no extra flab around his middle. His sandy hair is thinning slightly on top, a barely noticeable loss. Hair plugs or maybe Rogaine, I think, uncharitably. He motions me to join him on the loveseat.

"Come sit next to me. It's more comfortable than that chair. Tell me what's on your mind." If I sit that close to him the tape recorder will be in closer range, but the idea of being in touching distance of him repels me. It dawns on me that Matthew may be setting the stage for seduction. I'm buying time. Jill should arrive within twenty minutes. I join him on the loveseat, a few inches away, careful not to accidentally brush against him.

"Where is Aaron? Working late again?" His arm casually brushes my shoulder. "It's a mistake to neglect a beautiful wife."

He should know. "I'm meeting him a little later for dinner, with some friends. At Trattoria Tivoli at six-thirty."

"Too bad. That means there's only time for a quick visit. Well, Claire, let's drink to our friendship. Past and present." We click glasses.

Again, I bring the tumbler to my lips without sipping, noticing Matthew's self-satisfied smile as he gazes fondly at me.

"Matthew, I've been over this in my mind so many times, and I still can't figure it out. Can you help me understand how Lydia became so unhappy that she'd kill herself?"

"Oh, Claire, everything has to be so black and white for you, doesn't it? There's always a logical reason for what people do. And you always have to have the answers. You knew us so well, didn't you? The happy couple, the perfect family. I saw the way you looked at us across the dinner table, at those barbecues and brunches. Tell me, now that you've been married awhile. Could anyone live up to your ideal of domestic bliss?"

"Maybe I was young and naive, but what you guys had still seems pretty good to me. You seemed happy. You had a solid career, a beautiful child, a lovely home, nice friends. Neither of you had much to worry about. Maybe Lydia got bored at home, but at least she was her own boss. She didn't have to suffer the Sunday-night dread about next week's deadlines, or worry about spending her old age alone. Your lives were settled. Your refrigerator was always stocked with milk and orange juice, like at my mother's house or Sallie's. Lydia used to open my refrigerator and laugh. 'What's for dinner tonight, Claire, flat seltzer with desiccated lime? The mold on those sesame noodles looks delicious.'"

"I know that's how it looked to you. I'm talking about how it felt. Did you ever think that maybe we were too young to be impersonating Ward and June Cleaver? That maybe we'd wake up one day when we were thirty or thirty-five, and wonder whether we had made a series of mistakes? We were locked into a life that neither of us found fulfilling. You didn't marry until you were thirty. You had plenty of time on your own to make your own choices. Lydia and I were kids pretending to be grown-ups. It was fun, until we woke up one day and realized that we really *were* grown-ups. It was too late. We had thrown away our opportunity to be spontaneous, reckless, hedonistic."

"Oh please. You loved each other. You were happy. You had Colin. Are you telling me now that it was all a big act?" Matthew's version of events is revisionist history. He moves closer to me on the couch. I don't pull away this time. I want to make sure my hidden tape recorder is picking up our conversation.

"It's true that we were happy at first, for years even, when we first moved here, when Colin was a baby. Not for the last, I don't know, five or ten years. You should be glad Lydia shut you out. At least you can remember her the way she used to be. Before her life had become such a burden that she couldn't get through the day without her medications. You never came home to find her upstairs in bed, weeping as if she had lost everything."

"Why was she so unhappy? Tell me."

"You know, Claire, there were two Lydias: the self she displayed to the outside world, to Colin and Sallie, the neighbors, the PTA, to my business associates. The charming, gracious hostess. Devoted wife and mother. Beautiful, every hair on her head perfectly in place. But there was another Lydia, too. The miserable one."

He's gotten up during his recitation and is standing at the window, fingering the cords of the blinds. As soon as his back is turned, I lean over and spill most of my drink into the potted plant on the coffee table, then raise the glass to my lips as if I gulped it down. "This vermouth is delicious. What's it called again?"

He's too absorbed in his diatribe to answer. "Moody, depressed, cold, angry. Nothing could give her pleasure. Nothing. When I tried to touch her, she recoiled. Finally I stopped trying. Some marriage; we hadn't had sex in years. Sometimes she'd get better, but never for long. The only person capable of giving her joy was Colin. But, in the end, even her own son couldn't sustain her. Her life was unbearable. And no one understood. How could they? To the rest of the world, Lydia looked like she was blessed with everything." His voice is choked with tears.

"What was making her so unhappy?" I repeat, bewildered by the Lydia he is describing.

"Simple. She didn't love me anymore. She felt trapped."

Jill should be here already. I think I hear a faint click and pray that it's Jill unlocking the front door, and not my imagination. Matthew continues to speak, as if he hadn't heard the click.

"She didn't love you. You didn't love her. I know you're Catholic, but did you guys ever hear of divorce?"

He looks at me in disbelief. "She wouldn't consider it. She thought it would destroy Colin's life."

"So you killed her," I say softly. "As the only way out of a dead marriage? A smart guy like you couldn't find a gentler solution?" He looks at me, with a wounded expression.

Looking straight into his eyes, I speak in my iciest tone. "Matthew, let's cut the crap. We both know you killed Lydia."

He stares at me as if I have made an inappropriate comment about the weather. "Claire, I know Lydia's death has been a great shock to you, and that you've been suffering. Have you called any of the psychiatrists Randy recommended?"

"Don't patronize me, Matthew. I know all about it: your affair with Jill, the money you made with your insider trading on Theragenics, how you killed Lydia."

"Poor Claire," he says in a low voice. "I've always admired how you managed to hold everything together. So much energy and ambition packed into that petite frame. Career, family, entertaining your friends. No wonder Lydia envied you. But the last few weeks have taken their toll, haven't they? Why don't you lie down? I'll call Aaron to pick you up. Take a rest. I know you're not yourself lately."

I'd love to slap the smug expression off his face. "I don't need a rest, Matthew. In fact, I've never felt more alert." I realize the truth of this statement. Fear certainly beats caffeine as a picker-upper. "There's just one nagging question I can't get out of my head, Matthew. Why did you kill her?"

"Claire, please. Stop talking nonsense."

"Why?" I repeat. "You notice, Matthew, that I don't ask how. That's because I already know how. I know all about the carfentanyl in the toothpaste, about the new blender and the food you bought at Potomac Place. How you snuck back home that night with your

Ewald tube to force-feed her. I just can't figure out why. So, please, tell me."

Matthew's words are calm, but the color has drained from his face. "What a creative mind you have, Claire. No wonder you're such a successful writer. How did you dream up this absurd fantasy?"

"It's no fantasy, Matthew. I've collected plenty of evidence now, enough for the police to arrest you. Let's see, there's the lab analysis of the toothpaste with the carfentanyl, the receipts from Potomac Place for the blender and wine and cheese. Am I leaving anything out? Probably. It was a clever scheme, Matthew, but you're not going to get away with it."

"Oh, Claire." He shakes his head, as if I'm an amusing child. "How well I know you. You're bluffing. If you had any of this so-called evidence, you wouldn't be here, would you? You'd be at the police station. All you have are some half-baked notions based on medical terms you don't understand. I admire your bravado. Really. I always have. But the simple fact is that Lydia killed herself."

"You're right, Matthew. We do know each other well. That's what makes this so sad. We used to share the person in our lives who meant the most to us. That was a very long time ago, wasn't it? Before you started to hate Lydia. Before you killed her. Go on, tell me about it, Matthew. Remember how close we once were?"

"I keep telling you Claire, I didn't kill Lydia. She killed herself. Why can't you accept that? Is suicide too messy to fit into your compartmentalized version of reality? The warped reality portrayed every week on the pages of your simplistic magazine?"

And here I'd thought that Matthew was one of my biggest fans. Another illusion shattered. I unzip a compartment in my purse and remove Rob's letter to Lydia, careful not to jostle the tape recorder. "You know, Matthew, murder is a lot messier than suicide. Especially the way you did it, but maybe this letter will jog your memory."

I hand him Rob's letter. "It's a letter from my brother to Lydia, dated fourteen years ago. It was written after the night they conceived Colin. Don't bother ripping it up, it's a copy."

He grabs the letter and reads it. I look away, waiting for him to speak. He fumbles around his desk, looking for Kleenex, I presume. When I look up, however, he's pointing a syringe filled with a colorless liquid in my direction.

"What've you got there, Matthew?" I pretend to be only casually interested.

"Potassium. When I inject it into you it will make your heart stop."

"Do you think I'm going to allow you to inject me? I'm small but I'm strong."

He doesn't answer at first. Then he laughs. "I think I'm stronger, especially when that drink starts to hit you." So he did put something in my drink. I'll play along as if I'm really getting tired. I let the remark about the drink pass, as if I hadn't noticed it.

I'm focused on the syringe. I wonder how long it will take Matthew to realize I didn't drink the vermouth. "Don't you think a friend found dead in your office is going to arouse suspicion? Quite a coincidence so soon after your wife's death." Now that I know he's doctored my drink and expects me to pass out, I have a little leverage. Which doesn't mean that I'm not terrified. I don't know how I'm keeping up my end of the conversation, but I have to keep him talking until Jill walks in.

"Once you pass out I'm going to inject this right between your toes. No marks. You simply suffered a heart attack, poor girl. All that stress."

"Don't think that'll be so easy, Matthew." I stifle a big yawn for effect. "Aaron and Jill know what you did. You'll be arrested. And I bet the autopsy will show the potassium."

"Don't you think I know when you're bluffing? It doesn't matter. You'll be very sleepy soon."

I yawn again, relieved that he thinks he has time to spare. "So, Matthew, while we wait, I still have some questions."

He smiles. "Okay, Claire. We'll do it your way. That old letter doesn't prove a thing. So Rob is Colin's biological father. That's old news."

I'm startled. It never occurred to me that Matthew already knew about Lydia and Rob. It seems unnecessary to tell Matthew that until that moment, the "old news" was merely an unconfirmed guess on my part.

"How long have you known?"

"It was a few months ago, in February. I came home late one night, and Lydia began badgering me about giving her a divorce."

By some miracle, my voice only cracks a little. "So, Lydia *did* want a divorce. But you didn't, right? Too risky. If she hired a good lawyer, she might have uncovered your secret money stash."

"That night, we got into an ugly argument," he continues. "Colin was sleeping; he didn't hear it, thank God. That kid sleeps like a log. No, I didn't want a divorce. It wasn't just the money. Jill had made it clear that she wanted no role in the dissolution of our marriage. She said that we have to live with the choices we've already made."

"People want different things at different times," I say in an encouraging tone. It's amazing how fear can transform even the most hostile audience into a sympathetic listener.

"It's more than that. Jill's too much like me. Her work always comes first. That's why we didn't get together twenty years ago. I valued the wrong things: Lydia's looks, the way she placed my career and needs ahead of her own. I had no idea that those very qualities would make her so unhappy later. I wanted a wife, a hostess, a full-time mother for our kids. I didn't know that she would grow to hate me for turning her into that woman. As if she wasn't there every step of the way, making those same choices."

"The night of your argument with Lydia. What happened?" My tone has softened. If only he'd drop the damn syringe.

"Lydia said she'd spoken to a lawyer and was in the process of looking over our financial records. She didn't want to gouge me, she said, she just wanted a fair settlement, enough for her and Colin to be comfortable. We could sell the house; she didn't care, as long as Colin could stay at his school. I had hidden the bank records, but not very carefully. It had been years since Lydia paid any attention to our finances. She signed the tax returns, or any other papers I put in front of her, without reading them. But enough small talk, Claire." He glances meaningfully at the syringe.

"You're not actually planning to kill me, are you, Matthew? You'll be charged with double murder." Why hasn't Jill come in to help me yet?

Matthew's voice sounds disembodied, as if he's left the planet. "Life is so unpredictable. Two old friends sharing a drink after work and one suddenly has a heart attack." He clicks his tongue. "Imagine CPR not working." He's standing at his desk now, his back to the door.

I'm too paralyzed to speak, as I see Randy appear in the doorway and grab Matthew from behind, then twist his head and neck into a lock. The syringe drops to the floor. I run over and stomp the syringe into tiny pieces with my heel. I hope the potassium burns a big hole in Matthew's carpet.

"It's too late, Matthew. You'd have to kill me, too. And there is no way on earth you can explain away the deaths of your wife, Claire, and me. Now, come sit in this chair while we wait for the police. One move and I won't hesitate to use this." Randy takes a small handgun out of his jacket pocket and grasps it firmly.

"A Jewish guy with a gun?" I gasp. Today is turning out to be loaded with more surprise twists than a Hitchcock flick.

"Self-protection. There've been a few break-ins in my building lately. Drug addicts looking for narcotics. I keep it locked in my office safe."

I exhale, thrilled to be breathing. "I was wrong about you, Randy. Thanks for saving my life." My voice finally breaks. I curl up

231

on the loveseat, wrapping my arms tightly around myself. Once the tears start, I can't control them.

"I owe you an apology, too. Lydia *was* murdered. You just had the wrong guy."

I stop crying long enough to ask how he figured it out. Keeping his gaze and gun fixed on Matthew, he answers: "It was the journal article you threw at me. I'd never read that issue, or even seen it before. Matthew borrowed it a few months ago and never returned it. I just finished it, and finally realized what had happened. I tried to call your cell. When I couldn't reach you, Claire, I came right over. I wanted to hear what Matthew had to say."

"Just one more question, Randy. Did you break into my house looking for Lydia's camera?"

He looks down, embarrassed. "I'm so sorry, Claire. I know what a stupid move that was. I was out of my mind with worry over you seeing those pictures. Please, forgive me."

I think of how scared I was, my children's fear and upset. The mess. "Forgive you? You terrified my children. It was an idiotic stunt. I'm only sorry you didn't leave fingerprints. I would have loved to see you arrested for breaking and entering."

"I said I was sorry. Haven't you ever done something you regretted?" Randy looks more sad than contrite. I have to admit, in the scheme of things, the break-in seems like small stuff.

"I just saved your life. Doesn't that count for something?" Randy continues. "And you accused me of things I didn't do. Like murdering Lydia." He lowers his voice, realizing how that must sound. "I'm not trying to excuse what I did. It was inexcusable."

I'm still angry, but I have to let it go. Mostly, I feel relief. Relief that this ordeal is finally over. Matthew is the real bad guy, not Randy. "Saving my life counts for a little. I won't be pressing charges. And I won't be talking about it to Karen."

"Thank you, Claire." He turns his attention back to Matthew.

"Just sit tight, and don't move. Or I will use this. You can count on that." Randy calls in the direction of the waiting room: "You can come in now, Jill. It's safe."

Jill, her face streaked with tears, sits next to me on the loveseat, clasping my hand. She avoids looking at Matthew.

"The police will be here any minute," Jill says.

Randy is standing guard a few inches from Matthew's chair, a most welcome sight. "If we're just killing time, I have a few more questions," I say, turning to Matthew. "Lydia was onto your insider trading, right?"

He doesn't answer me. "Please, Matthew," I ask softly.

"No, not yet, but she was getting close. That must be why she called you, to help her poke around."

Of course, that had to be the reason. Finally, the reason she called me. I recall her words from our last phone conversation: *"In a strange way, you're the only person I can trust now."*

I take a few steps closer to Matthew's chair, emboldened by Randy's weapon and Jill's presence. "So, your real fear was that she'd discover the insider trading scam. Not that Lydia would turn you in to the authorities, or fleece you in a divorce, but that Lydia would tell Jill what you'd done, how you betrayed her."

Now Matthew turns to Jill. "I didn't want to lose you. Please, Jill, try to understand," he pleads.

"It's a flimsy excuse for murder, isn't it?" Randy says.

"You still don't understand. None of you," Matthew says. "I did it for only one reason. To keep my son. The night of our argument, I told Lydia to forget about a divorce. We could stay married and live separate lives, at least until Colin was older. I told her that, if she went ahead with the divorce proceedings, I would fight her for custody."

"We argued. She became hysterical. She told me I would never get Colin. She said she could prove he wasn't my biological son. That's when she told me about Rob."

"So that's why you killed her? Because she betrayed you?" I'm alone in trying to unravel his motives. Randy and Jill seem too drained to care.

"Don't you see? She destroyed the most important thing in my life. My only pure relationship." Jill looks up, shocked.

"I'm a good doctor. I help people, very sick people. But, along the way, I've cut corners, sacrificed little pieces of my integrity. I could have lived with loving a woman who wasn't my wife, and despising the woman I had married. My life was already a series of compromises. Except for Colin. When Lydia said she'd take that away from me, it was too much. She killed the only thing I had left."

"Oh, Matthew," I say, feeling a stir of compassion before my disgust returns in full force. "Why didn't you go to court and take your chances? No judge would have taken Colin away from you. You're his father. You raised him. Why were you so afraid of losing him?"

"I wanted to protect him. If we started divorce proceedings, who knows what would have come out. I couldn't let that happen."

"Back to that night of the argument," I say.

"I had to face facts. Our marriage was over, and a divorce was out of the question." He looks me in the eye. "I could have forgiven her for keeping her secret all those years, but not for revealing it. I didn't want to live with that hanging over me. I had to protect my son. No matter what."

"You loved her once. Enough to marry her. She was Colin's mother. How could you kill her that way?"

"It was the best way, the only way, to make it look like a suicide." He shrugs. "Anyway, she was unconscious. She didn't feel any pain."

Jill and I exchange glances. "Matthew, if you love Jill, as you say you do, why did you betray her?"

"Oh, it was stupid." He turns to Jill, who won't return his gaze. "I thought financial security was the only thing I could give you. If the acquisition went through, you would be set. If it didn't, I wanted a backup, enough money to keep Theragenics afloat."

"So, you sabotaged the acquisition to set yourself up as a hero later?" Jill looks puzzled.

"It didn't start as sabotage. I was trying to protect you. It just got out of hand."

Out of hand. Matthew doesn't see himself as evil or malicious, even now. He was just a man doing what he had to do to protect his loved ones. At last I've heard enough.

"The police will be here any second, Matthew. Are you ready to turn yourself in?" Randy asks in a gentler tone than before.

"Turn myself in?" he repeats.

"Matthew, your options are extremely limited. If you want to protect Colin, it's the best way."

"No matter what happens, Matthew, I promise to take care of Colin. You know I love him," I say, looking at Matthew crumpled in his chair, his desolation so sharp it nearly pierces me. Then, I think about Lydia.

Suddenly, the air fills with the crackle of walkie-talkies and the voices of men in blue uniforms.

"I'm ready," Matthew says, nodding to Randy, who accompanies him out.

Jill and I hold each other tightly. "The worst is over," I tell her. "We'll get through this." She doesn't believe it any more than I do.

We're still clinging to each other, faces buried in each other's shoulders, as Val, Rob, and Aaron arrive within minutes of each other, each of them frantic until they see that, physically, I am safe.

TWENTY-THREE

Proust can keep his madelines. Just give me smooth, white sand and the crash of waves pounding the shore. Like every other morning for the past six weeks, I slip out of bed early and carry my coffee mug to a patch high in the dunes.

No one inside the house—an East Hampton estate Rob rented for July and August—is stirring yet. Not Aaron, Rob, Trini, or any of the four children. By eight, Paulo, the caretaker who lives in the guest house, is stationed in the gleaming kitchen, squeezing oranges, grinding coffee beans, and mixing batter for banana waffles, Colin's favorite. When I return from my four-mile walk, I join the family at the kitchen table, leafing through the maple-syrup–stained pages of *The New York Times*.

For now, my four-newspapers-per-day habit is the only remnant of my *Nationweek* routine. I've been on leave since June, nearly ten weeks now. I miss seeing Val almost every day, the office camaraderie, the rush of deadlines, but not as much as I expected.

It's been a few months since that spring night when Matthew turned himself in. The healing has barely begun. The surreptitiously taped confession I handed over to the police was not admissible in court, of course, but it helped persuade Matthew to plead guilty, sparing Colin the public spectacle of a trial. Matthew's lawyers had hoped to cut a good deal, a light sentence at one of the tonier federal lockups, but that proved impossible.

Murder, unlike insider trading, isn't a federal crime. Matthew's been sentenced to twenty years in the Maryland state prison in Jessup. With exemplary behavior he could get out in thirteen years. Matthew won't be free again until Colin is an adult. As free, that is, as any of us is ever free of the past.

Certainly Colin will never be free of his family's terrible history. He lives with us now. We've all agreed on that—Aaron, Rob, Matthew, Sallie, Colin, and Colin's shrink, Dr. Marcy Jones-Harlan. The consensus is that he's been through enough upheaval this year to last a lifetime. We're not going to spring any more surprises on him, so we haven't told him yet that Rob is his biological father. In the meantime, Colin's getting to know Rob as a loving uncle, a close relative intimately involved in the texture of our family life.

If repairing that family life has led us all the way to East Hampton, well, there are worse places. Sallie commutes here by train most weekends. Aaron shuttles back and forth between trials and depositions, and Rob comes and goes but, for once in his adult life, mostly he stays. We chose East Hampton for convenience; half of Hollywood decamps here for July and August, as if there are no beautiful beaches on the other coast. I'm accustomed to the sight of Rob conducting deals poolside—holding his cell phone above the water as he ducks splashes from the kids.

Despite the luxurious surroundings, our daily life is not all fun and water games. Colin's demeanor is stormy, filled with moody silences and eruptions of anger. Dr. Marcy, as we call her in therapy sessions, both family and individual, counsels patience. On good days, and we've had one or two lately, I think I see signs of the old Colin trying to emerge: the affectionate, warm and trusting boy I remember. He'll be back someday. I know it.

My children are also having trouble adjusting to the new family configuration. We've worked through some tense moments with Allison, who resents relinquishing her position as senior sibling. Slowly, though, she and Colin are forging their own tentative bond. Last evening, after dinner, Colin and Allison rode their bikes to town for ice cream—a distance of half a mile. As I warned them to be careful—for the fifth time—they exchanged the kind of glance that used to pass between Rob and me whenever our parents were being especially overbearing.

The twins, so far, don't question the half-truths we've told them—that Colin lives with us because his mother died and his father is too sick to take care of him. Allison, like Colin, knows more of the truth, or at least the parts we couldn't avoid revealing. It's difficult sorting out what, when, and how much to tell the children. Despite my shelves of parenting guides, there are none to consult about family secrets of this enormity.

It makes me smile to think of those nursery-school parents—and I include our former selves in the joke—fretting over cartoons or toys they deem too violent for their children's fragile psyches. No longer do we enjoy the luxury of obsessing over such trite, abstract threats. In mundane ways, anyway, tragedy can be liberating.

With all the time we spend together, often the sole adults in residence, my brother and I are closer than ever, sometimes, it seems, to the exclusion of Aaron. After hours of tense negotiations, the three of us hammered out some practical issues pertaining to Colin's upbringing. Aaron and I eventually succumbed to Rob's insistence on making a financial contribution to our household. Hence the East Hampton house, which costs far more per week than our monthly mortgage in Bethesda, but appears to be chump change to my high-living brother. Likewise Paulo's salary, which Rob also pays.

Sallie, the other member of our newly extended family, plans to sell her house and the bakery and retire to Washington next year. She's looking for a condo or townhouse, where she can provide Colin with a temporary refuge from our household whenever he needs it. She knows the truth about Rob and Colin, and has been a rock. Rob wants to tell our parents the entire story over Thanksgiving. Maybe we will. I no longer plan that far ahead.

Aaron and I are going through a rough patch. Not noticeable enough for the kids to discern, but there's definitely a distance between us. He's angry about what he calls my "rash and irresponsible behavior" in pursuit of the truth. I see his point, but I'm angry too, mostly at his anger.

Sure, I understand it. In my zeal to solve the puzzle of Lydia's death, I underestimated the damage my investigation might wreak upon our formerly harmonious marriage. Yes, I transgressed a few legal and moral boundaries. I took some stupid risks, but I had to know the truth. Aaron should be more forgiving. Nothing I did was particularly out of character. I just pushed the envelope a little further than usual.

To be fair, I realize that Aaron is trying to make things right again. A few days ago, he threw me a small peace offering by blaming himself for being unavailable when I needed him. I know better than to tell him that his presence wouldn't have changed my behavior one iota. Once in awhile, when he drops his armor of moral superiority, he grudgingly admits that he's proud of me. For the end, if not the means. So, for now, I'm resigned to putting our relationship on automatic pilot, while we focus on getting the kids back on track. There'll be time for us later.

Although Colin bears the brunt of the emotional damage, nobody's emerged unscathed. Jill, financed in part by Rob's deep pockets, is scrambling to save Theragenics, which may not survive for long. Rob is her biggest shareholder now.

If I could overlook the trauma to my nearest and dearest—and I can't—I'd have to call the whole ugly mess a career booster. I had my fifteen minutes of fame: interview requests from respectable newspapers and sleazy tabloids, book offers, a nibble from a well-known producer about writing a screenplay based on the actual events. I haven't said *no* so many times per day since the twins were two. The vultures finally moved on to the next scandal, leaving me to rethink my antipathy toward people who instinctively hate the press.

At first, I went back to work for several weeks, but my heart wasn't in it. Leslie encouraged me to take a short but indefinite leave of absence. As far as Calvin is concerned, she assured me, my place at *Nationweek* is guaranteed. The murder case, and my role in solving it, has garnered more favorable publicity for the magazine than five years of our political columnists shrieking at each other on those stupid Sunday talking-head-a-thons.

I ran into Calvin a few weeks ago, while waiting for an iced cafe latte at the East Hampton Farmer's Market, where espresso qualifies as an agricultural product. He wheeled his overflowing cart next to me; apparently he was buying a few hundred dollars' worth of necessities for his weekend hosts. "If you can afford to shop here, Claire, then I overpay you," he joked. We chatted for awhile. "Don't get me wrong, we need you back as soon as you're ready," he said, patting my arm, "but don't shortchange your family. My kids are in college now and I can't buy back their childhoods." Not your typical mogul comment. Who knew an actual heart beats underneath that cash register in his chest?

Calvin is not the only person whom I may have pegged wrong. It turns out that the people we think we know best may sometimes be the biggest strangers. Just about everything I thought I knew about Lydia, my closest friend for twenty-three years, was wrong. Except for a single revealing detail: My Lydia would never kill herself.

My Lydia. I guess she never existed the way I imagined her. Lydia had personality traits and character quirks I never knew about or even suspected. My perception of our friendship was as narrow as the view outside my office window on the days when clouds and fog obscure the White House. When I look down at the buses and taxis stopped in traffic, at the well-dressed people walking by swinging their briefcases, what I see is true enough, an accurate depiction of reality. When viewed from the same perch on a bright, clear day, however, the scene from that window is just a narrow slice of a wider picture.

I see now that, when Lydia dropped me five years ago, the not knowing why, the lack of closure, haunted me as much as the loss of our friendship. It's ironic, really. Now I see that I've spent most of my life building a career searching for answers, yet it took me forty years to learn a lesson older than Adam and Eve. Sometimes knowledge exacts a much higher price than blessed ignorance.

Our daily struggle to build a life—an indestructible edifice—is based on a simple premise: that we can keep evil at bay, a stranger to us and our loved ones. That's why, at a certain stage in our lives, we move to leafy, tree-lined suburbs and construct sturdy picket fences around our property. Yet, unless we are unusually lucky, sooner or later, we'll encounter evil, and discover that it's not an alien invader. It's planted in our own backyards, embedded deep into the soil, underneath the blossoming scarlet azaleas.

The scariest part is that sometimes we don't recognize evil when it's staring directly at us. We're so blinded by love and preconceptions and prejudices that it's hidden in plain sight. We don't suspect that evil could be as recognizable as our next-door neighbor, as familiar as the reflection staring back at us from the bathroom mirror.

I've been reflecting lately on Lydia's legacy, what she's left me and the other people who loved her. Once the immediate pain subsides, how are we going to remember her? It's different, naturally, for each of us—Colin, Matthew, Sallie, Rob, Jill, Randy, Karen. (Karen and I are becoming friendly. Under the circumstances, she was understanding when I canceled the dinner party.) For me, discovering the truth about Lydia's death has released me from the ache of our unfinished business.

Still, the grief hasn't disappeared. Maybe it never will. I realize now that she was never the friend I held her out to be. What I excused or overlooked as moody was really something worse. During most of the years of our long friendship, Lydia was withholding something from me—her affection, her emotions, or the truth. None of these flaws can erase how much I once loved her or the happy memories I cherish.

And now Lydia has left me with a far more valuable bequest, to raise her beloved son, my own nephew. The other night, at dinner, we were eating hamburgers on the deck. Zach asked for the ketchup and, instead of hurling the bottle at him the way Allison does, Colin got up and carefully smeared a few dots of ketchup on his bun, in the center, exactly how Zach likes it. It was an act of brotherly kindness. I realized then that Lydia and I have at last achieved our childhood wish. We're sisters now, or at least relatives, linked through our children, who will grow old together, their destinies forever intertwined.

This morning, as the waves rise and crash and rise again, I think once more of Lydia's legacy, about the triumph of loyalty and friendship over the bad stuff. "I couldn't save you, Lydia. It was too late. But we're going to save Colin. All of us. So thank you. Thank you for that," I whisper into the roaring surf.

Sorting out Lydia's legacy isn't going to be easy. But there's one thing I already know. I've gotten worse gifts. At least this one is bound to prove more useful than some of her previous presents, like that ugly orange vest, still hanging unworn in the back of my closet.